WHERE BEASTS RULED MEN

Tarzan stepped forward and put his eyes to the aperture. Before him lay a large chamber, at one end of which was a raised dais. The central figure upon the dais was a huge, black-maned lion, now fastened by golden chains to rings upon the floor. Upon golden thrones behind the lion sat three magnificently ornamented gorillas. At the foot of the steps was La, High Priestess of the Flaming God of Opar, the last colony of ancient, sunken Atlantis.

Suddenly the gorilla occupying the central golden throne cried in a loud voice: "Drag the woman to your emperor!"

Instantly the lion became frantic, lashing its tail and straining at its stout chains as it sought to leap upon La, who was now being forcibly conducted up the steps of the dais toward the bejeweled man-eater so impatiently awaiting her.

Edgar Rice Burroughs
TARZAN NOVELS

COMPLETE AND UNABRIDGED!

TARZAN
AND THE
GOLDEN LION

Edgar Rice Burroughs

BALLANTINE BOOKS • NEW YORK

Copyright © 1922, 1923, Edgar Rice Burroughs

All rights reserved. Published in the United States by Ballantine Books, a division of Random House, Inc., New York, and simultaneously in Canada by Random House of Canada, Limited, Toronto, Canada.

ISBN 0-345-28998-6

This authorized edition published by arrangement with Edgar Rice Burroughs, Inc.

Manufactured in the United States of America

First Edition: July 1963
Ninth Printing: April 1981

Cover art by Boris Vallejo

CONTENTS

1

The Golden Lion

SABOR, the lioness, suckled her young—a single fuzzy ball, spotted like Sheeta, the leopard. She lay in the warm sunshine before the rocky cavern that was her lair, stretched out upon her side with half closed eyes, yet Sabor was alert. There had been three of these little, fuzzy balls at first—two daughters and a son—and Sabor and Numa, their sire, had been proud of them; proud and happy. But kills had not been plentiful, and Sabor, undernourished, had been unable to produce sufficient milk to nourish properly three lusty cubs, and then a cold rain had come, and the little ones had sickened. Only the strongest survived—the two daughters had died. Sabor had mourned, pacing to and fro beside the pitiful bits of bedraggled fur, whining and moaning. Now and again she would nose them with her muzzle as though she would awaken them from the long sleep that knows no waking. At last, however, she abandoned her efforts, and now her whole savage heart was filled with concern for the little male cub that remained to her. That was why Sabor was more alert than usual.

Numa, the lion, was away. Two nights before he had made a kill and dragged it to their lair and last night he had fared forth again, but he had not returned. Sabor was thinking, as she half dozed, of Wappi, the plump antelope, that her splendid mate might this very minute be dragging through the tangled jungle to her. Or perhaps it would be Pacco, the zebra, whose flesh was the best beloved of her kind—juicy, succulent Pacco. Sabor's mouth watered.

Ah, what was that? The shadow of a sound had come to those keen ears. She raised her head, cocking it first upon one side and then the other, as with up-pricked ears she sought to catch the faintest repetition of that which had disturbed her. Her nose sniffed the air. There was but the suggestion of a breeze, but what there was moved toward her from the direction of the sound she had heard, and which she still heard in a slightly increasing volume that told her that whatever was making it was approaching her. As it drew closer the beast's nervousness increased and she rolled over on her belly, shutting off the milk supply from the cub, which vented its disapproval in miniature growls until a low, querulous whine from the lioness silenced him, then he stood at her side, looking first at her and then in the direction toward which she looked, cocking his little head first on one side and then on the other.

Evidently there was a disturbing quality in the sound that Sabor heard—something that inspired a certain restlessness, if not actual apprehension—though she could not be sure as yet that it boded ill. It might be her great lord returning, but it did not sound like the movement of a lion, certainly not like a lion dragging a heavy kill. She glanced at her cub, breathing as she did so a plaintive whine. There was always the fear that some danger menaced him—this last of her little family—but she, Sabor the lioness, was there to defend him.

Presently the breeze brought to her nostrils the scent-spoor of the thing that moved toward her through the jungle. Instantly the troubled mother-face was metamorphosed into a bare-fanged, glittering-eyed mask of savage rage, for the scent that had come up to her through the jungle was the hated man-scent. She rose to her feet, her head flattened, her sinuous tail twitching nervously. Through that strange medium by which animals communicate with one another she cautioned her cub to lie down and remain where he was until she returned, then she moved rapidly and silently to meet the intruder.

The cub had heard what its mother heard and now he caught the smell of man—an unfamiliar smell that had never impinged upon his nostrils before, yet a smell that he knew at once for that of an enemy—a smell that brought a reaction as typical as that which marked the attitude of the grown lioness, bringing the hairs along his little spine erect and baring his tiny fangs. As the adult moved quickly and stealthily into the underbrush the small cub, ignoring her injunction, followed after her, his hind quarters wobbling from side to side, after the manner of the very young of his kind, the ridiculous gait comporting ill with the dignified bearing of his fore quarters; but the lioness, intent upon that which lay before her, did not know that he followed her.

There was dense jungle before the two for a hundred

yards, but through it the lions had worn a tunnel-like path to their lair; and then there was a small clearing through which ran a well-worn jungle trail, out of the jungle at one end of the clearing and into the jungle again at the other. As Sabor reached the clearing she saw the object of her fear and hatred well within it. What if the man-thing were not hunting her or hers? What if he even dreamed not of their presence? These facts were as nothing to Sabor, the lioness, today. Ordinarily she would have let him pass unmolested, so long as he did not come close enough to threaten the safety of her cub; or, cubless, she would have slunk away at the first intimation of his approach. But today the lioness was nervous and fearful—fearful because of the single cub that remained to her—her maternal instinct centered three-fold, perhaps, upon this lone and triply loved survivor—and so she did not wait for the man to threaten the safety of her little one; but instead she moved to meet him and to stop him. From the soft mother she had become a terrifying creature of destruction, her brain obsessed by a single thought—to kill.

She did not hesitate an instant at the edge of the clearing, nor did she give the slightest warning. The first intimation that the black warrior had that there was a lion within twenty miles of him, was the terrifying apparition of this devil-faced cat charging across the clearing toward him with the speed of an arrow. The black was not searching for lions. Had he known that there was one near he would have given it a wide berth. He would have fled now had there been anywhere to flee. The nearest tree was farther from him than was the lioness. She could overhaul him before he would have covered a quarter of the distance. There was no hope and there was only one thing to do. The beast was almost upon him and behind her he saw a tiny cub. The man bore a heavy spear. He carried it far back with his right hand and hurled it at the very instant that Sabor rose to seize him. The spear passed through the savage heart and almost simultaneously the giant jaws closed upon the face and skull of the warrior. The momentum of the lioness carried the two heavily to the ground, dead except for a few spasmodic twitchings of their muscles.

The orphaned cub stopped twenty feet away and surveyed the first great catastrophe of his life with questioning eyes. He wanted to approach his dam but a natural fear of the man-scent held him away. Presently he commenced to whine in a tone that always brought his mother to him hurriedly; but this time she did not come—she did not even rise and look

toward him. He was puzzled—he could not understand it.
He continued to cry, feeling all the while more sad and more
lonely. Gradually he crept closer to his mother. He saw that
the strange creature she had killed did not move and after a
while he felt less terror of it, so that at last he found the
courage to come quite close to his mother and sniff at her.
He still whined to her, but she did not answer. It dawned
on him at last that there was something wrong—that his
great, beautiful mother was not as she had been—a change
had come over her; yet still he clung to her, crying much
until at last he fell asleep, cuddled close to her dead body.

It was thus that Tarzan found him—Tarzan and Jane,
his wife, and their son, Korak the Killer, returning from the
mysterious land of Pal-ul-don from which the two men had
rescued Jane Clayton. At the sound of their approach the cub
opened his eyes and rising, flattened his ears and snarled at
them, backing close against his dead mother. At sight of
him the ape-man smiled.

"Plucky little devil," he commented, taking in the story of
the tragedy at a single glance. He approached the spitting
cub, expecting it to turn and run away; but it did nothing of
the sort. Instead it snarled more ferociously and struck at
his extended hand as he stooped and reached for it.

"What a brave little fellow," cried Jane. "Poor little
orphan!"

"He's going to make a great lion, or he would have if his
dam had lived," said Korak. "Look at that back—as straight
and strong as a spear. Too bad the rascal has got to die."

"He doesn't have to die," returned Tarzan.

"There's not much chance for him—he'll need milk for a
couple of months more, and who's going to get it for him?"

"I am," replied Tarzan.

"You're going to adopt him?"

Tarzan nodded.

Korak and Jane laughed. "That'll be fine," commented
the former.

"Lord Greystoke, foster mother to the son of Numa,"
laughed Jane.

Tarzan smiled with them, but he did not cease his at-
tentions toward the cub. Reaching out suddenly he caught the
little lion by the scruff of its neck and then stroking it gently
he talked to it in a low, crooning tone. I do not know what
he said; but perhaps the cub did, for presently it ceased its
struggles and no longer sought to scratch or bite the caressing
hand. After that he picked it up and held it against his
breast. It did not seem afraid now, nor did it even bare its

fangs against this close proximity to the erstwhile hated
man-scent.

"How do you do it?" exclaimed Jane Clayton.

Tarzan shrugged his broad shoulders. "Your kind are not
afraid of you—these are really my kind, try to civilize me
as you will, and perhaps that is why they are not afraid of me
when I give them the signs of friendship. Even this little rascal seems to know it, doesn't he?"

"I can never understand it," commented Korak. "I think
I am rather familiar with African animals, yet I haven't
the power over them or the understanding that you have.
Why is it?"

"There is but one Tarzan," said Lady Greystoke, smiling at
her son teasingly, and yet her tone was not without a note of
pride.

"Remember that I was born among beasts and raised by
beasts," Tarzan reminded him. "Perhaps after all my father
was an ape—you know Kala always insisted that he was."

"John! How can you?" exclaimed Jane. "You know perfectly well who your father and mother were."

Tarzan looked solemnly at his son and closed one eye.
"Your mother never can learn to appreciate the fine qual-
ities of the anthropoids. One might almost think that she
objected to the suggestion that she had mated with one of
them."

"John Clayton, I shall never speak to you again if you
don't stop saying such hideous things. I am ashamed of
you. It is bad enough that you are an unregenerate wild-man,
without trying to suggest that you may be an ape into the
bargain."

The long journey from Pal-ul-don was almost completed—
inside the week they should be again at the site of their
former home. Whether anything now remained of the ruins
the Germans had left was problematical. The barns and out-
houses had all been burned and the interior of the bungalow
partially wrecked. Those of the Waziri, the faithful native
retainers of the Greystokes, who had not been killed by
Hauptman Fritz Schneider's soldiers, had rallied to the beat
of the war-drum and gone to place themselves at the disposal
of the English in whatever capacity they might be found use-
ful to the great cause of humanity. This much Tarzan had
known before he set out in search of Lady Jane; but how
many of his warlike Waziri had survived the war and what
further had befallen his vast estates he did not know. Wan-
dering tribes of natives, or raiding bands of Arab slavers

might have completed the demolition inaugurated by the Hun, and it was likely, too, that the jungle had swept up and reclaimed its own, covering his clearings and burying amidst its riot of lush verdure every sign of man's brief trespass upon its world-old preserves.

Following the adoption of the tiny Numa, Tarzan was compelled to an immediate consideration of the needs of his *protégé* in planning his marches and his halts, for the cub must have sustenance and that sustenance could be naught but milk. Lion's milk was out of the question, but fortunately they were now in a comparatively well peopled country where villages were not infrequent and where the great Lord of the Jungle was known, feared, and respected, and so it was that upon the afternoon of the day he had found the young lion Tarzan approached a village for the purpose of obtaining milk for the cub.

At first the natives appeared sullen and indifferent, looking with contempt upon whites who traveled without a large safari—with contempt and without fear. With no safari these strangers could carry no presents for them, nor anything wherewith to repay for the food they would doubtless desire, and with no askari they could not demand food, or rather they could not enforce an order, nor could they protect themselves should it seem worth while to molest them. Sullen and indifferent the natives seemed, yet they were scarce unconcerned, their curiosity being aroused by the unusual apparel and ornamentation of these whites. They saw them almost as naked as themselves and armed similarly except that one, the younger man, carried a rifle. All three wore the trappings of Pal-ul-don, primitive and barbaric, and entirely strange to the eyes of the simple blacks.

"Where is your chief?" asked Tarzan as he strode into the village amongst the women, the children, and the yapping dogs.

A few dozing warriors rose from the shadows of the huts where they had been lying and approached the newcomers.

"The chief sleeps," replied one. "Who are you to awaken him? What do you want?"

"I wish to speak to your chief. Go and fetch him!"

The warrior looked at him in wide-eyed amaze, and then broke into a loud laugh.

"The chief must be brought to him," he cried, addressing his fellows, and then, laughing loudly, he slapped his thigh and nudged those nearest him with his elbows.

"Tell him," continued the ape-man, "that Tarzan would speak with him."

Instantly the attitude of his auditors underwent a remarkable transformation—they fell back from him and they ceased laughing—their eyes very wide and round. He who had laughed loudest became suddenly solemn. "Bring mats," he cried, "for Tarzan and his people to sit upon, while I fetch Umanga the chief," and off he ran as fast as he could as though glad of the excuse to escape the presence of the mighty one he feared he had offended.

It made no difference now that they had no safari, no askari, nor any presents. The villagers were vying with one another to do them honor. Even before the chief came many had already brought presents of food and ornaments. Presently Umanga appeared. He was an old man who had been a chief even before Tarzan of the Apes was born. His manner was patriarchal and dignified and he greeted his guest as one great man might greet another, yet he was undeniably pleased that the Lord of the Jungle had honored his village with a visit.

When Tarzan explained his wishes and exhibited the lion cub Umanga assured him that there would be milk a-plenty so long as Tarzan honored them with his presence—warm milk, fresh from the chief's own goats. As they palavered the apeman's keen eyes took in every detail of the village and its people, and presently they alighted upon a large bitch among the numerous curs that overran the huts and the street. Her udder was swollen with milk and the sight of it suggested a plan to Tarzan. He jerked a thumb in the direction of the animal. "I would buy her," he said to Umanga.

"She is yours, Bwana, without payment," replied the chief. "She whelped two days since and last night her pups were all stolen from her nest, doubtless by a great snake; but if you will accept them I will give you instead as many younger and fatter dogs as you wish, for I am sure that this one would prove poor eating."

"I do not wish to eat her," replied Tarzan. "I will take her along with me to furnish milk for the cub. Have her brought to me."

Some boys then caught the animal and tying a thong about its neck dragged it to the ape-man. Like the lion, the dog was at first afraid, for the scent of the Tarmangani was not as the scent of the blacks, and it snarled and snapped at its new master; but at length he won the animal's confidence so that it lay quietly beside him while he stroked its head. To get the lion close to it was, however, another matter, for here both were terrified by the enemy scent of the other—the lion snarling and spitting and the dog bare-fanged and growling. It required patience—infinite patience —but at last the thing was an accomplished fact and the cur bitch suckled the son of Numa. Hunger had succeeded in overcoming the natural suspicion of the lion, while the firm yet kindly attitude of the ape-man had won the confidence of the canine, which had been accustomed through life to more of cuffs and kicks than kindness.

That night Tarzan had the dog tied in the hut he occupied, and twice before morning he made her lie while the cub fed. The next day they took leave of Umanga and his people and with the dog still upon a leash trotting beside them they set off once more toward home, the young lion cuddled in the hollow of one of Tarzan's arms or carried in a sack slung across his shoulder.

They named the lion Jad-bal-ja, which in the language of the pithecanthropi of Pal-ul-don, means the Golden Lion, because of his color. Every day he became more accustomed to them and to his foster mother, who finally came to accept him as flesh of her flesh. The bitch they called Za, meaning girl. The second day they removed her leash and she followed them willingly through the jungle, nor ever after did she seek to leave them, nor was happy unless she was near one of the three.

As the moment approached when the trail should break from the jungle onto the edge of the rolling plain where their home had been, the three were filled with suppressed excitement, though none uttered a syllable of the hope and fear that was in the heart of each. What would they find? What *could* they find other than the same tangled mass of vegetation that the ape-man had cleared away to build his home when first he had come there with his bride?

At last they stepped from the concealing verdure of the forest to look out across the plain where, in the distance, the outlines of the bungalow had once been clearly discernible nestled amidst the trees and shrubs that had been retained or imported to beautify the grounds.

"Look!" cried Lady Jane. "It is there—it is still there!"

"But what are those other things to the left, beyond it?" asked Korak.

"They are the huts of natives," replied Tarzan.

"The fields are being cultivated!" exclaimed the woman.

"And some of the outbuildings have been rebuilt," said Tarzan. "It can mean but one thing—the Waziri have come back from the war—my faithful Waziri. They have restored what the Hun destroyed and are watching over our home until we return."

2

The Training of Jad-bal-ja

AND so Tarzan of the Apes, and Jane Clayton, and Korak came home after a long absence and with them came Jad-bal-ja, the golden lion, and Za, the bitch. Among the first to meet them and to welcome them home was old Muviro, father of Wasimbu, who had given his life in defense of the home and wife of the ape-man.

"Ah, Bwana," cried the faithful black, "my old eyes are made young again by the sight of you. It has been long that you have been gone, but though many doubted that you would return, old Muviro knew that the great world held nothing that might overcome his master. And so he knew, too, that his master would return to the home of his love and the land where his faithful Waziri awaited him; but that she, whom we have mourned as dead, should have returned is beyond belief, and great shall be the rejoicing in the huts of the Waziri tonight. And the earth shall tremble to the dancing feet of the warriors and the heavens ring with the glad cries of their women, since the three they love most on earth have come back to them."

And in truth, great indeed was the rejoicing in the huts of the Waziri. And not for one night alone, but for many nights did the dancing and the rejoicing continue until Tarzan was compelled to put a stop to the festivities that he and his family might gain a few hours of unbroken slumber. The ape-man found that not only had his faithful Waziri, under the equally faithful guidance of his English foreman, Jervis, completely rehabilitated his stables, corrals, and outbuildings as well as the native huts, but had restored the interior of the bungalow, so that in all outward appearances the place was precisely as it had been before the raid of the Germans. Jervis was at Nairobi on the business of the estate, and it was some days after their arrival that he returned to the ranch. His surprise and happiness were no less genuine than those of the Waziri. With the chief and warriors he sat for hours at the feet of the Big Bwana, listening to an account of the strange land of Pal-ul-don and the adventures that had befallen the three during Lady Greystoke's captivity there, and with the Waziri he marveled at the queer pets the ape-man had brought back with him. That Tarzan might have fancied a mongrel native cur was strange enough, but that he should have adopted a cub of his hereditary enemies, Numa and Sabor, seemed beyond all belief. And equally surprising to them all was the manner of Tarzan's education of the cub.

The golden lion and his foster mother occupied a corner of the ape-man's bedroom, and many was the hour each day that he spent in training and educating the little spotted, yellow ball—all playfulness and affection now, but one day to grow into a great, savage beast of prey.

As the days passed and the golden lion grew, Tarzan taught it many tricks—to fetch and carry, to lie motionless in hiding at his almost inaudible word of command, to move from point to point as he indicated, to hunt for hidden things by scent and to retrieve them, and when meat was added to its diet he fed it always in a way that brought grim smiles to the savage lips of the Waziri warriors, for Tarzan had built for him a dummy in the semblance of a man and the meat that the lion was to eat was fastened always at the throat of the dummy. Never did the manner of feeding vary. At a word from the ape-man the golden lion would crouch, belly to the ground, and then Tarzan would point at the dummy and whisper the single word "kill." However hungry he might be, the lion learned never to move toward his meat until that single word had been uttered by its master; and then with a rush and a savage growl it drove straight for the flesh. While it was little it had difficulty at first in clambering up the dummy to the savory morsel fastened at the figure's throat, but as it grew older and larger it gained the objective more easily, and finally a single leap would carry it to its goal and down would go the dummy upon its back with the young lion tearing at its throat.

There was one lesson that, of all the others, was most difficult to learn and it is doubtful that any other than Tarzan of the Apes, reared by beasts, among beasts, could have overcome the savage blood-lust of the carnivore and rendered his natural instinct subservient to the will of his master. It took weeks and months of patient endeavor to accomplish this single item of the lion's education, which consisted in teaching him that at the word "fetch" he must find any indicated object and return with it to his master, even the dummy with raw meat tied at its throat, and that he must not touch the meat nor harm the dummy nor any other article that he was fetching, but place them carefully at the ape-man's feet. Afterward he learned always to be sure of his reward, which usually consisted in a double portion of the meat that he loved best.

Lady Greystoke and Korak were often interested spectators of the education of the golden lion, though the former expressed mystification as to the purpose of such elaborate training of the young cub and some misgivings as to the wisdom of the ape-man's program.

"What in the world can you do with such a brute after he is grown?" she asked. "He bids fair to be a mighty Numa. Being accustomed to men he will be utterly fearless of them, and having fed always at the throat of a dummy he will look there at the throat of living men for his food hereafter."

"He will feed only upon what I tell him to feed," replied the ape-man.

"But you do not expect him to feed always upon men?" she interrogated, laughingly.

"He will never feed upon men."

"But how can you prevent it, having taught him from cub-hood always to feed upon men?"

"I am afraid, Jane, that you under-estimate the intelligence of a lion, or else I very much over-estimate it. If your theory is correct the hardest part of my work is yet before me, but if I am right it is practically complete now. However, we will experiment a bit and see which is right. We shall take Jad-bal-ja out upon the plain with us this afternoon. Game is plentiful and we shall have no difficulty in ascertaining just how much control I have over young Numa after all."

"I'll wager a hundred pounds," said Korak, laughing, "that he does just what he jolly well pleases after he gets a taste of live blood."

"You're on, my son," said the ape-man. "I think I am going to show you and your mother this afternoon what you or anyone else never dreamed could be accomplished."

"Lord Greystoke, the world's premier animal trainer!" cried Lady Greystoke, and Tarzan joined them in their laughter.

"It is not animal training," said the ape-man. "The plan upon which I work would be impossible to anyone but Tarzan of the Apes. Let us take a hypothetical case to illustrate what I mean. There comes to you some creature whom you hate, whom by instinct and heredity you consider a deadly enemy. You are afraid of him. You understand no word that he speaks. Finally, by means sometimes brutal he impresses upon your mind his wishes. You may do the thing he wants, but do you do it with a spirit of unselfish loyalty? You do not—you do it under compulsion, hating the creature that forces his will upon you. At any moment that you felt it was in your power to do so, you would disobey him. You would even go further—you would turn upon him and destroy him. On the other hand, there comes to you one with whom you are familiar; he is a friend, a protector. He understands and speaks the language that you understand and speak. He has fed you, he has gained your confidence by kindness and protection, he asks you to do something for him. Do you refuse? No, you obey willingly. It is thus that the golden lion will obey me."

"As long as it suits his purpose to do so," commented Korak.

"Let me go a step farther then," said the ape-man. "Suppose that this creature, whom you love and obey, has the power to punish, even to kill you, if it is necessary so to do to enforce his commands. How then about your obedience?"

"We'll see," said Korak, "how easily the golden lion will make one hundred pounds for me."

That afternoon they set out across the plain, Jad-bal-ja following Tarzan's horse's heels. They dismounted at a little clump of trees some distance from the bungalow and from there proceeded onward warily toward a swale in which antelopes were usually to be found, moving up which they came cautiously to the heavy brush that bordered the swale upon their side. There was Tarzan, Jane, and Korak, and close beside Tarzan the golden lion—four jungle hunters—and of the four Jad-bal-ja, the lion, was the least accomplished. Stealthily they crawled through the brush, scarce a leaf rustling to their passage, until at last they looked down into the swale upon a small herd of antelope grazing peacefully below. Closest to them was an old buck, and him Tarzan pointed out in some mysterious manner to Jad-bal-ja.

"Fetch him," he whispered, and the golden lion rumbled a scarce audible acknowledgment of the command.

Stealthily he worked his way through the brush. The antelopes fed on, unsuspecting. The distance separating the lion from his prey was over great for a successful charge, and so Jad-bal-ja waited, hiding in the brush, until the antelope should either graze closer to him or turn its back toward him. No sound came from the four watching the grazing herbivora, nor did the latter give any indication of a suspicion of the nearness of danger. The old buck moved closer to Jad-bal-ja. Almost imperceptibly the lion was gathering for the charge. The only noticeable movement was the twitching of his tail's tip, and then, as lightning from the sky, as an arrow from a bow, he shot from immobility to tremendous speed in an instant. He was almost upon the buck before the latter realized the proximity of danger, and then it was too late, for scarcely had the antelope wheeled than the lion rose upon its hind legs and seized it, while the balance of the herd broke into precipitate flight.

"Now," said Korak, "we shall see."

"He will bring the antelope to me," said Tarzan confidently.

The golden lion hesitated a moment, growling over the carcass of his kill. Then he seized it by the back and with his head turned to one side dragged it along the ground beside him, as he made his way slowly back toward Tarzan. Through the brush he dragged the slain antelope until he had dropped it at the feet of his master, where he stood, looking up at the face of the ape-man with an expression that could not have been construed into aught but pride in his achievement and a plea for commendation.

Tarzan stroked his head and spoke to him in a low voice, praising him, and then, drawing his hunting knife, he cut the jugular of the antelope and let the blood from the carcass. Jane and Korak stood close, watching Jad-bal-ja—what would the lion do with the smell of fresh, hot blood in his nostrils? He sniffed at it and growled, and with bared fangs he eyed the three wickedly. The ape-man pushed him away with his open palm and the lion growled again angrily and snapped at him.

Quick is Numa, quick is Bara, the deer, but Tarzan of the Apes is lightning. So swiftly did he strike, and so heavily, that Jad-bal-ja was falling on his back almost in the very instant that he had growled at his master. Swiftly he came to his feet again and the two stood facing one another.

"Down!" commanded the ape-man. "Lie down, Jad-bal-ja!" His voice was low and firm. The lion hesitated but for an instant, and then lay down as Tarzan of the Apes had taught him to do at the word of command. Tarzan turned and lifted the carcass of the antelope to his shoulder.

"Come," he said to Jad-bal-ja. "Heel!" and without another glance at the carnivore he moved off toward the horses.

"I might have known it," said Korak, with a laugh, "and saved my hundred pounds."

"Of course you might have known it," said his mother.

3

A Meeting of Mystery

A RATHER attractive-looking, though over-dressed, young woman was dining in a second-rate chop-house in London. She was noticeable, not so much for her fine figure and coarsely beautiful face as for the size and appearance of her companion, a large, well-proportioned man in the mid-twenties, with such a tremendous beard that it gave him the appearance of hiding in ambush. He stood fully three inches over six feet. His shoulders were broad, his chest deep, and his hips narrow. His physique, his carriage, everything about him, suggested indubitably the trained athlete.

The two were in close conversation, a conversation that occasionally gave every evidence of bordering upon heated argument.

"I tell you," said the man, "that I do not see what we need of the others. Why should they share with us—why divide into six portions that which you and I might have alone?"

"It takes money to carry the plan through," she replied, "and neither you nor I have any money. *They* have it and they will back us with it—me for my knowledge and you for your appearance and your strength. They searched for you, Esteban, for two years, and, now that they have found you, I should not care to be in your shoes if you betrayed them. They would just as soon slit your throat as not, Esteban, if they no more than thought they couldn't use you, now that you have all the details of their plan. But if you should try to take all the profit from them—" She paused, shrugging her shoulders. "No, my dear, I love life too well to join you in any such conspiracy as that."

"But I tell you, Flora, we ought to get more out of it than they want to give. You furnish all the knowledge and I take all the risk—why shouldn't we have more than a sixth apiece?"

"Talk to them yourself, then, Esteban," said the girl, with a shrug, "but if you will take my advice you will be satisfied with what you are offered. Not only have I the information, without which they can do nothing, but I found you into the bargain, yet I do not ask it all—I shall be perfectly satisfied with one-sixth, and I can assure you that if you do not muddle the thing, one-sixth of what you bring out will be enough for any one of us for the rest of his natural life."

The man did not seem convinced, and the young woman had a feeling that he would bear watching. Really, she knew very little about him, and had seen him in person only a few times since her first discovery of him some two months before, upon the screen of a London cinema house in a spectacular feature in which he had played the rôle of a Roman soldier of the Pretorian Guard.

Here his heroic size and perfect physique had alone entitled him to consideration, for his part was a minor one, and doubtless of all the thousands who saw him upon the silver sheet Flora Hawkes was the only one who took more than a passing interest in him, and her interest was aroused, not by his histrionic ability, but rather because for some two years she and her confederates had been searching for such a type as Esteban Miranda so admirably represented. To find him in the flesh bade fair to prove difficult of accomplishment, but after a month of seemingly fruitless searching she finally discovered him among a score of extra men at the studio of one of London's lesser producing companies. She needed no other credentials than her good looks to form his acquaintance, and while that was ripening into intimacy she made no mention to him of the real purpose of her association with him.

That he was a Spaniard and apparently of good family was evident to her, and that he was unscrupulous was to be guessed by the celerity with which he agreed to take part in the shady transaction that had been conceived in the mind of Flora Hawkes, and the details of which had been perfected by her and her four confederates. So, therefore, knowing that he was unscrupulous, she was aware that every precaution must be taken to prevent him taking advantage of the knowledge of their plan that he must one day have in detail, the key to which she, up to the present moment, had kept entirely to herself, not even confiding it to any one of her four other confederates.

They sat for a moment in silence, toying with the empty glasses from which they had been drinking. Presently she looked up to find his gaze fixed upon her and an expression in his eyes that even a less sophisticated woman than Flora Hawkes might readily have interpreted.

"You can make me do anything you want, Flora," he said, "for when I am with you I forget the gold, and think only of that other reward which you continually deny me, but which one day I shall win."

"Love and business do not mix well," replied the girl. "Wait until you have succeeded in this work, Esteban, and then we may talk of love."

"You do not love me," he whispered, hoarsely. "I know—I have seen—that each of the others loves you. That is why I could hate them. And if I thought that you loved one of them, I could cut his heart out. Sometimes I have thought that you did—first one of them and then another. You are too familiar with them, Flora. I have seen John Peebles squeeze your hand when he thought no one was looking, and when you dance with Dick Throck he holds you too close and you dance cheek to cheek. I tell you I do not like it, Flora, and one of these days I shall forget all about the gold and think only of you, and then something will happen and there will not be so many to divide the ingots that I shall bring back from Africa. And Bluber and Kraski are almost as bad; perhaps Kraski is the worst of all, for he is a good-looking devil and I do not like the way in which you cast sheep's eyes at him."

The fire of growing anger was leaping to the girl's eyes. With an angry gesture she silenced him.

"What business is it of yours, *Señor* Miranda, who I choose for my friends, or how I treat them or how they treat me? I will have you understand that I have known these men for years, while I have known you for but a few weeks, and if any has a right to dictate my behavior, which, thank God, none has, it would be one of them rather than you."

His eyes blazed angrily.

"It is as I thought!" he cried. "You love one of them." He half rose from the table and leaned across it toward her, menacingly. "Just let me find out which one it is and I will cut him into pieces!"

He ran his fingers through his long, black hair until it stood up on end like the mane of an angry lion. His eyes were blazing with a light that sent a chill of dread through the girl's heart. He appeared a man temporarily bereft of reason—if he were not a maniac he most certainly looked one, and the girl was afraid and realized that she must placate him.

"Come, come, Esteban," she whispered softly, "there is no need for working yourself into a towering rage over nothing. I have not said that I loved one of these, nor have I said that I do not love you, but I am not used to being wooed in such fashion. Perhaps your Spanish *señoritas* like it, but I am an English girl and if you love me treat me as an English lover would treat me."

"You have not said that you loved one of these others— no, but on the other hand you have not said that you do not love one of them—tell me, Flora, which one of them is it that you love?"

His eyes were still blazing, and his great frame trembling with suppressed passion.

"I do not love any of them, Esteban," she replied, "nor, as yet, do I love you. But I could, Esteban, that much I will tell you. I could love you, Esteban, as I could never love another, but I shall not permit myself to do so until after you have returned and we are free to live where and how we like. Then, maybe—but, even so, I do not promise."

"You had better promise," he said, sullenly, though evidently somewhat mollified. "You had better promise, Flora, for I care nothing for the gold if I may not have you also."

"Hush," she cautioned, "here they come now, and it is about time; they are fully a half-hour late."

The man turned his eyes in the direction of her gaze, and the two sat watching the approach of four men who had just entered the chop-house. Two of them were evidently Englishmen—big, meaty fellows of the middle class, who looked what they really were, former pugilists; the third, Adolph Bluber, was a short, fat German, with a round, red face and a bull neck; the other, the youngest of the four, was by far the best looking. His smooth face, clear complexion, and large dark eyes might of themselves have proven sufficient grounds for Miranda's jealousy, but supplementing these were a mop of wavy, brown hair, the figure of a Greek god and the grace of a Russian dancer, which, in truth, was what Carl Kraski was when he chose to be other than a rogue.

The girl greeted the four pleasantly, while the Spaniard vouchsafed them but a single, surly nod, as they found chairs and seated themselves at the table.

"Ale!" cried Peebles, pounding the table to attract the attention of a waiter, "let's 'ave ale."

The suggestion met with unanimous approval, and as they waited for their drink they spoke casually of unimportant things; the heat, the circumstance that had delayed them, the trivial occurrences since they had last met; throughout which Esteban sat in sullen silence, but after the waiter had returned and they drank to Flora, with which ceremony it had long been their custom to signalize each gathering, they got down to business.

"Now," cried Peebles, pounding the table with his meaty fist, " 'ere we are, and that's that! We 'ave everything, Flora —the plans, the money, *Señor* Miranda—and are jolly well ready, old dear, for your part of it."

"How much money have you?" asked Flora. "It is going to take a lot of money, and there is no use starting unless you have plenty to carry on with."

Peebles turned to Bluber. "There," he said, pointing a pudgy finger at him, "is the bloomin' treasurer. 'E can tell you 'ow much we 'ave, the fat rascal of a Dutchman."

Bluber smiled an oily smile and rubbed his fat palms together. "Vell," he said, "how much you t'ink, Miss Flora, ve should have?"

"Not less than two thousand pounds to be on the safe side," she replied quickly.

"*Ach, weh!*" exclaimed Bluber. "But dat is a lot of money —two t'ousand pounds."

The girl made a gesture of disgust. "I told you in the first place that I wouldn't have anything to do with a bunch of cheap screws, and that until you had enough money to carry the thing out properly I would not give you the maps and directions, without which you cannot hope to reach the vaults, where there is stored enough gold to buy this whole, tight, little island if half that what I have heard them say about it is true. You can go along and spend your own money, but you've got to show me that you have at least two thousand pounds to spend before I give up the information that will make you the richest men in the world."

"The blighter's got the money," growled Throck. "Blime if I know what he's beefin' about."

"He can't help it," growled the Russian, "he's that kind of chap; Bluber would try to bargain with the marriage license clerk if he were going to get married."

"Oh, vell," sighed Bluber, "for vy should we spend more money than is necessary? If ve can do it for von t'ousand pounds so much the better."

"Certainly," snapped the girl, "and if it doesn't take but one thousand, that is all that you will have to spend, but you've got to have the two thousand in case of emergencies, and from what I have seen of that country you are likely to run up against more emergencies than anything else."

"*Ach, weh!*" cried Bluber.

"'E's got the money all right," said Peebles, "now let's get busy."

"He may have it, but I want to see it first," replied the girl.

"Vat you t'ink; I carry all dat money around in my pocket?" cried Bluber.

"Can't you take our word for it?" grumbled Throck.

"You're a nice bunch of crooks to ask me that," she replied, laughing in the face of the burly ruffians. "I'll take Carl's word for it, though; if he tells me that you have it, and that it is in such shape that it can, and will, be used to pay all the necessary expenses of our expedition, I will believe him."

Peebles and Throck scowled angrily, and Miranda's eyes closed to two narrow, nasty slits, as he directed his gaze upon the Russian. Bluber, on the contrary, was affected not at all; the more he was insulted, the better, apparently, he liked it. Toward one who treated him with consideration or respect he would have become arrogant, while he fawned upon the hand that struck him. Kraski, alone, smiled a self-satisfied smile that set the blood of the Spaniard boiling.

"Bluber has the money, Flora," he said; "each of us has contributed his share. We'll make Bluber treasurer, because we know that he will squeeze the last farthing until it shrieks before he will let it escape him. It is our plan now to set out from London in pairs."

He drew a map from his pocket, and unfolding it, spread it out upon the table before them. With his finger he indicated a point marked X. "Here we will meet and here we will equip our expedition. Bluber and Miranda will go first; then Peebles and Throck. By the time that you and I arrive everything will be in shape for moving immediately into the interior, where we shall establish a permanent camp, off the beaten track and as near our objective as possible. Miranda will disport himself behind his whiskers until he is ready to set out upon the final stage of his long journey. I understand that he is well schooled in the part that he is to play and that he can depict the character to perfection. As he will have only ignorant natives and wild beasts to deceive it should not tax his histrionic ability too greatly." There was a veiled note of sarcasm in the soft, drawling tone that caused the black eyes of the Spaniard to gleam wickedly.

"Do I understand," asked Miranda, his soft tone belying his angry scowl, "that you and Miss Hawkes travel alone to X?"

"You do, unless your understanding is poor," replied the Russian.

The Spaniard half rose from the table and leaned across it menacingly toward Kraski. The girl, who was sitting next to him, seized his coat.

"None of that!" she said, dragging him back into his chair. "There has been too much of it among you already, and if there is any more I shall cut you all and seek more congenial companions for my expedition."

"Yes, cut it out; 'ere we are, and that's that!" exclaimed Peebles belligerently.

"John's right," rumbled Throck, in his deep bass, "and I'm here to back him up. And if there is any more of it, blime if I don't bash a couple of you pretty 'uns," and he looked first at Miranda and then at Kraski.

"Now," soothed Bluber, "let's all shake hands and be good friends."

"Right-o," cried Peebles, "that's the talk. Give 'im your 'and, Esteban. Come, Carl, bury the 'atchet. We can't start in on this thing with no hanimosities, and 'ere we are, and that's that."

The Russian, feeling secure in his position with Flora, and therefore in a magnanimous mood, extended his hand across the table toward the Spaniard. For a moment Esteban hesitated.

"Come, man, shake!" growled Throck, "or you can go back to your job as an extra man, blime, and we'll find some-one else to do your work and divvy the swag with."

Suddenly the dark countenance of the Spaniard was lighted by a pleasant smile. He extended his hand quickly and clasped Kraski's. "Forgive me," he said, "I am hot-tempered, but I mean nothing. Miss Hawkes is right, we must all be friends, and here's my hand on it, Kraski, as far as I am concerned."

"Good," said Kraski, "and I am sorry if I offended you;" but he forgot that the other was an actor, and if he could have seen into the depths of that dark soul he would have shuddered.

"Und now, dat we are all good friends," said Bluber, rubbing his hands together unctuously, "vy not arrange for vhen ve shall commence starting to finish up everyt'ings? Miss Flora, she gives me the map und der directions und we start commencing immediately."

"Loan me a pencil, Carl," said the girl, and when the man had handed her one she searched out a spot upon the map some distance into the interior from X, where she drew a tiny circle. "This is O," she said. "When we all reach here you shall have the final directions and not before."

Bluber threw up his hands. "*Ach!* Miss Flora, vat you t'ink, ve spend two t'ousand pounds to buy a pig in a poke? *Ach, weh!* you vouldn't ask us to do dat? Ve must see everyt'ing, ve must know everyt'ing before ve spend vun farthing."

"Yes, and 'ere we are, and that's that!" roared John Peebles, striking the table with his fist.

The girl rose leisurely from her seat. "Oh, very well," she said with a shrug. "If you feel that way about it we might as well call it all off."

"Oh, vait, vait, Miss Flora," cried Bluber, rising hurriedly. "Don't be ogcited. But can't you see vere ve are? Two t'ousand pounds is a lot of money, and ve are good business men. Ve shouldn't be spending it all vit'out getting not'ings for it."

"I am not asking you to spend it and get nothing for it," replied the girl, tartly; "but if anyone has got to trust anyone else in this outfit, it is you who are going to trust me. If I give you all the information I have, there is nothing in the world that could prevent you from going ahead and leaving me out in the cold, and I don't intend that that shall happen."

"But we are not fools, Miss Flora," insisted Bluber. "Ve vould not t'ink for vun minute of cheating you."

"You're not angels, either, Bluber, any of you," retorted the girl. "If you want to go ahead with this you've got to do it in my way, and I am going to be there at the finish to see that I get what is coming to me. You've taken my word for it, up to the present time, that I had the dope, and now you've got to take it the rest of the way or all bets are off. What good would it do me to go over into a bally jungle and suffer all the hardships that we are bound to suffer, dragging you along with me, if I were not going to be able to deliver the goods when I got there? And I am not such a softy as to think I could get away with it with a bunch of bandits like you if I tried to put anything of that kind over on you. And as long as I do play straight I feel perfectly safe, for I know that either Esteban or Carl will look after me, and I don't know but what the rest of you would, too. Is it a go or isn't it?"

"Vell, John, vot do you und Dick t'ink?" asked Bluber, addressing the two ex-prize-fighters. "Carl, I know he vill t'ink vhatever Flora t'inks. Hey? Vat?"

"Blime," said Throck, "I never was much of a hand at

trusting nobody unless I had to, but it looks now as though we had to trust Flora."

"Same 'ere," said John Peebles. "If you try any funny work, Flora—" He made a significant movement with his finger across his throat.

"I understand, John," said the girl with a smile, "and I know that you would do it as quickly for two pounds as you would for two thousand. But you are all agreed, then, to carry on according to my plans? You too, Carl?"

The Russian nodded. "Whatever the rest say goes with me," he remarked.

And so the gentle little coterie discussed their plans in so far as they could—each minutest detail that would be necessary to place them all at the O which the girl had drawn upon the map.

4

What the Footprints Told

WHEN Jad-bal-ja, the golden lion, was two years old, he was as magnificent a specimen of his kind as the Greystokes had ever looked upon. In size he was far above the average of that attained by mature males; in conformation he was superb, his noble head and his great black mane giving him the appearance of a full-grown male, while in intelligence he far outranked his savage brothers of the forest.

Jad-bal-ja was a never-ending source of pride and delight to the ape-man who had trained him so carefully, and nourished him cunningly for the purpose of developing to the full all the latent powers within him. The lion no longer slept at the foot of his master's bed, but occupied a strong cage that Tarzan had constructed for him at the rear of the bungalow, for who knew better than the ape-man that a lion, wherever he may be or however he may have been raised, is yet a lion—a savage flesh-eater. For the first year he had roamed at will about the house and grounds; after that he went abroad only in the company of Tarzan. Often the two roamed the plain and the jungle hunting together. In a way the lion was almost equally as familiar with Jane and Korak, and neither of them feared or mistrusted him, but toward Tarzan of the Apes did he show the greatest affection. The blacks of Tarzan's household he tolerated, nor did he ever offer to molest any of the domestic animals or fowl, after Tarzan had impressed upon him in his early cubhood that appropriate punishment followed immediately upon any predatory excursion into the corrals or henhouses. The fact that he was never permitted to become ravenously hungry was doubtless the deciding factor in safeguarding the live stock of the farm.

The man and the beast seemed to understand one another perfectly. It is doubtful that the lion understood all that Tarzan said to him, but be that as it may the ease with which he communicated his wishes to the lion bordered upon the uncanny. The obedience that a combination of sternness and affection had elicited from the cub had become largely habit in the grown lion. At Tarzan's command he would go to great distances and bring back antelope or zebra, laying his kill at his master's feet without offering to taste the flesh himself, and he had even retrieved living animals without harming them. Such, then, was the golden lion that roamed the primeval forest with his godlike master.

It was at about this time that there commenced to drift in to the ape-man rumors of a predatory band to the west and south of his estate; ugly stories of ivory-raiding, slave-running and torture, such as had not disturbed the quiet of the ape-man's savage jungle since the days of Sheik Amor Ben Khatour, and there came other tales, too, that caused Tarzan of the Apes to pucker his brows in puzzlement and thought, and then a month elapsed during which Tarzan heard no more of the rumors from the west.

The war had reduced the resources of the Greystokes to but a meager income. They had given practically all to the cause of the Allies, and now what little had remained to them had been all but exhausted in the rehabilitation of Tarzan's African estate.

"It looks very much, Jane," he said to his wife one night, "as though another trip to Opar were on the books."

"I dread to think of it. I do not want you to go," she said. "You have come away from that awful city twice, but barely with your life. The third time you may not be so fortunate. We have enough, John, to permit us to live here in comfort and in happiness. Why jeopardize those two things which are greater than all wealth in another attempt to raid the treasure vaults?"

"There is no danger, Jane," he assured her. "The last time Werper dogged my footsteps, and between him and the earthquake I was nearly done for. But there is no chance of any such combination of circumstances thwarting me again."

"You will not go alone, John?" she asked. "You will take Korak with you?"

"No," he said, "I shall not take him. He must remain here with you, for really my long absences are more dangerous to you than to me. I shall take fifty of the Waziri, as porters, to carry the gold, and thus we should be able to bring out enough to last us for a long time."

"And Jad-bal-ja," she asked, "shall you take him?"

"No, he had better remain here; Korak can look after him and take him out for a hunt occasionally. I am going to travel light and fast and it would be too hard a trip for him —lions don't care to move around too much in the hot sun, and as we shall travel mostly by day I doubt if Jad-bal-ja would last long."

And so it befell that Tarzan of the Apes set out once more upon the long trail that leads to Opar. Behind him marched fifty giant Waziri, the pick of the warlike tribe that had adopted Tarzan as its Chief. Upon the veranda of the bungalow stood Jane and Korak waving their adieux, while from the rear of the building there came to the ape-man's ears the rumbling roar of Jad-bal-ja, the golden lion. And as they marched away the voice of Numa accompanied them out upon the rolling plain, until at last it trailed off to nothingness in the distance.

His speed determined by that of the slowest of the blacks, Tarzan made but comparatively rapid progress. Opar lay a good twenty-five days' trek from the farm for men traveling light, as were these, but upon the return journey, laden as they would be with the ingots of gold, their progress would be slower. And because of this the ape-man had allotted two months for the venture. His safari, consisting of seasoned warriors only, permitted of really rapid progress. They carried no supplies, for they were all hunters and were moving through a country in which game was abundant—no need then for burdening themselves with the cumbersome inpedimenta of white huntsmen.

A thorn boma and a few leaves furnished their shelter for the night, while spears and arrows and the powers of their great white chief insured that their bellies would never go empty. With the picked men that he had brought with him

Tarzan expected to make the trip to Opar in twenty-one days, though had he been traveling alone he would have moved two or three times as fast, since, when Tarzan elected to travel with speed, he fairly flew through the jungle, equally at home in it by day or by night and practically tireless.

It was on a mid-afternoon the third week of the march that Tarzan, ranging far ahead of his blacks in search of game, came suddenly upon the carcass of Bara, the deer, a feathered arrow protruding from its flank. It was evident that Bara had been wounded at some little distance from where it had lain down to die, for the location of the missile indicated that the wound could not have caused immediate death. But what particularly caught the attention of the ape-man, even before he had come close enough to make a minute examination, was the design of the arrow, and immediately he withdrew it from the body of the deer he knew it for what it was, and was filled with such wonderment as might come to you or to me were we to see a native Swazi headdress upon Broadway or the Strand, for the arrow was precisely such as one may purchase in most any sporting-goods house in any large city of the world—such an arrow as is sold and used for archery practice in the parks and suburbs. Nothing could have been more incongruous than this silly toy in the heart of savage Africa, and yet that it had done its work effectively was evident by the dead body of Bara, though the ape-man guessed that the shaft had been sped by no practiced, savage hand.

Tarzan's curiosity was aroused and also his inherent jungle caution. One must know his jungle well to survive long in it, and if one would know it well he must let no unusual occurrence or circumstance go unexplained. And so it was that Tarzan set out upon the back track of Bara for the purpose of ascertaining, if possible, the nature of Bara's slayer. The bloody spoor was easily followed and the ape-man wondered why it was that the hunter had not tracked and overtaken his quarry, which had evidently been dead since the previous day. He found that Bara had traveled far, and the sun was already low in the west before Tarzan came upon the first indications of the slayer of the animal. These were in the nature of footprints that filled him with quite as much surprise as had the arrow. He examined them carefully, and, stooping low, even sniffed at them with his sensitive nostrils. Improbable, nay impossible though it seemed, the naked footprints were those of *a white man*—a large man, probably as large as Tarzan himself. As the foster-son of

Kala stood gazing upon the spoor of the mysterious stranger he ran the fingers of one hand through his thick, black hair in a characteristic gesture indicative of deep puzzlement.

What naked white man could there be in Tarzan's jungle who slew Tarzan's game with the pretty arrow of an archery club? It was incredible that there should be such a one, and yet there recurred to the ape-man's mind the vague rumors that he had heard weeks before. Determined to solve the mystery he set out now upon the trail of the stranger—an erratic trail which wound about through the jungle, apparently aimlessly, prompted, Tarzan guessed, by the ignorance of an inexperienced hunter. But night fell before he had arrived at a solution of the riddle, and it was pitch dark as the ape-man turned his steps toward camp.

He knew that his Waziri would be expecting meat and it was not Tarzan's intention to disappoint them, though he then discovered that he was not the only carnivore hunting the district that night. The coughing grunt of a lion close by apprised him of it first, and then, from the distance, the deep roar of another. But of what moment was it to the ape-man that others hunted? It would not be the first time that he had pitted his cunning, his strength, and his agility against the other hunters of his savage world—both man and beast.

And so it was that Tarzan made his kill at last, snatching it almost from under the nose of a disappointed and infuriated lion—a fat antelope that the latter had marked as his own. Throwing his kill to his shoulder almost in the path of the charging Numa, the ape-man swung lightly to the lower terraces and with a taunting laugh for the infuriated cat, vanished noiselessly into the night.

He found the camp and his hungry Waziri without trouble, and so great was their faith in him that they not for a moment doubted but that he would return with meat for them.

Early the following morning Tarzan set out again toward Opar, and directing his Waziri to continue the march in the most direct way, he left them that he might pursue further his investigations of the mysterious presence in his jungle that the arrow and the footsteps had apprised him of. Coming again to the spot at which darkness had forced him to abandon his investigations, he took up the spoor of the stranger. Nor had he followed it far before he came upon further evidence of the presence of this new and malign personality—stretched before him in the trail was the body of a giant ape, one of the tribe of great anthropoids among whom Tarzan had been raised. Protruding from the hairy abdomen of the Mangani was another of the machine-made arrows of civilization. The ape-man's eyes narrowed and a scowl darkened his brow. Who was this who dared invade his sacred preserves and slaughter thus ruthlessly Tarzan's people?

A low growl rumbled in the throat of the ape-man. Sloughed with the habiliments of civilization was the thin veneer of civilization that Tarzan wore among white men. No English lord was this who looked upon the corpse of his hairy cousin, but another jungle beast in whose breast raged the unquenchable fire of suspicion and hatred for the man-thing that is the heritage of the jungle-bred. A beast of prey viewed the bloody work of ruthless man. Nor was there in the consciousness of Tarzan any acknowledgement of his blood relationship to the killer.

Realizing that the trail had been made upon the second day before, Tarzan hastened on in pursuit of the slayer. There was no doubt in his mind but that plain murder had been committed, for he was sufficiently familiar with the traits of the Mangani to know that none of them would provoke assault unless driven to it.

Tarzan was traveling up wind, and some half-hour after he had discovered the body of the ape his keen nostrils caught the scent-spoor of others of its kind. Knowing the timidity of these fierce denizens of the jungle he moved forward now with great wariness, lest, warned of his approach, they take flight before they were aware of his identity. He did not see them often, yet he knew that there were always those among them who recalled him, and that through these he could always establish amicable relations with the balance of the tribe.

Owing to the denseness of the undergrowth Tarzan chose the middle terraces for his advance, and here, swinging freely and swiftly among the leafy boughs, he came presently upon the giant anthropoids. There were about twenty of them in the band, and they were engaged, in a little natural clearing, in their never-ending search for caterpillars and beetles, which formed important items in the diet of the Mangani.

A faint smile overspread the ape-man's face as he paused upon a great branch, himself hidden by the leafy foliage about him, and watched the little band below him. Every action, every movement of the great apes, recalled vividly to Tarzan's mind the long years of his childhood, when, protected by the fierce mother-love of Kala, the she-ape, he had ranged the jungle with the tribe of Kerchak. In the romping young, he saw again Neeta and his other childhood playmates and in the adults all the great, savage brutes he had feared in youth and conquered in manhood. The ways of man may change but the ways of the ape are the same, yesterday, today and forever.

He watched them in silence for some minutes. How glad they would be to see him when they discovered his identity! For Tarzan of the Apes was known the length and the breadth of the great jungle as the friend and protector of the Mangani. At first they would growl at him and threaten him, for they would not depend solely on either their eyes or their ears for confirmation of his identity. Not until he had entered the clearing, and bristling bulls with bared fighting fangs had circled him stiffly until they had come close enough for their nostrils to verify the evidence of their eyes and ears, would they finally accept him. Then doubtless there would be great excitement for a few minutes, until, following the instincts of the ape mind, their attention was weaned from him by a blowing leaf, a caterpillar, or a bird's egg, and then they would move about their business, taking no further notice of him more than of any other member of the tribe. But this would not come until after each individual had smelled of him, and perhaps, pawed his flesh with calloused hands.

Now it was that Tarzan made a friendly sound of greeting, and as the apes looked up stepped from his concealment into plain view of them. "I am Tarzan of the Apes," he said, "mighty fighter, friend of the Mangani. Tarzan comes in friendship to his people," and with these words he dropped lightly to the lush grass of the clearing.

Instantly pandemonium reigned. Screaming warnings, the shes raced with the young for the opposite side of the clearing, while the bulls, bristling and growling, faced the intruder.

"Come," cried Tarzan, "do you not know me? I am Tarzan of the Apes, friend of the Mangani, son of Kala, and king of the tribe of Kerchak."

"We know you," growled one of the old bulls; "yesterday we saw you when you killed Gobu. Go away or we shall kill you."

"I did not kill Gobu," replied the ape-man. "I found his dead body yesterday and I was following the spoor of his slayer, when I came upon you."

"We saw you," repeated the old bull; "go away or we shall kill you. You are no longer the friend of the Mangani."

The ape-man stood with brows contracted in thought. It was evident that these apes really believed that they had seen him kill their fellow. What was the explanation? How could it be accounted for? Did the naked footprints of the great white man whom he had been following mean more, then, than he had guessed? Tarzan wondered. He raised his eyes and again addressed the bulls.

"It was not I who killed Gobu," he insisted. "Many of you have known me all your lives. You know that only in fair fight, as one bull fights another, have I ever killed a Mangani. You know that, of all the jungle people, the Mangani are my best friends, and that Tarzan of the Apes is the best friend the Mangani have. How, then, could I slay one of my own people?"

"We only know," replied the old bull, "that we saw you kill Gobu. With our own eyes we saw you kill him. Go away quickly, therefore, or we shall kill you. Mighty fighter is Tarzan of the Apes, but mightier even than he are all the great bulls of Pagth. I am Pagth, king of the tribe of Pagth. Go away before we kill you."

Tarzan tried to reason with them but they would not listen, so confident were they that it was he who had slain their fellow, the bull Gobu. Finally, rather than chance a quarrel in which some of them must inevitably be killed, he turned sorrowfully away. But more than ever, now, was he determined to seek out the slayer of Gobu that he might demand an accounting of one who dared thus invade his life-long domain.

Tarzan trailed the spoor until it mingled with the tracks of many men—barefooted blacks, mostly, but among them the footprints of booted white men, and once he saw the footprints of a woman or a child, which, he could not tell. The trail led apparently toward the rocky hills which protected the barren valley of Opar.

Forgetful now of his original mission and imbued only with a savage desire to wrest from the interlopers a full accounting for their presence in the jungle, and to mete out to the slayer of Gobu his just deserts, Tarzan forged ahead upon the now broad and well-marked trail of the considerable party which could not now be much more than a half-day's march ahead of him, which meant that they were now already upon the rim of the valley of Opar, if this was their ultimate destination. And what other they could have in view Tarzan could not imagine.

He had always kept closely to himself the location of Opar. In so far as he knew no white person other than Jane, and their son, Korak, knew of the location of the forgotten city of the ancient Atlantians. Yet what else could have drawn these white men, with so large a party, into the savage, unexplored wilderness which hemmed Opar upon all sides?

Such were the thoughts that occupied Tarzan's mind as he followed swiftly the trail that led toward Opar. Darkness fell, but so fresh was the spoor that the ape-man could follow it by scent even when he could not see the imprints upon the ground, and presently, in the distance, he saw the light of a camp ahead of him.

5

The Fatal Drops

A T HOME, the life in the bungalow and at the farm followed its usual routine as it had before the departure of Tarzan. Korak, sometimes on foot and sometimes on horseback, followed the activities of the farm hands and the herders, sometimes alone, but more often in company with the white foreman, Jervis, and often, especially when they rode, Jane accompanied them.

The golden lion Korak exercised upon a leash, since he was not at all confident of his powers of control over the beast, and feared lest, in the absence of his master, Jad-bal-ja might take to the forest and revert to his natural savage state. Such a lion, abroad in the jungle, would be a distinct menace to human life, for Jad-bal-ja, reared among men, lacked that natural timidity of men that is so marked a trait of all wild beasts. Trained as he had been to make his kill at the throat of a human effigy, it required no considerable powers of imagination upon the part of Korak to visualize what might occur should the golden lion, loosed from all restraint, be thrown upon his own resources in the surrounding jungle.

It was during the first week of Tarzan's absence that a runner from Nairobi brought a cable message to Lady Greystoke, announcing the serious illness of her father in London. Mother and son discussed the situation. It would be five or six weeks before Tarzan could return, even if they sent a runner after him, and, were Jane to await him,

there would be little likelihood of her reaching her father
in time. Even should she depart at once, there seemed only
a faint hope that she should see him alive. It was decided, therefore, that she should set out immediately, Korak
accompanying her as far as Nairobi, and then returning
to the ranch and resuming its general supervision until his
father's return.

It is a long trek from the Greystoke estate to Nairobi,
and Korak had not yet returned when, about three weeks
after Tarzan's departure, a black, whose duty it was to feed
and care for Jad-bal-ja, carelessly left the door of the cage
unfastened while he was cleaning it. The golden lion paced
back and forth while the black wielded his broom within the
cage. They were old friends, and the Waziri felt no fear of
the great lion, with the result that his back was as often
turned to him as not. The black was working in the far
corner of the cage when Jad-bal-ja paused a moment at the
door at the opposite end. The beast saw that the gate hung
slightly ajar upon its hinges. Silently he raised a great padded
paw and inserted it in the opening—a slight pull and the
gate swung in. Instantly the golden lion inserted his snout
in the widened aperture, and as he swung the barrier aside
the horrified black looked up to see his charge drop softly
to the ground outside.

"Stop, Jad-bal-ja! Stop!" screamed the frightened black,
leaping after him. But the golden lion only increased his pace,
and leaping the fence, loped off in the direction of the forest.

The black pursued him with brandishing broom, emitting
loud yells that brought the inmates of the Waziri huts into
the open, where they joined their fellow in pursuit of the
lion. Across the rolling plains they followed him, but might as
well have sought to snare the elusive will-o'-the-wisp as this
swift and wary fugitive, who heeded neither their blandish-
ments nor their threats. And so it was that they saw the golden
lion disappear into the primeval forest and, though they
searched diligently until almost dark, they were forced at
length to give up their quest and return crestfallen to the
farm.

"Ah," cried the unhappy black, who had been responsible
for the escape of Jad-bal-ja, "what will the Big Bwana say
to me, what will he do to me when he finds that I have permitted the golden lion to get away!"

"You will be banished from the bungalow for a long time,
Keewazi," old Muviro assured him. "And doubtless you will
be sent to the grazing ground far to the east to guard the herd
there, where you will have plenty of lions for company,

though they will not be as friendly as was Jad-bal-ja. It is not half what you deserve, and were the heart of the Big Bwana not filled with love for his black children—were he like other white Bwanas old Muviro has seen—you would be lashed until you could not stand, perhaps until you died."

"I am a man," replied Keewazi. "I am a warrior and a Waziri. Whatever punishment the Big Bwana inflicts I will accept as a man should."

It was that same night that Tarzan approached the camp-fires of the strange party he had been tracking. Unseen by them, he halted in the foliage of a tree directly in the center of their camp, which was surrounded by an enormous thorn boma, and brilliantly lighted by numerous fires which blacks were diligently feeding with branches from an enormous pile of firewood that they had evidently gathered earlier in the day for this purpose. Near the center of the camp were several tents, and before one, in the light of a fire, sat four white men. Two of them were great, bull-necked, red-faced fellows, apparently Englishmen of the lower class, the third appeared to be short, fat, and Teutonic, while the fourth was a tall, slender, handsome fellow, with dark, wavy brown hair and regular features. He and the German were most meticulously garbed for Central African traveling, after the highly idealized standard of motion pictures, in fact either one of them might have stepped directly from a screen-ing of the latest jungle thriller. The young man was evidently not of English descent and Tarzan mentally cataloged him, almost immediately, as a Slav. Shortly after Tarzan's arrival this one arose and entered one of the nearby tents, from which Tarzan immediately heard the sound of voices in low conversation. He could not distinguish the words, but the tones of one seemed quite distinctly feminine. The three remaining at the fire were carrying on a desultory conversa-tion, when suddenly from near at hand beyond the boma wall, a lion's roar broke the silence of the jungle.

With a startled shriek Bluber leaped to his feet, so sud-denly that he cleared the ground a good foot, and then, stepping backward, he lost his balance, tripped over his camp-stool, and sprawled upon his back.

"My Gord, Adolph!" roared one of his companions. "If you do that again, damn me if I don't break your neck. 'Ere we are, and that's that."

"Blime if 'e ain't worse'n a bloomin' lion," growled the other.

Bluber crawled to his feet. "*Mein Gott!*" he cried, his voice quavering, "I t'ought sure he vas coming over der fence.

S'elp me if I ever get out of diss, neffer again—not for all der gold in Africa vould I go t'rough vat I haf been t'rough dese past t'ree mont's. *Ach, weh!* ven I t'ink of it, *Ach, du lieber!* Lions, und leopards, und rhinoceroses und hippopotamuses."

His companions laughed. "Dick and I tells you right along from the beginning that you 'adn't oughter come into the interior," said one of them.

"But for vy I buy all dese clo's?" wailed the German. "*Mein Gott,* dis suit, it stands me tventy guineas, vot I stand in. Ach, had I know somet'ing, vun guinea vould have bought me my whole vardrobe—tventy guineas for dis und no vun to see it but savages und lions."

"And you look like 'ell in it, besides," commented one of his friends.

"Und look at it, it's all dirty and torn. How should I know it I spoil dis suit? Mit mine own eyes I see it at der Princess Teayter, how der hero spend t'ree mont's in Africa hunting lions und killing cannibals, und ven he comes oud he hasn't even got a greast spot on his pants—how should I know it Africa was so dirty und full of thorns?"

It was at this point that Tarzan of the Apes elected to drop quietly into the circle of firelight before them. The two Englishmen leaped to their feet, quite evidently startled, and Bluber turned and took a half step as though in flight, but immediately his eyes rested upon the ape-man he halted, a look of relief supplanting that of terror which had overspread his countenance, as Tarzan had dropped upon them apparently from the heavens.

"*Mein Gott,* Esteban," shrilled the German, "vy you come back so soon, and for vy you come back like dot, sudden—don't you suppose ve got nerves?"

Tarzan was angry, angry at these raw intruders, who dared enter without his permission, the wide domain in which he kept peace and order. When Tarzan was angry there flamed upon his forehead the scar that Bolgani, the gorilla, had placed there upon that long-gone day when the boy Tarzan had met the great beast in mortal combat, and first learned the true value of his father's hunting knife—the knife that had placed him, the comparatively weak little Tarmangani, upon an even footing with the great beasts of the jungle.

His gray eyes were narrowed, his voice came cold and level as he addressed them. "Who are you," he demanded, "who dare thus invade the country of the Waziri, the land of Tarzan, without permission from the Lord of the Jungle?"

"Where do you get that stuff, Esteban," demanded one of

the Englishmen, "and wat in 'ell are you doin' back 'ere alone and so soon? Where are your porters, and where is the bloomin' gold?"

The ape-man eyed the speaker in silence for a moment. "I am Tarzan of the Apes," he said. "I do not know what you are talking about. I only know that I come in search of him who slew Gobu, the great ape; him who slew Bara, the deer, without my permission."

"Oh, 'ell," exploded the other Englishman, "stow the guff, Esteban—if you're tryin' for to be funny we don't see the joke, 'ere we are, and that's that."

Inside the tent, which the fourth white man had entered while Tarzan was watching the camp from his hiding place in the tree above, a woman, evidently suddenly stirred by terror, touched the arm of her companion frantically, and pointed toward the tall, almost naked figure of the ape-man as he stood revealed in the full light of the beast fires. "God, Carl," she whispered, in trembling tones, "look!"

"What's wrong, Flora?" inquired her companion. "I see only Esteban."

"It is not Esteban," hissed the girl. "It is Lord Greystoke himself—it is Tarzan of the Apes!"

"You are mad, Flora," replied the man, "it cannot be he."

"It is he, though," she insisted. "Do you suppose that I do not know him? Did I not work in his town house for years? Did I not see him nearly every day? Do you suppose that I do not know Tarzan of the Apes? Look at that red scar flaming on his forehead—I have heard the story of that scar and I have seen it burn scarlet when he was aroused to anger. It is scarlet now, and Tarzan of the Apes is angry."

"Well, suppose it *is* Tarzan of the Apes, what can he do?"

"You do not know him," replied the girl. "You do not guess the tremendous power he wields here—the power of life and death over man and beast. If he knew our mission here not one of us would ever reach the coast alive. The very fact that he is here now makes me believe that he may have discovered our purpose, and if he has, God help us—unless—unless——"

"Unless what?" demanded the man.

The girl was silent in thought for a moment. "There is only one way," she said finally. "We dare not kill him. His savage blacks would learn of it, and no power on earth could save us then. There is a way, though, if we act quickly." She turned and searched for a moment in one of her bags, and presently she handed the man a small bottle, containing liquid. "Go out and talk to him," she said, "make friends with him. Lie to him. Tell him anything. Promise anything. But get on friendly enough terms with him so that you can offer him coffee. He does not drink wine or anything with alcohol in it, but I know that he likes coffee. I have often served it to him in his room late at night upon his return from the theater or a ball. Get him to drink coffee and then you will know what to do with this." And she indicated the bottle which the man still held in his hand.

Kraski nodded. "I understand," he said, and, turning, left the tent.

He had taken but a step when the girl recalled him. "Do not let him see me. Do not let him guess that I am here or that you know me."

The man nodded and left her. Approaching the tense figures before the fire he greeted Tarzan with a pleasant smile and a cheery word.

"Welcome," he said, "we are always glad to see a stranger in our camp. Sit down. Hand the gentleman a stool, John," he said to Peebles.

The ape-man eyed Kraski as he had eyed the others. There was no answering friendly light in his eyes responding to the Russian's greeting.

"I have been trying to find out what your party is doing here," he said sharply to the Russian, "but they still insist that I am someone whom I am not. They are either fools or knaves, and I intend to find out which, and deal with them accordingly."

"Come, come," cried Kraski, soothingly. "There must be some mistake, I am sure. But tell me, who are you?"

"I am Tarzan of the Apes," replied the ape-man. "No hunters enter this part of Africa without my permission. That fact is so well known that there is no chance of your having passed the coast without having been so advised. I seek an explanation, and that quickly."

"Ah, you are Tarzan of the Apes," exclaimed Kraski. "Fortunate indeed are we, for now may we be set straight upon our way, and escape from our frightful dilemma is assured. We are lost, sir, inextricably lost, due to the ignorance or knavery of our guide, who deserted us several weeks ago. Surely we knew of you; who does not know of Tarzan of the Apes? But it was not our intention to cross the boundaries of your territory. We were searching farther south for specimens of the fauna of the district, which our good friend and employer, here, Mr. Adolph Bluber, is collecting at great expense for presentation to a museum in his home city in America. Now I am sure that you can tell us where we are and direct us upon our proper course."

Peebles, Throck, and Bluber stood fascinated by Kraski's glib lies, but it was the German who first rose to the occasion. Too thick were the skulls of the English pugs to grasp quickly the clever ruse of the Russian.

"Vy yes," said the oily Bluber, rubbing his palms together, "dot iss it, yust vot I vas going to tell you."

Tarzan turned sharply upon him. "Then what was all this talk about Esteban?" he asked. "Was it not by that name that these others addressed me?"

"Ah," cried Bluber, "John will haf his leetle joke. He iss ignorant of Africa; he has neffer been here before. He t'ought perhaps dat you vere a native. John he calls all der natives Esteban, und he has great jokes by himself mit dem, because he knows dey cannot onderstand vot he says. Hey John, iss it not so, vot it iss I say?" But the shrewd Bluber did not wait for John to reply. "You see," he went on, "ve are lost, und you take us oud mit dis jungle, ve pay you anyt'ing—you name your own price."

The ape-man only half believed him, yet he was somewhat mollified by their evidently friendly intentions. Perhaps after all they were telling him a half-truth and had, really, wandered into his territory unwittingly. That, however, he would find out definitely from their native carriers, from whom his own Waziri would wean the truth. But the matter of his having been mistaken for Esteban still piqued his curiosity, also he was still desirous of learning the identity of the slayer of Gobu, the great ape.

"Please sit down," urged Kraski. "We were about to have coffee and we should be delighted to have you join us. We meant no wrong in coming here, and I can assure you that we will gladly and willingly make full amends to you, or to whomever else we may have unintentionally wronged."

To take coffee with these men would do no harm. Perhaps he had wronged them, but however that might be a cup of their coffee would place no great obligation upon him. Flora had been right in her assertion that if Tarzan of the Apes had any weakness whatsoever it was for an occasional cup of black coffee late at night. He did not accept the proffered camp stool, but squatted, ape-fashion, before them, the flickering light of the beast fires playing upon his bronzed hide and bringing into relief the gracefully contoured muscles of his godlike frame. Not as the muscles of the blacksmith or the professional strong man were the muscles of Tarzan of the Apes, but rather as those of Mercury or Apollo, so symmetri-

cally balanced were their proportions, suggesting only the great
strength that lay in them. Trained to speed and agility were
they as well as to strength, and thus, clothing as they did
his giant frame, they imparted to him the appearance of a
demi-god.

Throck, Peebles, and Bluber sat watching him in spell-
bound fascination, while Kraski walked over to the cook
fire to arrange for the coffee. The two Englishmen were as
yet only half awakened to the fact that they had mistaken
this newcomer for another, and as it was, Peebles still
scratched his head and grumbled to himself in inarticulate
half-denial of Kraski's assumption of the new identity of
Tarzan. Bluber was inwardly terror-stricken. His keener
intelligence had quickly grasped the truth of Kraski's recog-
nition of the man for what he was rather than for what
Peebles and Throck thought him to be, and, as Bluber knew
nothing of Flora's plan, he was in quite a state of funk as
he tried to visualize the outcome of Tarzan's discovery of
them at the very threshold of Opar. He did not realize, as
did Flora, that their very lives were in danger—that it was
Tarzan of the Apes, a beast of the jungle, with whom they
had to deal, and not John Clayton, Lord Greystoke, an
English peer. Rather was Bluber considering the two thousand pounds that they stood to lose through this deplorable
termination of their expedition, for he was sufficiently familiar with the reputation of the ape-man to know that they
would never be permitted to take with them the gold that
Esteban was very likely, at this moment, pilfering from the
vaults of Opar. Really Bluber was almost upon the verge
of tears when Kraski returned with the coffee, which he
brought himself.

From the dark shadows of the tent's interior Flora Hawkes
looked nervously out upon the scene before her. She was
terrified at the possibility of discovery by her former employer,
for she had been a maid in the Greystokes' London town
house as well as at the African bungalow and knew that
Lord Greystoke would recognize her instantly should he
chance to see her. She entertained for him, now, in his
jungle haunts, a fear that was possibly greater than Tarzan's
true character warranted, but none the less real was it to
the girl whose guilty conscience conjured all sorts of possible
punishments for her disloyalty to those who had always
treated her with uniform kindliness and consideration.

Constant dreaming of the fabulous wealth of the treasure
vaults of Opar, concerning which she had heard so much
in detail from the conversations of the Greystokes, had

aroused within her naturally crafty and unscrupulous mind a desire for possession, and in consequence thereof she had slowly visualized a scheme whereby she might loot the treasure vaults of a sufficient number of the golden ingots to make her independently wealthy for life. The entire plan had been hers. She had at first interested Kraski, who had in turn enlisted the coöperation of the two Englishmen and Bluber, and these four had raised the necessary money to defray the cost of the expedition. It had been Flora who had searched for a type of man who might successfully impersonate Tarzan in his own jungle, and she had found Esteban Miranda, a handsome, powerful, and unscrupulous Spaniard, whose histrionic ability aided by the art of make-up, of which he was a past master, permitted him to impersonate almost faultlessly the character their desired him to portray, in so far, at least, as outward appearances were concerned.

The Spaniard was not only powerful and active, but physically courageous as well, and since he had shaved his beard and donned the jungle habiliments of a Tarzan, he had lost no opportunity for emulating the ape-man in every way that lay within his ability. Of jungle craft he had none of course, and personal combats with the more savage jungle beasts caution prompted him to eschew, but he hunted the lesser game with spear and arrow and practiced continually with the grass rope that was a part of his make-up.

And now Flora Hawkes saw all her well-laid plans upon the verge of destruction. She trembled as she watched the men before the fire, for her fear of Tarzan was very real, and then she became tense with nervous anticipation as she saw Kraski approaching the group with the coffee pot in one hand and cups in the other. Kraski set the pot and the cups upon the ground a little in the rear of Tarzan, and, as he filled the latter, she saw him pour a portion of the contents of the bottle she had given him into one of the cups. A cold sweat broke out upon her forehead as Kraski lifted this cup and offered it to the ape-man. Would he take it? Would he suspect? If he did suspect what horrible punishment would be meted to them all for their temerity? She saw Kraski hand another cup to Peebles, Throck, and Bluber, then return to the circle with the last one for himself. As the Russian raised it before his face and bowed politely to the ape-man, she saw the five men drink. The reaction which ensued left her weak and spent. Turning, she collapsed upon her cot, and lay there trembling, her face buried in her arm. And, outside, Tarzan of the Apes drained his cup to the last drop.

6

Death Steals Behind

D URING the afternoon of the day that Tarzan discovered the camp of the conspirators, a watcher upon the crumbling outer wall of the ruined city of Opar descried a party of men moving downward into the valley from the summit of the encircling cliff. Tarzan, Jane Clayton, and their black Waziri were the only strangers that the denizens of Opar had ever seen within their valley during the lifetime of the oldest among them, and only in half-forgotten legends of a by-gone past was there any suggestion that strangers other than these had ever visited Opar. Yet from time immemorial a guard had always remained upon the summit of the outer wall. Now a single knurled and crippled man-like creature was all that recalled the numerous, lithe warriors of lost Atlantis. For down through the long ages the race had deteriorated and finally, through occasional mating with the great apes, the men had become the beast-like things of modern Opar. Strange and inexplicable had been the providence of nature that had confined this deterioration almost solely to the males, leaving the females straight, well-formed, often of comely and even beautiful features, a condition that might be largely attributable to the fact that female infants possessing ape-like characteristics were immediately destroyed, while, on the other hand, boy babies who possessed purely human attributes were also done away with.

Typical indeed of the male inhabitants of Opar was the lone watcher upon the outer city wall, a short, stocky man with matted hair and beard, his tangled locks growing low upon a low, receding forehead; small, close-set eyes and fang-like teeth bore evidence of his simian ancestry, as did his short, crooked legs and long, muscular ape-like arms, all scantily hair-covered as was his torso.

As his wicked, blood-rimmed eyes watched the progress

45

of the party across the valley toward Opar, evidences of his growing excitement were manifested in the increased rapidity of his breathing, and low, almost inaudible growls that issued from his throat. The strangers were too far distant to be recognizable only as human beings, and their number roughly to be approximated as between two and three score. Having assured himself of these two facts the watcher descended from the outer wall, crossed the space between it and the inner wall, through which he passed, and at a rapid trot crossed the broad avenue beyond and disappeared within the crumbling but still magnificent temple beyond.

Cadj, the High Priest of Opar, squatted beneath the shade of the giant trees which now overgrew what had once been one of the gardens of the ancient temple. With him were a dozen members of the lesser priesthood, the intimate cronies of the High Priest, who were startled by the sudden advent of one of the inferior members of the clan of Opar. The fellow hurried breathlessly to Cadj.

"Cadj," he cried, "strange men descend upon Opar! From the northwest they have come into the valley from beyond the barrier cliffs—fifty of them at least, perhaps half again that number. I saw them as I watched from the summit of the outer wall, but further than they are men I cannot say, for they are still a great distance away. Not since the great Tarmangani came among us last have there been strangers within Opar."

"It has been many moons since the great Tarmangani who called himself Tarzan of the Apes was among us," said Cadj. "He promised us to return before the rain to see that no harm had befallen La, but he did not come back and La has always insisted that he is dead. Have you told any other of what you have seen?" he demanded, turning suddenly upon the messenger.

"No," replied the latter.

"Good!" exclaimed Cadj. "Come, we will all go to the outer wall and see who it is who dares enter forbidden Opar, and let no one breathe a word of what Blagh has told us until I give permission."

"The word of Cadj is law until La speaks," murmured one of the priests.

Cadj turned a scowling face upon the speaker. "I am High Priest of Opar," he growled. "Who dares disobey me?"

"But La is High Priestess," said one, "and the High Priestess is the queen of Opar."

"But the High Priest can offer whom he will as sacrifice

in the Chamber of the Dead or to the Flaming God," Cadj reminded the other meaningly.

"We shall keep silence, Cadj," replied the priest, cringing.

"Good!" growled the High Priest and led the way from the garden through the corridors of the temple back toward the outer wall of Opar. From here they watched the approaching party that was in plain view of them, far out across the valley. The watchers conversed in low gutturals in the language of the great apes, interspersed with which were occasional words and phrases of a strange tongue that were doubtless corrupted forms of the ancient language of Atlantis handed down through countless generations from their human progenitors—that now extinct race whose cities and civilization lie buried deep beneath the tossing waves of the Atlantic, and whose adventurous spirit had, in remote ages, caused them to penetrate into the heart of Africa in search of gold and to build there, in duplication of their far home cities, the magnificent city of Opar.

As Cadj and his followers watched from beneath shaggy brows the strangers plodding laboriously beneath the now declining equatorial sun across the rocky, barren valley, a gray little monkey eyed them from amidst the foliage of one of the giant trees that had forced its way through the pavement of the ancient avenue behind them. A solemn, sad-faced little monkey it was, but like all his kind overcome by curiosity, and finally to such an extent that his fear of the fierce males of Opar was so considerably overcome that he at last swung lightly from the tree to the pavement, made his way through the inner wall and up the inside of the outer wall to a position in their rear where he could hide behind one of the massive granite blocks of the crumbling wall in comparative safety from detection, the while he might overhear the conversation of the Oparians, all of which that was carried on in the language of the great apes he could understand perfectly.

The afternoon was drawing to a close before the slowly moving company approaching Opar was close enough for individuals to be recognizable in any way, and then presently one of the younger priests exclaimed excitedly:

"It is he, Cadj. It is the great Tarmangani who calls himself Tarzan of the Apes. I can see him plainly; the others are all black men. He is urging them on, prodding them with his spear. They act as though they were afraid and very tired, but he is forcing them forward."

"You are sure," demanded Cadj, "you are sure that it is Tarzan of the Apes?"

"I am positive," replied the speaker, and then another of the priests joined his assurances to that of his fellow. At last they were close enough so that Cadj himself, whose eye-sight was not as good as that of the younger members of the company, realized that it was indeed Tarzan of the Apes who was returning to Opar. The High Priest scowled angrily in thought. Suddenly he turned upon the others.

"He must not come," he cried; "he must not enter Opar. Hasten and fetch a hundred fighting men. We will meet them as they come through the outer wall and slay them one by one."

"But La," cried he who had aroused Cadj's anger in the garden, "I distinctly recall that La offered the friendship of Opar to Tarzan of the Apes upon that time, many moons ago, that he saved her from the tusks of infuriated Tantor."

"Silence," growled Cadj, "he shall not enter; we shall slay them all, though we need not know their identity until it is too late. Do you understand? And know, too, that whosoever attempts to thwart my purpose shall die—and he die not as a sacrifice, he shall die at my hands, but die he shall. You hear me?" And he pointed an unclean finger at the trembling priest.

Manu, the monkey, hearing all this, was almost bursting with excitement. He knew Tarzan of the Apes—as all the migratory monkeys the length and breadth of Africa knew him—he knew him for a friend and protector. To Manu the males of Opar were neither beast, nor man, nor friend. He knew them as cruel and surly creatures who ate the flesh of his kind, and he hated them accordingly. He was therefore greatly exercised at the plot that he had heard discussed which was aimed at the life of the great Tarmangani. He scratched his little gray head, and the root of his tail, and his belly, as he attempted mentally to digest what he had heard, and bring forth from the dim recesses of his little brain a plan to foil the priests and save Tarzan of the Apes. He made grotesque grimaces that were aimed at the unsuspecting Cadj and his followers, but which failed to perturb them, possibly because a huge granite block hid the little monkey from them. This was quite the most momentous thing that had occurred in the life of Manu. He wanted to jump up and down and dance and screech and jabber—to scold and threaten the hated Oparians, but something told him that nothing would be gained by this, other than, perhaps, to launch in his direction a shower of granite missiles, which the priests knew only too well how to throw with accuracy. Now Manu is not a deep thinker, but upon this occasion

he quite outdid himself, and managed to concentrate his
mind upon the thing at hand rather than permit its being distracted by each falling leaf or buzzing insect. He even permitted a succulent caterpillar to crawl within his reach and
out again with impunity.

Just before darkness fell, Cadj saw a little gray monkey
disappear over the summit of the outer wall fifty paces from
where he crouched with his fellows, waiting for the coming of
the fighting men. But so numerous were the monkeys about
the ruins of Opar that the occurrence left Cadj's mind almost as quickly as the monkey disappeared from his view,
and in the gathering gloom he did not see the little gray
figure scampering off across the valley toward the band of
intruders who now appeared to have stopped to rest
at the foot of a large kopje that stood alone out in the valley,
about a mile from the city.

Little Manu was very much afraid out there alone in the
growing dusk, and he scampered very fast with his tail
bowed up and out behind him. All the time he cast affrightened
glances to the right and left. The moment he reached the kopje
he scampered up its face as fast as he could. It was really
a huge, precipitous granite rock with almost perpendicular
sides, but sufficiently weather-worn to make its ascent easy
to little Manu. He paused a moment at the summit to get
his breath and still the beatings of his frightened little heart,
and then he made his way around to a point where he could
look down upon the party beneath.

There, indeed, was the great Tarmangani Tarzan, and
with him were some fifty Gomangani. The latter were splicing
together a number of long, straight poles, which they had
laid upon the ground in two parallel lines. Across these two,
at intervals of a foot or more, they were lashing smaller
straight branches about eighteen inches in length, the whole
forming a crude but substantial ladder. The purpose of all
this Manu, of course, did not understand, nor did he know
that it had been evolved from the fertile brain of Flora
Hawkes as a means of scaling the precipitous kopje, at the
summit of which lay the outer entrance to the treasure vaults
of Opar. Nor did Manu know that the party had no intention of entering the city of Opar and were therefore in no
danger of becoming victims of Cadj's hidden assassins. To
him, the danger to Tarzan of the Apes was very real, and so,
having regained his breath, he lost no time in delivering his
warning to the friend of his people.

"Tarzan," he cried, in the language that was common to
both.

The white man and the blacks looked up at the sound of his chattering voice.

"It is Manu, Tarzan," continued the little monkey, "who has come to tell you not to go to Opar. Cadj and his people await within the outer wall to slay you."

The blacks, having discovered that the author of the disturbance was nothing but a little gray monkey, returned immediately to their work, while the white man similarly ignored his words of warning. Manu was not surprised at the lack of interest displayed by the blacks, for he knew that they did not understand his language, but he could not comprehend why Tarzan failed to pay any attention whatsoever to him. Again and again he called Tarzan by name. Again and again he shrieked his warning to the ape-man, but without eliciting any reply or any information that the great Tarmangani had either heard or understood him. Manu was mystified. What had occurred to render Tarzan of the Apes so indifferent to the warnings of his old friend.?

At last the little monkey gave it up and looked longingly back in the direction of the trees within the walled city of Opar. It was now very dark and he trembled at the thought of recrossing the valley, where he knew enemies might prowl by night. He scratched his head and he hugged his knees, then sat there whimpering, a very forlorn and unhappy little ball of a monkey. But however uncomfortable he was upon the high kopje, he was comparatively safe, and so he decided to remain there during the night rather than venture the terrifying return trip through the darkness. Thus it was that he saw the ladder completed and erected against the side of the kopje; and when the moon rose at last and lighted the scene, he saw Tarzan of the Apes urging his men to mount the ladder. He had never seen Tarzan thus rough and cruel with the blacks who accompanied him. Manu knew how ferocious the great Tarmangani could be with an enemy, whether man or beast, but he had never seen him accord such treatment to the blacks who were his friends.

One by one and with evident reluctance the blacks ascended the ladder, continually urged forward to greater speed by the sharp spear of the white man; when they had all ascended Tarzan followed, and Manu saw them disappear apparently into the heart of the great rock.

It was only a short time later that they commenced to reappear, and now each was burdened by two heavy objects which appeared to Manu to be very similar to some of the smaller stone blocks that had been used in the construction of the buildings in Opar. He saw them take the blocks to the edge of the kopje and cast them over to the ground beneath, and when the last of the blacks had emerged with his load and cast it to the valley below, one by one the party descended the ladder to the foot of the kopje. But this time Tarzan of the Apes went first. Then they lowered the ladder and took it apart and laid its pieces close to the foot of the cliff, after which they took up the blocks which they had brought from the heart of the kopje, and following Tarzan, who set out in the lead, they commenced to retrace their steps toward the rim of the valley.

Manu would have been very much mystified had he been a man, but being only a monkey he saw only what he saw without attempting to reason very much about it. He knew that the ways of men were peculiar, and oftentimes unaccountable. For example, the Gomangani who could not travel through the jungle and the forest with the ease of any other of the animals which frequented them, added to their difficulties by loading themselves down with additional weights in the form of metal anklets and armlets, with necklaces and girdles, and with skins of animals, which did nothing more than impede their progress and render life much more complicated than that which the untrammeled beasts enjoyed. Manu, whenever he gave the matter a thought, congratulated himself that he was not a man—he pitied the foolish, unreasonable creatures.

Manu must have slept. He thought that he had only closed his eyes a moment, but when he opened them the rosy light of dawn had overspread the desolate valley. Just disappearing over the cliffs to the northeast he could see the last of Tarzan's party commencing the descent of the barrier, then Manu turned his face toward Opar and prepared to descend from the kopje, and scamper back to the safety of his trees within the walls of Opar. But first he would reconnoiter—Sheeta, the panther, might be still abroad, and so he scampered around the edge of the kopje to a point where he could see the entire valley floor between himself and Opar. And there it was that he saw again that which filled him with greatest excitement. For, debouching from the ruined outer wall of Opar was a large company of Opar's frightful men—fully a hundred of them Manu could have counted had Manu been able to count.

They seemed to be coming toward the kopje, and he sat and watched them as they approached, deciding to defer his return to the city until after the path was cleared of hated Oparians. It occurred to him that they were coming after him, for the egotism of the lower animals is inordinate. Because he was a monkey, the idea did not seem at all ridiculous and so he hid behind a jutting rock, with only one little, bright eye exposed to the enemy. He saw them come closer and he grew very much excited, though he was not at all afraid, for he knew that if they ascended one side of the kopje he could descend the other and be half-way to Opar before they could possibly locate him again.

On and on they came, but they did not stop at the kopje —as a matter of fact they did not come very close to it, but continued on beyond it. Then it was that the truth of the matter flashed into the little brain of the monkey—Cadj and his people were pursuing Tarzan of the Apes to slay him. If Manu had been offended by Tarzan's indifference to him upon the night before, he had evidently forgotten it, for now he was quite as excited about the danger which he saw menace the ape-man as he had been upon the afternoon previous. At first he thought of running ahead, and again warning Tarzan, but he feared to venture so far from the trees of Opar, even if the thought of having to pass the hated Oparians had not been sufficient to deter him from carrying out this plan. For a few minutes he sat watching them, until they had all passed the kopje, and then it became quite clear to him that they were heading directly for the spot at which the last of Tarzan's party had disappeared from the valley—there could be no doubt that they were in pursuit of the ape-man.

Manu scanned the valley once more toward Opar. There was nothing in sight to deter him from an attempted return, and so, with the agility of his kind, he scampered down the vertical face of the kopje and was off at great speed toward the city's wall. Just when he formulated the plan that he eventually followed it is difficult to say. Perhaps he thought it all out as he sat upon the kopje, watching Cadj and his people upon the trail of the ape-man, or perhaps it occurred to him while he was scampering across the barren waste toward Opar. It may just have popped into his mind from a clear sky after he had regained the leafy sanctuary of his own trees. Be that however as it may, the fact remains that as La, High Priestess and princess of Opar, in company with several of her priestesses, was bathing in a pool in one of the temple gardens, she was startled by the screaming of a monkey, swinging frantically by his tail from the branch of a great tree which overspread the pool—it was a little gray monkey with a face so wise and serious that one might easily have imagined that the fate of nations lay constantly upon the shoulders of its owner.

"La, La," it screamed, "they have gone to kill Tarzan. They have gone to kill Tarzan."

At the sound of that name La was instantly all attention. Standing waist deep in the pool she looked up at the little monkey questioningly. "What do you mean, Manu?" she asked. "It has been many moons since Tarzan was at Opar. He is not here now. What are you talking about?"

"I saw him," screamed Manu, "I saw him last night with many Gomangani. He came to the great rock that lies in the valley before Opar; with all his men he climbed to the top of it, went into the heart of it, and came out with stones which they threw down into the valley. Afterward they descended from the rock, and picked up the stones again and left the valley—there," and Manu pointed toward the northeast with one of his hairy little fingers.

"How do you know it was Tarzan of the Apes?" asked La.

"Does Manu not know his cousin and his friend?" demanded the monkey. "With my eyes I saw him—it was Tarzan of the Apes."

La of Opar puckered her brows in thought. Deep in her heart smoldered the fires of her great love for Tarzan. Fires that had been quenched by the necessity that had compelled her marriage with Cadj since last she had seen the ape-man. For it is written among the laws of Opar that the high Priestess of the Flaming God must take a mate within a certain number of years after her consecration. For many moons La longed to make Tarzan that mate. The ape-man had not loved her, and finally she had come to a realization that he could never love her. Afterward she had bowed to the frightful fate that had placed her in the arms of Cadj.

As month after month had passed and Tarzan had not returned to Opar, as he had promised he would do, to see that no harm befell La, she had come to accept the opinion of Cadj that the ape-man was dead, and though she hated the repulsive Cadj none the less, her love for Tarzan had gradually become little more than a sorrowful memory. Now to learn that he was alive and had been so near was like reopening an old wound. At first she comprehended little else than that Tarzan had been close to Opar, but presently the cries of Manu aroused her to a realization that the ape-man was in danger—just what the danger was, she did not know.

"Who has gone to kill Tarzan of the Apes?" she demanded suddenly.

"Cadj, Cadj!" shrieked Manu. "He has gone with many, many men, and is following upon the spoor of Tarzan."

La sprang quickly from the pool, seized her girdle and ornaments from her attendant and adjusting them hurriedly, sped through the garden and into the temple.

7

"You Must Sacrifice Him"

WARILY Cadj and his hundred frightful followers, armed with their bludgeons and knives, crept stealthily down the face of the barrier into the valley below, upon the trail of the white man and his black companions. They made no haste, for they had noted from the summit of Opar's outer wall, that the party they were pursuing moved very slowly, though why, they did not know, for they had been at too great a distance to see the burden that each of the blacks carried. Nor was it Cadj's desire to overtake his quarry by daylight, his plans contemplating a stealthy night attack, the suddenness of which, together with the great number of his followers, might easily confuse and overwhelm a sleeping camp.

The spoor they followed was well marked. There could be no mistaking it, and they moved slowly down the now gentle declivity, toward the bottom of the valley. It was close to noon that they were brought to a sudden halt by the discovery of a thorn boma recently constructed in a small clearing just ahead of them. From the center of the boma arose the thin smoke of a dying fire. Here, then, was the camp of the ape-man.

Cadj drew his followers into the concealment of the thick bushes that bordered the trail, and from there he sent ahead a single man to reconnoiter. It was but a few moments later that the latter returned to say that the camp was deserted, and once again Cadj moved forward with his men. Entering the boma they examined it in an effort to estimate the size of the party that accompanied Tarzan. As they were thus occupied Cadj saw something lying half concealed by bushes at the far end of the boma. Very warily he approached it, for there was that about it which not only aroused his curiosity but prompted him to caution, for it resembled indistinctly the figure of a man, lying huddled upon the ground.

With ready bludgeons a dozen of them approached the thing that had aroused Cadj's curiosity, and when they had come close to it they saw lying before them the lifeless figure of Tarzan of the Apes.

"The Flaming God has reached forth to avenge his desecrated altar," cried the High Priest, his eyes glowing with the maniacal fires of fanaticism. But another priest, more practical, perhaps, or at least more cautious, kneeled beside the figure of the ape-man and placed his ear against the latter's heart.

"He is not dead," he whispered; "perhaps he only sleeps."

"Seize him, then, quickly," cried Cadj, and an instant later Tarzan's body was covered by the hairy forms of as many of the frightful men as could pile upon him. He offered no resistance—he did not even open his eyes, and presently his arms were securely bound behind him.

"Drag him forth where the eye of the Flaming God may rest upon him," cried Cadj. They dragged Tarzan out into the center of the boma into the full light of the sun, and Cadj, the High Priest, drawing his knife from his loin cloth, raised it above his head and stood over the prostrate form of his intended victim. Cadj's followers formed a rough circle about the ape-man and some of them pressed close behind their leader. They appeared uneasy, looking alternately at Tarzan and their High Priest, and then casting furtive glances at the sun, riding high in a cloud-mottled sky. But whatever the thoughts that troubled their half-savage brains, there was only one who dared voice his, and he was the same priest who, upon the preceding day, had questioned Cadj's proposal to slay the ape-man.

"Cadj," he said now, "who are you to offer up a sacrifice to the Flaming God? It is the privilege alone of La, our High Priestess and our queen, and indeed will she be angry when she learns what you have done."

"Silence, Dooth!" cried Cadj; "I, Cadj, am the High Priest of Opar. I, Cadj, am the mate of La, the queen. My word, too, is law in Opar. And you would remain a priest, and you would remain alive, keep silence."

"Your word is not law," replied Dooth, angrily, "and if you anger La, the High Priestess, or if you anger the

Flaming God, you may be punished as another. If you make this sacrifice both will be angry."

"Enough," cried Cadj; "the Flaming God has spoken to me and has demanded that I offer up as sacrifice this defiler of his temple."

He knelt beside the ape-man and touched his breast above the heart with the point of his sharp blade, and then he raised the weapon high above him, preparatory to the fatal plunge into the living heart. At that instant a cloud passed before the face of the sun and a shadow rested upon them. A murmur rose from the surrounding priests.

"Look," cried Dooth, "the Flaming God is angry. He has hidden his face from the people of Opar."

Cadj paused. He cast a half-defiant, half-frightened look at the cloud obscuring the face of the sun. Then he rose slowly to his feet, and extending his arms upward toward the hidden god of day, he remained for a moment silent in apparently attentive and listening attitude. Then, suddenly, he turned upon his followers.

"Priests of Opar," he cried, "the Flaming God has spoken to his High Priest, Cadj. He is not angered. He but wishes to speak to me alone, and he directs that you go away into the jungle and wait until he has come and spoken to Cadj, after which I shall call you to return. Go!"

For the most part they seemed to accept the word of Cadj as law, but Dooth and a few others, doubtless prompted by a certain skepticism, hesitated.

"Be gone!" commanded Cadj. And so powerful is the habit of obedience that the doubters finally turned away and melted into the jungle with the others. A crafty smile lighted the cruel face of the High Priest as the last of them disappeared from sight, and then he once again turned his attention to the ape-man. That, deep within his breast however, lurked an inherent fear of his deity, was evidenced by the fact that he turned questioning glances toward the sky. He had determined to slay the ape-man while Dooth and the others were absent, yet the fear of his god restrained his hand until the light of his deity should shine forth upon him once more and assure him that the thing he contemplated might meet with favor.

It was a large cloud that overcast the sun, and while Cadj waited his nervousness increased. Six times he raised his knife for the fatal blow, yet in each instance his superstition prevented the consummation of the act. Five, ten, fifteen minutes passed, and still the sun remained obscured. But now at last Cadj could see that it was nearing the edge of the cloud, and once again he took his position kneeling beside the ape-man with his blade ready for the moment that the sunlight should flood again, for the last time, the living Tarzan. He saw it sweeping slowly across the boma toward him, and as it came a look of demoniacal hatred shone in his close-set, wicked eyes. Another instant and the Flaming God would have set the seal of his approval upon the sacrifice. Cadj trembled in anticipation. He raised the knife a trifle higher, his muscles tensed for the downward plunge, and then the silence of the jungle was broken by a woman's voice, raised almost to a scream.

"Cadj!" came the single word, but with all the suddenness and all the surprising effect of lightning from a clear sky.

His knife still poised on high, the High Priest turned in the direction of the interruption to see at the clearing's edge the figure of La, the High Priestess, and behind her Dooth and a score of the lesser priests.

"What means this, Cadj?" demanded La, angrily, approaching rapidly toward him across the clearing. Sullenly the High Priest rose.

"The Flaming God demanded the life of this unbeliever," he cried.

"Speaker of lies," retorted La, "the Flaming God communicates with men through the lips of his High Priestess only. Too often already have you attempted to thwart the will of your queen. Know, then, Cadj, that the power of life and death which your queen holds is as potent over you as another. During the long ages that Opar has endured, our legends tell us that more than one High Priest has been offered upon the altar to the Flaming God. And it is not unlikely that yet another may go the way of the presumptuous. Curb, therefore, your vanity and your lust for power, lest they prove your undoing."

Cadj sheathed his knife and turned sullenly away, casting a venomous look at Dooth, to whom he evidently attributed his undoing. That he was temporarily abashed by the presence of his queen was evident, but to those who knew Cadj there was little doubt that he still harbored his intention to despatch the ape-man, and if the opportunity ever presented itself that he would do so, for Cadj had a strong following among the people and priests of Opar. There were many who doubted that La would ever dare to incur the displeasure and anger of so important a portion of her followers as to cause the death or degradation of their high priest, who occupied his office by virtue of laws and customs so old that their origin had been long lost in antiquity.

For years she had found first one excuse and then another to delay the ceremonies that would unite her in marriage to the High Priest. She had further aroused the antagonism of her people by palpable proofs of her infatuation for the ape-man, and even though at last she had been compelled to mate with Cadj, she had made no effort whatsoever to conceal her hatred and loathing for the man. How much further she could go with impunity was a question that often troubled those whose position in Opar depended upon her favor, and, knowing all these conditions as he did, it was not strange that Cadj should entertain treasonable thoughts toward his queen. Leagued with him in his treachery was Oah, a priestess who aspired to the power and offices of La. If La could be done away with, then Cadj had the influence to see that Oah became High Priestess. He also had Oah's promise to mate with him and permit him to rule as king, but as yet both were bound by the superstitious fear of their flaming deity, and because of this fact was the life of La temporarily made safe. It required, however, but the slightest spark to ignite the flames of treason that were smoldering about her.

So far, she was well within her rights in forbidding the sacrifice of Tarzan by the High Priest. But her fate, her very life, perhaps, depended upon her future treatment of the prisoner. Should she spare him, should she evidence in any way a return of the great love she had once almost publicly avowed for him, it was likely that her doom would be sealed. It was even questionable whether or not she might with impunity spare his life and set him at liberty.

Cadj and the others watched her closely now as she crossed to the side of Tarzan. Standing there silently for several moments she looked down upon him.

"He is already dead?" she asked.

"He was not dead when Cadj sent us away," volunteered Dooth. "If he is dead now it is because Cadj killed him while we were away."

"I did not kill him," said Cadj. "That remains, as La, our queen, has told you, for her to do. The eye of the Flaming God looks down upon you, High Priestess of Opar. The knife is at your hip, the sacrifice lies before you."

La ignored the man's words and turned toward Dooth. "If he still lives," she said, "construct a litter and bear him back to Opar."

Thus, once more, came Tarzan of the Apes into the an-

cient colonial city of the Atlantians. The effects of the narcotic that Kraski had administered to him did not wear off
for many hours. It was night when he opened his eyes, and for
a moment he was bewildered by the darkness and the silence that surrounded him. All that he could scent at first
was that he lay upon a pile of furs and that he was uninjured; for he felt no pain. Slowly there broke through the fog
of his drugged brain recollection of the last moment before
unconsciousness had overcome him, and presently he realized
the trick that had been played upon him. For how long
he had been unconscious and where he then was he could
not imagine. Slowly he arose to his feet, finding that except
for a slight dizziness he was quite himself. Cautiously he felt
around in the darkness, moving with care, a hand outstretched,
and always feeling carefully with his feet for secure footing.
Almost immediately a stone wall stopped his progress, and
this he followed around four sides of what he soon realized
was a small room in which there were but two openings, a
door upon each of the opposite sides. Only his senses of touch
and smell were of value to him here. These told him only at
first that he was imprisoned in a subterranean chamber,
but as the effects of the narcotic diminished, the keenness of
the latter returned, and with its return there was borne in
upon Tarzan's brain an insistent impression of familiarity in
certain fragrant odors that impinged upon his olfactory organs
—a haunting suggestion that he had known them before under similar circumstances. Presently from above, through
earth and masonry, came the shadow of an uncanny scream
—just the faintest suggestion of it reached the keen ears
of the ape-man, but it was sufficient to flood his mind with
vivid recollections, and, by association of ideas, to fix the
identity of the familiar odors about him. He knew at last
that he was in the dark pit beneath Opar.

Above him, in her chamber in the temple, La, the High
Priestess, tossed upon a sleepless couch. She knew all too
well the temper of her people and the treachery of the High
Priest, Cadj. She knew the religious fanaticism which prompted the ofttime maniacal actions of her bestial and ignorant followers, and she guessed truly that Cadj would inflame
them against her should she fail this time in sacrificing the
ape-man to the Flaming God. And it was the effort to find
an escape from her dilemma that left her sleepless, for it
was not in the heart of La to sacrifice Tarzan of the Apes.
High Priestess of a horrid cult though she was, the queen
of a race of half-beasts, yet she was a woman, too, a woman
who had loved but once and given that love to the godlike

ape-man who was again within her power. Twice before had he escaped her sacrificial knife; in the final instance love had at last triumphed over jealousy and fanaticism, and La, the woman, had realized that never again could she place in jeopardy the life of the man she loved, however hopeless she knew that love to be.

Tonight she was faced with a problem that she felt almost beyond her powers of solution. The fact that she was mated with Cadj removed the last vestige of hope that she had ever had of becoming the wife of the ape-man. Yet she was no less determined to save Tarzan if it were possible. Twice had he saved her life, once from a mad priest, and once from Tantor in *must*. Then, too, she had given her word that when Tarzan came again to Opar he came in friendship and would be received in friendship. But the influence of Cadj was great, and she knew that that influence had been directed unremittingly against the ape-man—she had seen it in the attitude of her followers from the very moment that they had placed Tarzan upon a litter to bear him back to Opar—she had seen it in the evil glances that had been cast at her. Sooner or later they would dare denounce her—all that they needed was some slight, new excuse, that, she knew, they eagerly awaited in her forthcoming attitude toward Tarzan. It was well after midnight when there came to her one of the priestesses who remained always upon guard outside her chamber door.

"Dooth would speak with you," whispered the hand-maiden.

"It is late," replied La, "and men are not permitted in this part of the temple. How came he here, and why?"

"He says that he comes in the service of La, who is in great danger," replied the girl.

"Fetch him here then," said La, "and as you value your life see that you tell no one."

"I shall be as voiceless as the stones of the altar," replied the girl, as she turned and left the chamber.

A moment later she returned bringing Dooth, who halted a few feet from the High Priestess and saluted her. La signaled to the girl who had brought him, to depart, and then she turned questioningly to the man.

"Speak, Dooth!" she commanded.

"We all know," he said, "of La's love for the strange ape-man, and it is not for me, a lesser priest, to question the thoughts or acts of my High Priestess. It is only for me to serve, as those would do better to serve who now plot against you."

"What do you mean, Dooth? Who plots against me?"

"Even at this minute are Cadj and Oah and several of the priests and priestesses carrying out a plan for your undoing. They are setting spies to watch you, knowing that you would liberate the ape-man, because there will come to you one who will tell you that to permit him to escape will be the easiest solution of your problem. This one will be sent by Cadj, and then those who watch you will report to the people and to the priests that they have seen you lead the sacrifice to liberty. But even that will avail you nothing, for Cadj and Oah and the others have placed upon the trail from Opar many men in hiding, who will fall upon the ape-man and slay him before the Flaming God has descended twice into the western forest. In but one way only may you save yourself, La of Opar."

"And what is that way?" she asked.

"You must, with your own hands, upon the altar of our temple, sacrifice the ape-man to the Flaming God."

8

Mystery of the Past

LA HAD breakfasted the following morning, and had sent Dooth with food for Tarzan, when there came to her a young priestess, who was the sister of Oah. Even before the girl had spoken La knew that she was an emissary from Cadj, and that the treachery of which Dooth had warned her was already under way. The girl was ill at ease and quite evidently frightened, for she was young and held in high revere the queen whom she had good reason to know was all-powerful, and who might even inflict death upon her if she so wished. La, who had already determined upon a plan of action that she knew would be most embarrassing to Cadj and his conspirators, waited in silence for the girl to speak. But it was some time before the girl could muster up her courage or find a proper opening. Instead, she spoke of many things that had no bearing whatsoever upon her subject, and La, the High Priestess, was amused at her discomfiture.

"It is not often," said La, "that the sister of Oah comes to the apartments of her queen unless she is bidden. I am glad to see that she at last realizes the service that she owes to the High Priestess of the Flaming God."

"I come," said the girl, at last, speaking almost as one who has learned a part, "to tell you that I have overheard that which may be of interest to you, and which I am sure that you will be glad to hear."

"Yes?" interrogated La, raising her arched eyebrows.

"I overheard Cadj speaking with the lesser priests," the girl continued, "and I distinctly heard him say that he would be glad if the ape-man escaped, as that would relieve you, and Cadj as well, of much embarrassment. I thought that La, the queen, would be glad to know this, for it is known by all of us that La has promised friendship to the ape-man and therefore does not wish to sacrifice him upon the altar of the Flaming God."

"My duty is plain to me," replied La, in a haughty voice, "and I do not need Cadj nor any hand-maiden to interpret it to me. I also know the prerogatives of a High Priestess, and that the right of sacrifice is one of them. For this reason I prevented Cadj from sacrificing the stranger. No other hand than mine may offer his heart's blood to the Flaming God, and upon the third day he shall die beneath my knife upon the altar of our temple."

The effect of these words upon the girl were precisely what La had anticipated. She saw disappointment and chagrin written upon the face of Cadj's messenger, who now had no answer, for her instructions had not foreseen this attitude upon the part of La. Presently the girl found some lame pretext upon which to withdraw, and when she had left the presence of the High Priestess, La could scarcely restrain a smile. She had no intention of sacrificing Tarzan, but this, of course, the sister of Oah did not know. So she returned to Cadj and repeated as nearly as she could recall it, all that La had said to her. The High Priest was much chagrined, for his plan had been now, not so much to encompass the destruction of Tarzan as to lead La into the commission of an act that would bring upon her the wrath of the priests and people of Opar, who, properly instigated, would demand her life in expiation. Oah, who was present when her sister returned, bit her lips, for great was her disappointment. Never before had she seen so close at hand the longed-for possibility of becoming High Priestess. For several minutes she paced to and fro in deep thought, and then, suddenly, she halted before Cadj.

"La loves this ape-man," she said, "and even though she may sacrifice him, it is only because of fear of her people. She loves him still—loves him better, Cadj, than she has ever loved you. The ape-man knows it, and trusts her, and because he knows it there is a way. Listen, Cadj, to Oah. We will send one to the ape-man who shall tell him that she comes from La, and that La has instructed her to lead him out of Opar and set him free. This one shall lead him into our ambush and when he is killed we shall go, many of us, before La, and accuse her of treachery. The one who led the ape-man from Opar shall say that La ordered her to do it, and the priests and the people will be very angry, and then you shall demand the life of La. It will be very easy and we shall be rid of both of them."

"Good!" exclaimed Cadj. "We shall do this thing at dawn upon the morrow, and before the Flaming God goes to his rest at night he shall look upon a new High Priestess in Opar."

That night Tarzan was aroused from his sleep by a sound at one of the doors of his prison cell. He heard the bolt slipped back and the door creak slowly open upon its ancient hinges. In the inky darkness he could discern no presence, but he heard the stealthy movement of sandaled feet upon the concrete floor, and then, out of the darkness, his name was whispered, in a woman's voice.

"I am here," he replied. "Who are you and what do you want of Tarzan of the Apes?"

"Your life is in danger," replied the voice. "Come, follow me."

"Who sent you?" demanded the ape-man, his sensitive nostrils searching for a clue to the identity of the nocturnal visitor, but so heavily was the air laden with the pungent odor of some heavy perfume with which the body of the woman seemed to have been anointed, that there was no distinguishing clue by which he might judge as to whether she was one of the priestesses he had known upon the occasion of his former visits to Opar, or an entire stranger to him.

"La sent me," she said, "to lead you from the pits of Opar to the freedom of the outside world beyond the city's walls." Groping in the darkness she finally found him. "Here are your weapons," she said, handing them to him, and then she took his hand, turned and led him from the dungeon, through a long, winding, and equally black corridor, down flights of age-old concrete steps, through passages and corridors, opening and closing door after door that creaked and groaned upon rusty hinges. How far they traveled thus, and in what direction, Tarzan could not guess. He had gleaned enough from Dooth, when the latter brought him his food, to believe that in La he had a friend who would aid him, for Dooth had told him that she had saved him from Cadj when the latter had discovered him unconscious in the deserted boma of the Europeans who had drugged and left him. And so, the woman having said that she came from La, Tarzan followed her willingly. He could not but recall Jane's prophecy of the evils that he might expect to befall him should he persist in undertaking this third trip to Opar, and he wondered if, after all, his wife were right, that he should never again escape from the toils of the fanatical priests of the Flaming God. He had not, of course, expected to enter Opar, but there seemed to hang over the accursed city a guardian demon that threatened the life of whosoever dared approach the forbidden spot or wrest from the forgotten treasure vaults a portion of their great hoard.

For more than an hour his guide led him through the Stygian darkness of underground passages, until ascending a flight of steps they emerged into the center of a clump of bushes, through which the pale light of the moon was barely discernible. The fresh air, however, told him that they had reached the surface of the ground, and now the woman, who had not spoken a word since she had led him from his cell, continued on in silence, following a devious trail that wound hither and thither in an erratic fashion through a heavy forest choked with undergrowth, and always upward.

From the location of the stars and moon, and from the upward trend of the trail, Tarzan knew that he was being led into the mountains that lie behind Opar—a place he had never thought of visiting, since the country appeared rough and uninviting, and not likely to harbor game such as Tarzan cared most to hunt. He was already surprised by the nature of the vegetation, for he had thought the hills barren except for stunted trees and scraggy bush. As they continued upon their way, climbing ever upward, the moon rose higher in the heavens, until its soft light revealed more clearly to the keen eyes of the ape-man the topography of the country they were traversing, and then it was that he saw they were ascending a narrow, thickly wooded gorge, and he understood why the heavy vegetation had been invisible from the plain before Opar. Himself naturally uncommunicative, the woman's silence made no particular impression upon Tarzan. Had he had anything to say he should have said it, and likewise he assumed that there was no necessity for her speaking unless there was some good reason for speaking, for those who travel far and fast have no breath to waste upon conversation.

The eastern stars were fading at the first hint of coming dawn when the two scrambled up a precipitous bank that formed the upper end of the ravine, and came out upon comparatively level ground. As they advanced the sky lightened, and presently the woman halted at the edge of a declivity, and as the day broke Tarzan saw below him a wooded basin in the heart of the mountain, and, showing through the trees at what appeared to be some two or three miles distant, the outlines of a building that glistened and sparkled and scintillated in the light of the new sun. Then he turned and looked at his companion, and surprise and consternation were writ upon his face, for standing before him was La, the High Priestess of Opar.

"You?" he exclaimed. "Now indeed will Cadj have the excuse that Dooth said he sought to put you out of the way."

"He will never have the oppportunity to put me out of the way," replied La, "for I shall never return to Opar."

"Never return to Opar!" he exclaimed, "then where are you going? Where can you go?"

"I am going with you," she replied. "I do not ask that you love me. I only ask that you take me away from Opar and from the enemies who would slay me. There was no other way. Manu, the monkey, overheard them plotting, and he came to me and told me all that they would do. Whether I saved you or sacrificed you, it had all been the same with me. They were determined to do away with me, that Oah might be High Priestess and Cadj king of Opar. But I should not have sacrificed you, Tarzan, under any circumstances, and this, then, seemed the only way in which we might both be saved. We could not go to the north or the west across the plain of Opar for there Cadj has placed warriors in ambush to waylay you, and though you be Tarzan and a mighty fighter, they would overwhelm you by their very numbers and slay you."

"But where are you leading me?" asked Tarzan.

"I have chosen the lesser of two evils; in this direction lies an unknown country, filled for us Oparians with legends of grim monsters and strange people. Never has an Oparian ventured here and returned again to Opar. But if there lives in all the world a creature who could win through this unknown valley, it be you, Tarzan of the Apes."

"But if you know nothing of this country, or its inhabitants," demanded Tarzan, "how is it that you so well know the trail that leads to it?"

"We well know the trail to the summit, but that is as far as I have ever been before. The great apes and the lions use this trail when they come down into Opar. The lions, of course, cannot tell us where it leads, and the great apes will not, for usually we are at war with them. Along this trail they come down into Opar to steal our people, and upon this trail we await to capture them, for often we offer a great ape in sacrifice to the Flaming God, or rather that was our former custom, but for many years they have been too wary for us, the toll being upon the other side, though we do not know for what purpose they steal our people, unless it be that they eat them. They are a very powerful race, standing higher than Bolgani, the gorilla, and infinitely more cunning, for, as there is ape blood in our veins, so is there human blood in the veins of these great apes that dwell in the valley above Opar."

"Why is it, La, that we must pass through this valley in order to escape from Opar? There must be some other way."

"There is no other way, Tarzan of the Apes," she replied. "The avenues across the valley are guarded by Cadj's people. Our only chance of escape lies in this direction, and I have brought you along the only trail that pierces the precipitous cliffs that guard Opar upon the south. Across or around this valley we must go in an attempt to find an avenue across the mountain and down upon the other side."

The ape-man stood gazing down into the wooded basin below them, his mind occupied with the problems of the moment. Had he been alone he would not have come this way, for he was sufficiently confident of his own prowess to believe that he might easily have crossed the valley of Opar in comparative safety, regardless of Cadj's plans to the contrary. But he was not alone. He had now to think of La, and he realized that in her efforts to save him she had placed him under a moral obligation which he might not disregard.

To skirt the basin, keeping as far as possible from the building, which he could see in the distance, seemed the wisest course to pursue, since, of course, his sole purpose was to find a way across the mountain and out of this inhospitable country. But the glimpses he caught of the edifice, half concealed as it was amid the foliage of great trees, piqued his curiosity to such an extent that he felt an almost irresistible urge to investigate. He did not believe that the basin was inhabited by other than wild beasts, and he attributed the building which he saw to the handiwork of an extinct or departed people, either contemporaneous with the ancient Atlantians who had built Opar or, perhaps, built by the original Oparians themselves, but now forgotten by their descendants. The glimpses which he caught of the building suggested such size and magnificence as might belong to a palace.

The ape-man knew no fear, though he possessed to a reasonable extent that caution which is inherent in all wild beasts. He would not have hesitated to pit his cunning and his prowess against the lower orders, however ferocious they might be, for, unlike man, they could not band together to his undoing. But should men elect to hunt him in numbers he knew that a real danger would confront him, and that, in the face of their combined strength and intelligence, his own might not avail him. There was little likelihood, however, he reasoned, that the basin was inhabited by human beings. Doubtless closer investigation of the building he saw would reveal that it was but a deserted ruin, and that the most formidable foes he would encounter would be the great apes and the lions. Of neither of these had he any fear; with the former it was even reasonable to imagine that he might establish amicable relations. Believing as he did that he must look for egress from the basin upon its opposite side, it was only natural that he should wish to choose the most direct route across the basin. Therefore his inclinations to explore the valley were seconded by considerations of speed and expediency.

"Come," he said to La, and started down the declivity which led into the basin in the direction of the building ahead of them.

"You are not going that way?" she cried in astonishment.

"Why not?" he said. "It is the shortest way across the valley, and in so far as I can judge our trail over the mountains is more likely to lie in that direction than elsewhere."

"But I am afraid," she said. "The Flaming God alone knows what hideous dangers lurk in the depths of that forest below us."

"Only Numa and the Mangani," he said. "Of these we need have no fear."

"You fear nothing," she said, "but I am only a woman."

"We can die but once," replied Tarzan, "and that once we must die. To be always fearing, then, would not avert it, and would make life miserable. We shall go the short way, then, and perhaps we shall see enough to make the risk well worth while."

They followed a well-worn trail downward among the brush, the trees increasing in both size and number as they approached the floor of the basin, until at last they were walking beneath the foliage of a great forest. What wind there was was at their back, and the ape-man, though he moved at a swinging walk, was constantly on the alert. Upon the hard-packed earth of the trail there were few signs to indicate the nature of the animals that had passed to and fro, but here and there the spoor of a lion was in evidence. Several times Tarzan stopped and listened, often he raised his head and his sensitive nostrils dilated as he sought for whatever the surrounding air might hold for him.

"I think there are men in this valley," he said presently. "For some time I have been almost positive that we are being watched. But whoever is stalking us is clever beyond words, for it is only the barest suggestion of another presence that I can scent."

La looked about apprehensively and drew close to his side. "I see no one," she said, in a low voice.

"Nor I," he replied. "Nor can I catch any well-defined scent spoor, yet I am positive that someone is following us. Someone or something that trails by scent, and is clever enough to keep its scent from us. It is more than likely that, whatever it is, it is passing through the trees, at a sufficient height to keep its scent spoor always above us. The air is right for that, and even if he were up wind from us we might not catch his scent at all. Wait here, I will make sure," and he swung lightly into the branches of a nearby tree and swarmed upward with the agility of Manu, the monkey. A moment later he descended to the girl's side.

"I was right," he said, "there is someone, or something, not far off. But whether it is man or Mangani I cannot say, for the odor is a strange one to me, suggesting neither, yet both. But two can play at that game. Come!" And he swung the girl to his shoulder and a moment later had carried her high into the trees. "Unless he is close enough to watch us, which I doubt," he said, "our spoor will be carried over his head and it will be some time before he can pick it up again, unless he is wise enough to rise to a higher level."

La marveled at the strength of the ape-man as he carried her easily from tree to tree, and at the speed with which he traversed the swaying, leafy trail. For half an hour he continued onward, and then quite suddenly he stopped, poised high upon a swaying bough.

"Look!" he said, pointing ahead and below them. Looking in the direction that he indicated the girl saw through the leafy foliage a small, heavily stockaded compound, in which were some dozen huts that immediately riveted her surprised attention, nor no less was the ape-man's curiosity piqued by what he glimpsed vaguely through the foliage. Huts they evidently were, but they seemed to be moving to and fro in the air, some moving gently backward and forward, while others jumped up and down in more or less violent agitation. Tarzan swung to a nearer tree and descended to a sturdy branch, to which he lowered La from his shoulder. Then he crept forward stealthily, the girl following, for she was, in common with the other Oparians, slightly arboreal. Presently they reached a point where they could see plainly the village below them, and immediately the seeming mystery of the dancing huts was explained.

They were of the bee-hive type, common to many African tribes, and were about seven feet in diameter by six or seven in height, but instead of resting on the ground, each hut was suspended by a heavy hawser-like grass rope to a branch of one of the several giant trees that grew within the stockade. From the center of the bottom of each hut trailed another lighter rope. From his position above them Tarzan saw no openings in any of the huts large enough to admit the body of a man, though there were several openings four or five inches in diameter in the sides of each hut about three feet above the floor. Upon the ground, inside the compound, were several of the inhabitants of the village, if the little collection of swinging houses could be dignified by such a name. Nor were the people any less strange to Tarzan than their peculiar domiciles. That they were negroes was evident, but of a type entirely unfamiliar to the ape-man. All were naked, and without any ornamentation whatsoever other than a few daubs of color, placed apparently at random upon their bodies. They were tall, and very muscular appearing, though their legs seemed much too short and their arms too long for perfect symmetry, while their faces were almost bestial in contour, their jaws being exaggeratedly prognathous while above their beetling brows there was no forehead, the skull running back in an almost horizontal plane to a point.

As Tarzan stood looking at them he saw another descend one of the ropes that dangled from the bottom of a hut, and immediately he understood the purpose of the ropes and the location of the entrances to the dwellings. The creatures squatting about upon their haunches were engaged in feeding. Several had bones from which they were tearing the uncooked flesh with their great teeth, while others ate fruit and tubers. There were individuals of both sexes and of various ages, from childhood to maturity, but there was none that seemed very old. They were practically hairless, except for scraggy,

reddish brown locks upon their heads. They spoke but sel-
dom and then in tones which resembled the growling of
beasts, nor once, while Tarzan watched them, did he see one
laugh or even smile, which, of all their traits, rendered them
most unlike the average native of Africa. Though Tarzan's
eyes searched the compound carefully he saw no indication
of cooking utensils or of any fire. Upon the ground about
them lay their weapons, short javelin-like spears and a sort
of battle-ax with a sharpened, metal blade. Tarzan of the
Apes was glad that he had come this way, for it had permitted him to see such a type of native as he had not
dreamed existed—a type that bordered closely upon the brute.
Even the Waz-dons and Ho-dons of Pal-ul-don were far
advanced in the scale of evolution compared to these.

As he looked at them he could not but wonder that they
were sufficiently intelligent to manufacture the weapons they
possessed, which he could see, even at a distance, were of
fine workmanship and design. Their huts, too, seemed well
and ingeniously made, while the stockade which surrounded
the little compound was tall, strong, and well-built, evidently
for the purpose of safeguarding them against the lions which
infested the basin.

As Tarzan and La watched these people they became
presently aware of the approach of some creature from their
left, and a moment later they saw a man similar to those of
the compound swing from a tree that overhung the stockade
and drop within. The others acknowledged his coming with
scarce more than indifferent glances. He came forward and,
squatting among them, appeared to be telling them of something, and though Tarzan could not hear his words he judged
from his gestures and the sign language which he used to
supplement his meager speech, that he was telling his fellows
of the strange creatures he had seen in the forest a short
time before, and the ape-man immediately judged that this
was the same whom he had been aware was following them
and whom he had successfully put off the scent. The narra-
tion evidently excited them, for some of them arose, and
leaping up and down with bent knees, slapped their arms
against their sides grotesquely. The expressions upon their
faces scarcely changed, however, and after a moment each
squatted down again as he had been before.

It was while they were thus engaged that there echoed
through the forest a loud scream that awakened in the mind
of the ape-man many savage memories.

"Bolgani," he whispered to La.

"It is one of the great apes," she said, and shuddered.

Presently they saw him, swinging down the jungle trail toward the compound. A huge gorilla, but such a gorilla as Tarzan of the Apes had never looked on before. Of almost gigantic stature, the creature was walking erect with the stride of a man, not ever once touching his knuckles to the ground. His head and face were almost those of a gorilla, and yet there was a difference, as Tarzan could note as the creature came nearer—it was Bolgani, with the soul and brain of a man—nor was this all that rendered the creature startling and unique. Stranger perhaps than aught else was the fact that it wore ornaments—and such ornaments! Gold and diamonds sparkled against its shaggy coat, above its elbows were numerous armlets and there were anklets upon its legs, while from a girdle about its middle there depended before and behind a long narrow strip that almost touched the ground and which seemed to be entirely constructed of golden spangles set with small diamonds. Never before had John Clayton, Lord Greystoke, seen such a display of barbaric finery, nor even amidst the jewels of Opar such a wealth of priceless stones.

Immediately after the hideous scream had first broken the comparative silence of the forest, Tarzan had noticed its effects upon the inmates of the compound. Instantly they had arisen to their feet. The women and children scurried behind the boles of the trees or clambered up the ropes into their swinging cages, while some of the men advanced to what Tarzan now saw was the gate of the compound. Outside this gate the gorilla halted and again raised his voice, but this time in speech rather than his hideous scream.

9

The Shaft of Death

A S THE huge, man-like gorilla entered the compound the warriors closed the gate, and fell back respectfully as he advanced to the center of the village where he stood for a moment, looking about.

"Where are the shes and the balus?" he asked, tersely. "Call them."

The women and the children must have heard the command, but they did not emerge from their hiding places. The warriors moved about uneasily, evidently torn by the conflicting emotions of fear of the creature who had issued the order, and reluctance to fulfil his commands.

"Call them," he repeated, "or go and fetch them." But at last one of the warriors mustered the courage to address him.

"This village has already furnished one woman within the moon," he said. "It is the turn of another village."

"Silence!" roared the gorilla-man, advancing threateningly toward him. "You are a rash Gomangani to threaten the will of a Bolgani—I speak with the voice of Numa, the Emperor; obey or die."

Trembling, the black turned and called the women and children, but none responded to his summons. The Bolgani gestured impatiently.

"Go and fetch them," he demanded. And the blacks, cringing, moved sullenly across the compound toward the hiding places of their women and children. Presently they returned, dragging them with them, by the arms sometimes, but usually by the hair. Although they had seemed loath to give them up, they showed no gentleness toward them, nor any indication of affection. Their attitude toward them, however, was presently explained to Tarzan by the next words of the warrior who had spoken previously.

"Great Bolgani," he said, addressing the gorilla-man, "if Numa takes always from this village, there will soon be not enough women for the warriors here, and there will be too few children, and in a little time there will be none of us left."

"What of that?" growled the gorilla-man. "There are already too many Gomangani in the world. For what other purpose were you created than to serve Numa, the emperor, and his chosen people, the Bolgani?" As he spoke he was examining the women and children, pinching their flesh and pounding upon their chests and backs. Presently he returned to a comparatively young woman, straddling whose hip was a small child.

"This one will do," he said, snatching the child from its mother and hurling it roughly across the compound, where it lay against the face of the palisade, moaning pitifully, and perchance broken and dying. The poor, stupid mother, apparently more beast than human, stood for a moment trembling in dumb anguish, and then she started to rush forward to her child. But the gorilla-man seized her with one of his great hands and hurled her to the ground. Simultaneously there arose from the silent foliage above them the fierce and terrible scream of the challenging bull ape. In terror the simple blacks cast affrighted glances upward, while the gorilla-man raised his hideous face in snarling anger toward the author of the bestial cry.

Swaying upon a leafy bough they beheld such a creature as none of them had ever looked upon before—a white man, a Tarmangani, with hide as hairless as the body of Histah, the snake. In the instant that they looked they saw the spear hand of the stranger drive forward, and the shaft, speeding with the swiftness of thought, bury itself in the breast of the Bolgani. With a single scream of rage and pain, the gorilla-man crumpled to the earth, where he struggled spasmodically for a moment and then lay still, in death.

The ape-man held no great love for the Gomangani as a race, but inherent in his English brain and heart was the spirit of fair play, which prompted him to spontaneous es-pousal of the cause of the weak. On the other hand Bolgani was his hereditary enemy. His first battle had been with Bolgani, and his first kill.

The poor blacks were still standing in stupefied wonder-ment when he dropped from the tree to the ground among them. They stepped back in terror, and simultaneously they raised their spears menacingly against him.

"I am a friend," he said. "I am Tarzan of the Apes. Lower your spears." And then he turned and withdrew his own weapon from the carcass of Bolgani. "Who is this creature, that may come into your village and slay your balus and steal your shes? Who is he, that you dare not drive your spears through him?"

"He is one of the great Bolgani," said the warrior, who seemed to be spokesman, and the leader in the village, "He is one of the chosen people of Numa, the Emperor, and when Numa learns that he has been killed in our village we shall all die for what you have done."

"Who is Numa?" demanded the ape-man, to whom Numa, in the language of the great apes, meant only lion.

"Numa is the Emperor," replied the black, "who lives with the Bolgani in the Palace of Diamonds."

He did not express himself in just these words, for the meager language of the great apes, even though amplified by the higher intelligence and greater development of the Oparians, is still primitive in the extreme. What he had really said was more nearly "Numa, the king of kings, who lives in the king's hut of glittering stones," which carried to the ape-man's mind the faithful impression of the fact. Numa, evidently, was the name adopted by the king of the Bolgani, and the title *emperor*, indicated merely his preeminence among the chiefs.

The instant that Bolgani had fallen the bereaved mother rushed forward and gathered her injured infant into her arms. She squatted now against the palisade, cuddling it to her breast, and crooning softly to pacify its cries, which Tarzan suddenly discovered were more the result of fright than injury. At first the mother had been frightened when he had attempted to examine the child, drawing away and baring her fighting fangs, much after the manner of a wild beast. But presently there had seemed to come to her dull brain a realization that this creature had saved her from Bolgani, that he had permitted her to recover her infant and that he was making no effort to harm either of them. Convinced at last that the child was only bruised, Tarzan turned again toward the warriors, who were talking together in an excited little group a few paces away. As they saw him advancing, they spread into a semi-circle and stood facing him.

"The Bolgani will send and slay us all," they said, "when they learn what has happened in our village, unless we can take to them the creature that cast the spear. Therefore, Tarmangani, you shall go with us to the Palace of Diamonds, and there we shall give you over to the Bolgani and perhaps Numa will forgive us."

The ape-man smiled. What kind of creature did the simple blacks think him, to believe that he would permit himself to be easily led into the avenging hands of Numa, the Emperor of the Bolgani. Although he was fully aware of the risk that he had taken in entering the village, he knew too that because he was Tarzan of the Apes there was a greater chance that he would be able to escape than that they could hold him. He had faced savage spearmen before and knew precisely what to expect in the event of hostilities. He preferred, however, to make peace with these people, for it had been in his mind to find some means of questioning them the moment that he had discovered their village hidden away in this wild forest.

"Wait," he said, therefore. "Would you betray a friend who enters your village to protect you from an enemy?"

"We will not slay you, Tarmangani. We will take you to the Bolgani for Numa, the Emperor."

"But that would amount to the same thing," returned Tarzan, "for you well know that Numa, the Emperor, will have me slain."

"That we cannot help," replied the spokesman. "If we

could save you we would, but when the Bolgani discover what has happened in our village, it is we who must suffer, unless, perhaps, they are satisfied to punish you instead."

"But why need they know that the Bolgani has been slain in your village?" asked Tarzan.

"Will they not see his body next time they come?" asked the spokesman.

"Not if you remove his body," replied Tarzan.

The blacks scratched their heads. Into their dull, ignorant minds had crept no such suggestion of a solution of their problem. What the stranger said was true. None but they and he knew that Bolgani had been slain within their palisade. To remove the body, then, would be to remove all suspicion from their village. But where were they to take it? They put the question to Tarzan.

"I will dispose of him for you," replied the Tarmangani. "Answer my questions truthfully and I will promise to take him away and dispose of him in such a manner that no one will know how he died, or where."

"What are your questions?" asked the spokesman.

"I am a stranger in your country. I am lost here," replied the ape-man. "And I would find a way out of the valley in that direction." And he pointed toward the southeast.

The black shook his head. "There may be a way out of the valley in that direction," he said, "but what lies beyond no man knows, nor do I know whether there be a way out or whether there be anything beyond. It is said that all is fire beyond the mountain, and no one dares to go and see. As for myself, I have never been far from my village—at most only a day's march to hunt for game for the Bolgani, and to gather fruit and nuts and plantains for them. If there is a way out I do not know, nor would any man dare take it if there were."

"Does no one ever leave the valley?" asked Tarzan.

"I know not what others do," replied the spokesman, "but those of this village never leave the valley."

"What lies in that direction?" asked Tarzan, pointing toward Opar.

"I do not know," replied the black, "only that sometimes the Bolgani come from that way, bringing with them strange creatures; little men with white skins and much hair, with short, crooked legs and long arms, and sometimes white shes, who do not look at all like the strange little Tarmangani. But where they get them I do not know, nor do they ever tell us. Are these all the questions that you wish to ask?"

"Yes, that is all," replied Tarzan, seeing that he could

gain no information whatsoever from these ignorant villagers. Realizing that he must find his own way out of the valley, and knowing that he could do so much more quickly and safely if he were alone, he decided to sound the blacks in relation to a plan that had entered his mind.

"If I take the Bolgani away, so that the others will not know that he was slain in your village, will you treat me as a friend?" he asked.

"Yes," replied the spokesman.

"Then," said Tarzan, "will you keep here for me my white she until I return again to your village? You can hide her in one of your huts if a Bolgani comes, and no one need ever know that she is among you. What do you say?"

The blacks looked around. "We do not see her," said the spokesman. "Where is she?"

"If you will promise to protect her and hide her, I will bring her here," replied the ape-man.

"I will not harm her," said the head man, "but I do not know about the others."

Tarzan turned toward the others who were clustered about, listening. "I am going to bring my mate into your village," he said, "and you are going to hide her, and feed her, and protect her until I return. I shall take away the body of Bolgani, so that no suspicion shall fall upon you, and when I come back I shall expect to find my mate safe and unharmed."

He had thought it best to describe La as his mate, since thus they might understand that she was under his protection, and if they felt either gratitude or fear toward him, La would be safer. Raising his face toward the tree where she was hidden, he called to La to descend, and a moment later she clambered down to the lower branches of one of the trees in the compound and dropped into Tarzan's arms.

"This is she," he said to the assembled blacks, "guard her well and hide her from the Bolgani. If, upon my return, I find that any harm has befallen her, I shall take word to the Bolgani that it was you who did this," and he pointed to the corpse of the gorilla-man.

La turned appealingly toward him, fear showing in her eyes. "You are not going to leave me here?" she asked.

"Temporarily only," replied Tarzan. "These poor people are afraid that if the death of this creature is traced to their village they shall all suffer the wrath of his fellows, and so I have promised that I will remove the evidence in such a way as to direct suspicion elsewhere. If they are sufficiently high in the scale of evolution to harbor sentiments of gratitude, which I doubt, they will feel obligated to me for having slain this beast, as well as for preventing suspicion falling upon them. For these reasons they should protect you, but to make assurance doubly sure I have appealed also to their fear of the Bolgani—a characteristic which I know they possess. I am sure that you will be as safe here as with me until I return, otherwise I would not leave you. But alone I can travel much faster, and while I am gone I intend to find a way out of this valley, then I shall return for you and together we may make our escape easily, or at least with greater assurance of success than were we to blunder slowly about together."

"You will come back?" she asked, a note of fear, longing, and appeal in her voice.

"I will come back," he replied, and then turning to the blacks: "Clear out one of these huts for my mate, and see that she is not molested, and that she is furnished with food and water. And remember what I said, upon her safety your lives depend."

Stooping, Tarzan lifted the dead gorilla-man to his shoulder, and the simple blacks marveled at his prowess. Of great physical strength themselves, there was not one of them but would have staggered under the weight of Bolgani, yet this strange Tarmangani walked easily beneath his burden, and when they had opened the gate in the palisade he trotted down the jungle trail as though he carried nothing but his own frame. A moment later he disappeared at a turn and was swallowed by the forest.

La turned to the blacks: "Prepare my hut," she said, for she was very tired and longed to rest. They eyed her askance and whispered among themselves. It was evident to her that there was a difference of opinion among them, and presently from snatches of conversation which she overheard she realized that while some of the blacks were in favor of obeying Tarzan's injunctions implicitly, there were others who objected strenuously and who wished to rid their village of her, lest she be discovered there by the Bolgani, and the villagers be punished accordingly.

"It would be better," she heard one of the blacks say, "to turn her over to the Bolgani at once and tell them that we saw her mate slay the messenger of Numa. We will say that we tried to capture the Tarmangani but that he escaped, and that we were only able to seize his mate. Thus will we win the favor of Numa, and perhaps then he will not take so many of our women and children."

"But the Tarmangani is great," replied one of the others. "He is more powerful even than Bolgani. He would make a terrible enemy, and, as the chances are that the Bolgani would not believe us we should then have not only them but the Tarmangani to fear."

"You are right," cried La, "the Tarmangani is great. Far better will it be for you to have him for friend than enemy. Single-handed he grapples with Numa, the lion, and slays him. You saw with what ease he lifted the body of the mighty Bolgani to his shoulder. You saw him trot lightly down the jungle trail beneath his burden. With equal ease will he carry the corpse through the trees of the forest, far above the ground. In all the world there is no other like him, no other like Tarzan of the Apes. If you are wise, Gomangani, you will have Tarzan for a friend."

The blacks listened to her, their dull faces revealing nothing of what was passing in their stupid brains. For a few moments they stood thus in silence, the hulking, ignorant blacks upon one side, the slender, beautiful white woman upon the other. Then La spoke.

"Go," she cried imperiously, "and prepare my hut." It was the High Priestess of the Flaming God; La, the queen of Opar, addressing slaves. Her regal mien, her commanding tones, wrought an instant change in the villagers, and La knew then that Tarzan was right in his assumption that they could be moved only through fear, for now they turned quickly, cowering like whipped dogs, and hastened to a nearby hut, which they quickly prepared for her, fetching fresh leaves and grasses for its floor, and fruit and nuts and plantains for her meal.

When all was ready, La clambered up the rope and through the circular opening in the floor of the hanging hut, which she found large and airy, and now reasonably clean. She drew the rope up after her and threw herself upon the soft bed they had prepared for her, and soon the gentle swaying of the swinging hut, the soft murmur of the leaves above her, the voices of the birds and insects combined with her own physical exhaustion to lull her into deep slumber.

10

Mad Treachery

T O THE northwest of the valley of Opar the smoke rose
from the cook fires of a camp in which some hundred
blacks and six whites were eating their evening meal.
The negroes squatted sullen and morose, mumbling together
in low tones over their meager fare, the whites, scowling and
apprehensive, kept their firearms close at hand. One of
them, a girl, and the only member of her sex in the party,
was addressing her fellows:

"We have Adolph's stinginess and Esteban's braggadocio
to thank for the condition in which we are," she said.

The fat Bluber shrugged his shoulder, the big Spaniard
scowled.

"For vy," asked Adolph, "am I to blame?"

"You were too stingy to employ enough carriers. I told
you at the time that we ought to have had two hundred
blacks in our party, but you wanted to save a little money,
and now what is the result? Fifty men carrying eighty pounds
of gold apiece and the other carriers are overburdened with
camp equipment, while there are scarce enough left for askari to guard us properly. We have to drive them like beasts
to make any progress and to keep them from throwing
away their loads, and they are fagged out and angry. They
don't require much of an excuse to kill us all on the spot.
On top of all this they are underfed. If we could keep their
bellies filled we could probably keep them happy and reasonably contented, but I have learned enough about natives
to know that if they are hungry they are neither happy nor
contented, even in idleness. If Esteban had not bragged so
much about his prowess as a hunter we should have brought
enough provisions to last us through, but now, though we

are barely started upon our return journey, we are upon less than half rations."

"I can't kill game when there isn't any game," growled the Spaniard.

"There is plenty of game," said Kraski, the Russian. "We see the tracks of it every day."

The Spaniard eyed him venomously. "If there is so much game," he said, "go out and get it yourself."

"I never claimed to be a hunter," replied Kraski, "though I could go out with a sling shot and a pea shooter and do as well as you have."

The Spaniard leaped to his feet menacingly, and instantly the Russian covered him with a heavy service revolver.

"Cut that business," cried the girl, sharply, leaping between them.

"Let the blighters fight," growled John Peebles. "If one of 'em kills the hother there'll be fewer to split the swag, and 'ere we are 'n that's that."

"For vy should ve quarrel?" demanded Bluber. "Dere is enough for all—over forty-tree t'ousand pounds apiece. Ven you get mad at me you call me names und say dat I am stingy, but *Mein Gott!* you English are vorser. You vould kill vun of your friends to get more money. *Ja wohl,* tank *Gott* dat I am not an Englisher."

"Shut up," growled Throck, "or we'll have forty-three thousand pounds more to divide."

Bluber eyed the big Englishman fearfully. "Come, come, Dick," he oozed, in his oiliest tones, "you wouldn't get mad at a leedle choke vould you, und me your best friend?"

"I'm sick of all this grousin'," said Throck. "I ain't no high-brow, I ain't nothin' but a pug. But I got sense enough to know that Flora's the only one in the bloomin' bunch whose brains wouldn't rattle around in a peanut shell. John, Bluber, Kraski and me, we're here because we could raise the money to carry out Flora's plan. The actor there"—and he indicated Esteban—"because his face and his figure filled the bill. There don't any of us need no brains for this work, and there ain't any of us got any more brains than we need. Flora's the brains of this outfit, and the sooner everyone understands that and takes orders from her, the better off we'll all be. She's been to Africa with this Lord Greystoke feller before—you wuz his wife's maid, wasn't you, Flora? And she knows somethin' about the country and the natives and the animals, and there don't none of us know nuttin'."

"Throck is right," said Kraski, quickly, "we've been muddling long enough. We haven't had a boss, and the thing to do is to make Flora boss from now on. If anyone can get us out of this, she can, and from the way those fellows over there are acting," and he nodded toward the blacks, "we'll be lucky if we ever get out with our skins, let alone taking any of the gold with us."

"*Ach, nein!* You don't mean to leave der gold?" almost shrieked Bluber.

"I mean that we do whatever Flora thinks best," replied Kraski. "If she says to leave the gold, we'll leave it."

"That we do," seconded Throck.

"I'm for it," said Peebles. "Whatever Flora says goes."

The Spaniard nodded his assent sullenly.

"The rest of us are all for it, Bluber. How about you?" asked Kraski.

"O vell—sure—if you say so," said Bluber, "und as John says 'und here ve ain't und vat's dat.' "

"And now, Flora," said Peebles, "you're the big 'un. What you say goes. What'll we do next?"

"Very well," said the girl; "we shall camp here until these men are rested, and early tomorrow we'll start out intelligently and systematically, and get meat for them. With their help we can do it. When they are rested and well fed we will start on again for the coast, moving very slowly, so as not to tire them too much. This is my first plan, but it hinges upon our ability to get meat. If we do not find it I shall bury the gold here, and we will do our best to reach the coast as quickly as possible. There we shall recruit new porters—twice as many as we have now—and purchase enough provisions to carry us in and out again. As we come back in, we will cache provisions at every camping place for our return trip, thus saving the necessity of carrying heavy loads all the way in and out again. In this way we can come out light, with twice as many porters as we actually need. And by working them in shifts we will travel much faster and there will be no grumbling. These are my two plans. I am not asking you what you think of them, because I do not care. You have made me chief, and I am going to run this from now on as I think best."

"Bully for you," roared Peebles; "that's the kind of talk I likes to hear."

"Tell the head man I want to see him, Carl," said the girl, turning to Kraski, and a moment later the Russian returned with a burly native.

"Owaza," said the girl, as the black halted before her, "we are short of food and the men are burdened with loads twice as heavy as they should carry. Tell them that we shall wait here until they are rested and that tomorrow we shall all go out and hunt for meat. You will send your boys out under three good men, and they will act as beaters and drive the game in to us. In this way we should get plenty of meat, and when the men are rested and well fed we will move on slowly. Where game is plentiful we will hunt and rest. Tell them that if they do this and we reach the coast in safety and with all our loads, I shall pay them twice what they agreed to come for."

"*Himmel!*" spluttered Bluber, "twice vat dey agreed to come for! Oh, Flora, vy not offer dem ten per cent? Dat would be fine interest on their money."

"Shut up, you fool," snapped Kraski, and Bluber subsided, though he rocked back and forth, shaking his head in disapproval.

The black, who had presented himself for the interview with sullen and scowling demeanor, brightened visibly now. "I will tell them," he said, "and I think that you will have no more trouble."

"Good," said Flora, "go and tell them now," and the black turned and left.

"There," said the girl, with a sigh of relief, "I believe that we can see light ahead at last."

"Twice vat ve promised to pay them!" bawled Bluber.

Early the following morning they prepared to set out upon the hunt. The blacks were now smiling and happy in anticipation of plenty of meat, and as they tramped off into the jungle they were singing gayly. Flora had divided them into three parties, each under a head man, with explicit directions for the position each party was to take in the line of beaters. Others had been detailed to the whites as gun-bearers, while a small party of the askari were left behind to guard the camp. The whites, with the exception of Esteban, were armed with rifles. He alone seemed inclined to question Flora's authority, insisting that he preferred to hunt with spear and arrows in keeping with the part he was playing. The fact that, though he had hunted assiduously for weeks, yet had never brought in a single kill, was not sufficient to dampen his egotism. So genuinely had he entered his part that he really thought he was Tarzan of the Apes, and with such fidelity had he equipped himself in every detail, and such a master of the art of make-up was he, that, in conjunction with his splendid figure and his handsome face that were almost a counterpart of Tarzan's, it was scarcely to be wondered at that he almost fooled himself as successfully as he had fooled others, for there were men among the carriers who had known the great ape-man, and even these were deceived, though they wondered at the change in him, since in little things he did not deport himself as Tarzan, and in the matter of kills he was disappointing.

Flora Hawkes, who was endowed with more than a fair share of intelligence, realized that it would not be well to cross any of her companions unnecessarily, and so she permitted Esteban to hunt that morning in his own way, though some of the others grumbled a little at her decision.

"What is the difference?" she asked them, after the Spaniard had set out alone. "The chances are that he could use a rifle no better than he uses his spear and arrows. Carl and Dick are really the only shots among us, and it is upon them we depend principally for the success of our hunt to-day. Esteban's egotism has been so badly bumped that it is possible that he will go to the last extremity to make a kill today—let us hope that he is successful."

"I hope he breaks his fool neck," said Kraski. "He has served our purpose and we would be better off if we were rid of him."

The girl shook her head negatively. "No," she said, "we must not think or speak of anything of that kind. We went into this thing together, let us stick together until the end. If you are wishing that one of us is dead, how do you know that others are not wishing that you were dead?"

"I haven't any doubt but that Miranda wishes I were dead," replied Kraski. "I never go to bed at night without thinking that the damned greaser may try to stick a knife into me before morning. And it don't make me feel any kinder toward him to hear you defending him, Flora. You've been a bit soft on him from the start."

"If I have, it's none of your business," retorted the girl.

And so they started out upon their hunt, the Russian scowling and angry, harboring thoughts of vengeance or worse against Esteban, and Esteban, hunting through the jungle, was occupied with his hatred and his jealousy. His dark mind was open to every chance suggestion of a means for putting the other men of the party out of the way, and taking the woman and the gold for himself. He hated them all; in each he saw a possible rival for the affections of Flora, and in the death of each he saw not only one less suitor for the girl's affections, but forty-three thousand additional pounds to be divided among fewer people. His mind was thus occupied to the exclusion of the business of hunting, which should have occupied him solely, when he came through a patch of heavy underbrush, and stepped into the glaring sunlight of a large clearing, face to face with a party of some fifty magnificent ebon warriors. For just an instant Esteban stood frozen in a paralysis of terror, forgetting momentarily the part he was playing—thinking of himself only as a lone white man in the heart of savage Africa facing a large band of war-like natives—cannibals, perhaps. It was that moment of utter silence and inaction that saved him, for, as he stood thus before them, the Waziri saw in the silent, majestic figure their beloved lord in a characteristic pose.

"O Bwana, Bwana," cried one of the warriors, rushing forward, "it is indeed you, Tarzan of the Apes, Lord of the Jungle, whom we had given up as lost. We, your faithful Waziri, have been searching for you, and even now we were about to dare the dangers of Opar, fearing that you might have ventured there without us and had been captured."

The black, who had at one time accompanied Tarzan to London as a body servant, spoke broken English, an accomplishment of which he was inordinately proud, losing no opportunity to air his attainment before his less fortunate fellows. The fact that it had been he whom fate had chosen to act as spokesman was indeed a fortunate circumstance to Miranda. Although the latter had applied himself assiduously to mastering the dialect of the west coast carriers, he would have been hard put to it to carry on a conversation with one of them, while he understood nothing of the Waziri tongue. Flora had schooled him carefully and well in the lore of Tarzan, so that he realized now that he was in the presence of a band of the ape-man's faithful Waziri. Never before had he seen such magnificent blacks—clean-cut, powerful men, with intelligent faces and well molded features, appearing as much higher in the scale of evolution as were the west coast blacks above the apes. Lucky indeed was Esteban Miranda that he was quick-witted and a consummate actor. Otherwise must he have betrayed his terror and his chagrin upon learning that this band of Tarzan's fierce and faithful followers was in this part of the country. For a moment longer he stood in silence before them, gathering his wits, and then he spoke, realizing that his very life depended upon his plausibility. And as he thought a great light broke upon the shrewd brain of the unscrupulous Spaniard.

"Since I last saw you," he said, "I discovered that a party of white men had entered the country for the purpose of robbing the treasure vaults of Opar. I followed them until I found their camp, and then I came in search of you, for there are many of them and they have many ingots of gold, for they have already been to Opar. Follow me, and we will raid their camp and take the gold from them. Come!" and he turned back toward the camp that he had just quitted.

As they made their way along the jungle trail, Usula, the Waziri who had spoken English to him, walked at Esteban's side. Behind them the Spaniard could hear the other warriors speaking in their native tongue, no word of which he understood, and it occurred to him that his position would be most embarrassing should he be addressed in the Waziri language, which, of course, Tarzan must have understood perfectly. As he listened to the chatter of Usula his mind was working rapidly, and presently, as though it were an inspiration, there recurred to him the memory of an accident that had befallen Tarzan, which had been narrated to him by Flora—the story of the injury he had received in the treasure vaults of Opar upon the occasion that he had lost his memory because of a blow upon the head. Esteban wondered if he had committed himself too deeply at first to attribute to amnesia any shortcomings in the portrayal of the rôle he was acting. At its worst, however, it seemed to him the best that he could do. He turned suddenly upon Usula.

"Do you remember," he asked, "the accident that befell me in the treasure vaults of Opar, depriving me of my memory?"

"Yes, Bwana, I remember it well," replied the black.

"A similar accident has befallen me," said Esteban. "A great tree fell in my path, and in falling a branch struck me upon the head. It has not caused me to lose my memory entirely, but since then it is with difficulty that I recall many things, and there are others which I must have forgotten entirely, for I do not know your name, nor do I understand the words that my other Waziri are speaking about me."

Usula looked at him compassionately. "Ah, Bwana, sad indeed is the heart of Usula to hear that this accident has befallen you. Doubtless it will soon pass away as did the other, and in the meantime I, Usula, will be your memory for you."

"Good," said Esteban, "tell the others that they may understand, and tell them also that I have lost the memory of other things besides. I could not now find my way home without you, and my other senses are dull as well. But as you say, Usula, it will soon pass off, and I shall be myself again."

"Your faithful Waziri will rejoice indeed with the coming of that moment," said Usula.

As they approached the camp, Miranda cautioned Usula to warn his followers to silence, and presently he halted them at the outskirts of the clearing where they could attain a view of the boma and the tents, guarding which was a little band of a half-dozen askari.

"When they see our greater numbers they will make no resistance," said Esteban. "Let us surround the camp, therefore, and at a signal from me we will advance together, when you shall address them, saying that Tarzan of the Apes comes with his Waziri for the gold they have stolen, but that he will spare them if they will leave the country at once and never return."

Had it fulfilled his purpose as well, the Spaniard would have willingly ordered his Waziri to fall upon the men guarding the camp and destroy them all, but to his cunning brain had been born a cleverer scheme. He wanted these men to see him with the Waziri and live to tell the others that they had seen him, and to repeat to Flora and her followers the thing that Esteban had in his mind to tell one of the askari, while the Waziri were gathering up the gold ingots from the camp.

In directing Usula to station his men about the camp, Esteban had to warn them that they were not to show themselves until he had crept out into the clearing and attracted the attention of the askari on guard. Fifteen minutes, perhaps, were consumed in stationing his men, and then Usula returned to Esteban to report that all was ready.

"When I raise my hand then you will know that they have recognized me and that you are to advance," Esteban cautioned him, and stepped forward slowly into the clearing. One of the askari saw him and recognized him as Esteban. The Spaniard took a few steps closer to the boma and then halted.

"I am Tarzan of the Apes," he said; "your camp is entirely surrounded by my warriors. Make no move against us and we shall not hurt you."

He waved his hand. Fifty stalwart Waziri stepped into view from the concealing verdure of the surrounding jungle. The askari eyed them in ill-concealed terror, fingering their rifles nervously.

"Do not shoot," cautioned Esteban, "or we shall slay you all." He approached more closely and his Waziri closed in about him, entirely surrounding the boma.

"Speak to them, Usula," said Esteban. The black stepped forward.

"We are the Waziri," he cried, "and this is Tarzan of the

Apes, Lord of the Jungle, our master. We have come to recover the gold of Tarzan that you have stolen from the treasure vaults of Opar. This time we shall spare you on condition that you leave the country and never return. Tell this word to your masters; tell them that Tarzan watches, and that his Waziri watch with him. Lay down your rifles."

The askari, glad to escape so easily, complied with the demands of Usula, and a moment later the Waziri had entered the boma, and at Esteban's direction were gathering up the golden ingots. As they worked, Esteban approached one of the askari, whom he knew spoke broken English.

"Tell your master," he said, "to give thanks for the mercy of Tarzan who has exacted a toll of but one life for this invasion of his country and theft of his treasure. The creature who presumes to pose as Tarzan I have slain, and his body I shall take away with me and feed to the lions. Tell them that Tarzan forgives even their attempt to poison him upon the occasion that he visited their camp, but only upon the condition that they never return to Africa, and that they divulge the secret of Opar to no others. Tarzan watches and his Waziri watch, and no man may enter Africa without Tarzan's knowledge. Even before they left London I knew that they were coming. Tell them that."

It took but a few minutes for the Waziri to gather up the golden ingots, and before the askari had recovered from the surprise of their appearance, they had gone again into the jungle, with Tarzan, their master.

It was late in the afternoon before Flora and the four white men returned from their hunt, surrounded by happy, laughing blacks, bearing the fruits of a successful chase.

"Now that you are in charge, Flora," Kraski was saying, "fortune is smiling upon us indeed. We have enough meat here for several days, and with plenty of meat in their bellies they ought to make good progress."

"I vill say it myself dot tings look brighter," said Bluber.

"Blime, they do that," said Throck. "I'm tellin' you Flora's a bright one."

"What the devil is this?" demanded Peebles, "what's wrong with them beggars?" And he pointed toward the boma which was now in sight, and from which the askari were issuing at a run, jabbering excitedly as they raced toward them.

"Tarzan of the Apes has been here," they cried excitedly. "He has been here with all his Waziri—a thousand great warriors—and though we fought, they overcame us, and taking the gold they went away. Tarzan of the Apes spoke strange words to me before they left. He said that he had

killed one of your number who had dared to call himself
Tarzan of the Apes. We do not understand it. He went
away alone to hunt when you went in the morning, and
he came back shortly with a thousand warriors, and he took
all the gold and he threatened to kill us and you if you ever
return to this country again."

"Vot, vot?" cried Bluber, "der gold iss gone? *Ach! Ach!*"
And then they all commenced to ask questions at once until
Flora silenced them.

"Come," she said to the leader of the askari, "we will
return to the boma and then you shall tell me slowly and
carefully all that has happened since we left."

She listened intently to his narrative, and then questioned him carefully upon various points several times. At
last she dismissed him. Then she turned to her confederates.

"It is all clear to me," she said. "Tarzan recovered from
the effects of the drug we administered. Then he followed
us with his Waziri, caught Esteban and killed him and,
finding the camp, has taken the gold away. We shall be
fortunate indeed if we escape from Africa with our lives."

"*Ach, weh!*" almost shrieked Bluber, "der dirty crook.
He steals all our gold, und ve lose our two t'ousand pounds
into der bargain."

"Shut up, you coward," growled Throck. "If it hadn't 'a'
been for you and the actor there 'ere thing would never 'a'
'appened. With 'im abraggin' about 'is 'unting and not bein'
able to kill anything, and you a-squeezin' every bloomin'
hapenny, we're in a rotten mess—that we are. This 'ere Tarzan bounder he bumped off Esteban, which is the best work
what 'e ever done. Too bloody bad you weren't 'ere to get
it too, and what I got a good mind to do is to slit your
throat meself."

"Stow the guff, Dick," roared Peebles; "it wasn't nobody's
fault, as far as I can see. Instead of talkin' what we oughter
do is to go after this 'ere Tarzan feller and take the bloomin'
gold away from 'im."

Flora Hawkes laughed. "We haven't a chance in the world,"
she said. "I know this Tarzan bloke. If he was all alone we
wouldn't be a match for him, but he's got a bunch of his
Waziri with him, and there are no finer warriors in Africa
than they. And they'd fight for him to the last man. You
just tell Owaza that you're thinking of going after Tarzan
of the Apes and his Waziri to take the gold away from
them, and see how long it'd be before we wouldn't have a
single porter with us. The very name of Tarzan scares these
west coast blacks out of a year's growth. They would sooner

face the devil. No, sir, we've lost, and all we can do is to get out of the country, and thank our lucky stars if we manage to get out alive. The ape-man will watch us. I should not be surprised if he were watching us this minute." Her companions looked around apprehensively at this, casting nervous glances toward the jungle. "And he'd never let us get back to Opar for another load, even if we could prevail upon our blacks to return there."

"Two t'ousand pounds, two t'ousand pounds!" wailed Bluber. "Und all dis suit, vat it cost me tventy guineas vat I can't vear it again in England unless I go to a fancy dress ball, vich I never do."

Kraski had not spoken, but had sat with eyes upon the ground, listening to the others. Now he raised his head. "We have lost our gold," he said, "and before we get back to England we stand to spend the balance of our two thousand pounds—in other words our expedition is a total loss. The rest of you may be satisfied to go back broke, but I am not. There are other things in Africa besides the gold of Opar, and when we leave the country there is no reason why we shouldn't take something with us that will repay us for our time and investment."

"What do you mean?" asked Peebles.

"I have spent a lot of time talking with Owaza," replied Kraski, "trying to learn their crazy language, and I have come to find out a lot about the old villain. He's as crooked as they make 'em, and if he were to be hanged for all his murders, he'd have to have more lives than a cat, but notwithstanding all that, he's a shrewd old fellow, and I've learned a lot more from him than just his monkey talk— I have learned enough, in fact, so that I feel safe in saying that if we stick together we can go out of Africa with a pretty good sized stake. Personally, I haven't given up the gold of Opar yet. What we've lost, we've lost, but there's plenty left where that came from, and some day after this blows over, I'm coming back to get my share."

"But how about this other thing?" asked Flora. "How can Owaza help us?"

"There's a little bunch of Arabs down here," explained Kraski, "stealing slaves and ivory. Owaza knows where they are working and where their main camp is. There are only a few of them, and their blacks are nearly all slaves who would turn on them in a minute. Now the idea is this: we have a big enough party to overpower them and take their ivory away from them if we can get their slaves to take our side. We don't want the slaves; we couldn't do anything with them if we had them, so we can promise them their freedom for their help, and give Owaza and his gang a share in the ivory."

"How do you know Owaza will help us?" asked Flora.

"The idea is his; that's the reason I know," replied Kraski.

"It sounds good to me," said Peebles; "I ain't fer goin' 'ome empty 'anded." And in turn the others signified their approval of the scheme.

11

Strange Incense Burns

AS TARZAN carried the dead Bolgani from the village of the Gomangani, he set his steps in the direction of the building he had seen from the rim of the valley, the curiosity of the man overcoming the natural caution of the beast. He was traveling up wind and the odors wafted down to his nostrils told him that he was approaching the habitat of the Bolgani. Intermingled with the scent spoor of the gorilla-men was that of Gomangani and the odor of cooked food, and the suggestion of a heavily sweet scent, which the ape-man could connect only with burning incense, though it seemed impossible that such a fragrance could emanate from the dwellings of the Bolgani. Perhaps it came from the great edifice he had seen—a building which must have been constructed by human beings, and in which human beings might still dwell, though never among the multitudinous odors that assailed his nostrils did he once catch the faintest suggestion of the man scent of whites.

When he perceived from the increasing strength of their odor, that he was approaching close to the Bolgani, Tarzan took to the trees with his burden, that he might thus stand a better chance of avoiding discovery, and presently, through the foliage ahead, he saw a lofty wall, and, beyond, the outlines of the weird architecture of a strange and mysterious pile— outlines that suggested a building of another world, so unearthly were they, and from beyond the wall came the odor of the Bolgani and the fragrance of the incense, intermingled with the scent spoor of Numa, the lion. The jungle was cleared away for fifty feet outside the wall surrounding the building, so that there was no tree overhanging the wall, but Tarzan approached as closely as he could, while still remaining reasonably well-concealed by the foliage. He had chosen a point at a sufficient height above the ground to permit him to see over the top of the wall.

The building within the enclosure was of great size, its different parts appearing to have been constructed at various periods, and each with utter disregard to uniformity, resulting in a conglomeration of connecting buildings and towers, no two of which were alike, though the whole presented a rather pleasing, if somewhat bizarre appearance. The building stood upon an artificial elevation about ten feet high, surrounded by a retaining wall of granite, a wide staircase leading to the ground level below. About the building were shrubbery and trees, some of the latter appearing to be of great antiquity, while one enormous tower was almost entirely covered by ivy. By far the most remarkable feature of the building, however, lay in its rich and barbaric ornamentation. Set into the polished granite of which it was composed was an intricate mosaic of gold and diamonds; glittering stones in countless thousands scintillated from façades, minarets, domes, and towers.

The enclosure, which comprised some fifteen or twenty acres, was occupied for the most part by the building. The terrace upon which it stood was devoted to walks, flowers, shrubs, and ornamental trees, while that part of the area below, which was within the range of Tarzan's vision, seemed to be given over to the raising of garden truck. In the garden and upon the terrace were naked blacks, such as he had seen in the village where he had left La. There were both men and women, and these were occupied with the care of growing things within the enclosure. Among them were several of the gorilla-like creatures such as Tarzan had slain in the village, but these performed no labor, devoting themselves rather, it seemed, to directing the work of the blacks, toward whom their manner was haughty and domineering, sometimes even brutal. These gorilla-men were trapped in rich ornaments, similar to those upon the body which now rested in a crotch of the tree behind the ape-man.

As Tarzan watched with interest the scene below him, two Bolgani emerged from the main entrance, a huge portal, some thirty feet in width, and perhaps fifteen feet high. The two wore head-bands, supporting tall, white feathers. As they emerged they took post on either side of the entrance, and cupping their hands before their mouths gave voice to a series of shrill cries that bore a marked resemblance to trumpet calls. Immediately the blacks ceased work and hastened to the foot of the stairs descending from the terrace to the garden. Here they formed lines on either side of the stairway, and similarly the Bolgani formed two lines upon the terrace from the main portal to the stairway, forming a living aisle from one to the other. Presently from the interior of the building came other trumpet-like calls, and a moment later Tarzan saw the head of a procession emerging. First came four Bolgani abreast, each bedecked with an ornate feather headdress, and each carrying a huge bludgeon erect before him. Behind these came two trumpeters, and twenty feet behind the trumpeters paced a huge, black-maned lion, held in leash by four sturdy blacks, two upon either side, holding what appeared to be golden chains that ran to a scintillant diamond collar about the beast's neck. Behind the lion marched twenty more Bolgani, four abreast. These carried spears, but whether they were for the purpose of protecting the lion from the people or the people from the lion Tarzan was at a loss to know.

The attitude of the Bolgani lining either side of the way between the portal and the stairway indicated extreme deference, for they bent their bodies from their waists in a profound bow while Numa was passing between their lines. When the beast reached the top of the stairway the procession halted, and immediately the Gomangani ranged below prostrated themselves and placed their foreheads on the ground. Numa, who was evidently an old lion, stood with lordly mien surveying the prostrate humans before him. His evil eyes glared glassily, the while he bared his tusks in a savage grimace, and from his deep lungs rumbled forth an ominous roar, at the sound of which the Gomangani trembled in unfeigned terror. The ape-man knit his brows in thought. Never before had he been called upon to witness so remarkable a scene of the abasement of man before a beast. Presently the procession continued upon its way descending the staircase and turning to the right along a path through the garden, and when it had passed them the Gomangani and the Bolgani arose and resumed their interrupted duties.

Tarzan remained in his concealment watching them, trying to discover some explanation for the strange, paradoxical conditions that he had witnessed. The lion, with his retinue, had turned the far corner of the palace and disappeared from sight. What was he to these people, to these strange creatures? What did he represent? Why this topsy-turvy arrangement of species? Here man ranked lower than the half-beast, and above all, from the deference that had been accorded him, stood a true beast—a savage carnivore.

He had been occupied with his thoughts and his observations for some fifteen minutes following the disappearance of Numa around the eastern end of the palace, when his attention was attracted to the opposite end of the structure by the sound of other shrill trumpet calls. Turning his eyes in that direction, he saw the procession emerging again into view, and proceeding toward the staricase down which they had entered the garden. Immediately the notes of the shrill call sounded upon their ears the Gomangani and the Bolgani resumed their original positions from below the foot of the staircase to the entrance to the palace, and once again was homage paid to Numa as he made his triumphal entry into the building.

Tarzan of the Apes ran his fingers through his mass of tousled hair, but finally he was forced to shake his head in defeat—he could find no explanation whatsoever for all that he had witnessed. His curiosity, however, was so keenly piqued that he determined to investigate the palace and surrounding grounds further before continuing on his way in search of a trail out of the valley.

Leaving the body of Bolgani where he had cached it, he started slowly to circle the building that he might examine it from all sides from the concealing foliage of the surrounding forest. He found the architecture equally unique upon all sides, and that the garden extended entirely around the building, though a portion upon the south side of the palace was given over to corrals and pens in which were kept numerous goats and a considerable flock of chickens. Upon this side, also, were several hundred swinging, beehive huts, such as he had seen in the native village of the Gomangani. These he took to be the quarters of the black slaves, who performed all the arduous and menial labor connected with the palace.

The lofty granite wall which surrounded the entire enclosure was pierced by but a single gate which opened opposite the east end of the palace. This gate was large and of massive construction, appearing to have been built to withstand the assault of numerous and well-armed forces. So strong did it appear that the ape-man could not but harbor the opinion that it had been constructed to protect the interior against forces equipped with heavy battering rams. That such a force had ever existed within the vicinity in historic times seemed most unlikely, and Tarzan conjectured, therefore, that the wall and the gate were of almost unthinkable antiquity, dating, doubtless, from the forgotten age of the Atlantians, and constructed, perhaps, to protect the builders of the Palace of Diamonds from the well-armed forces that had come from Atlantis to work the gold mines of Opar and to colonize central Africa.

While the wall, the gate, and the palace itself, suggested in many ways almost unbelievable age, yet they were in such an excellent state of repair that it was evident that they were still inhabited by rational and intelligent creatures; while upon the south side Tarzan had seen a new tower in process of construction, where a number of blacks working under the direction of Bolgani were cutting and shaping granite blocks and putting them in place.

Tarzan had halted in a tree near the east gate to watch the life passing in and out of the palace grounds beneath the ancient portal, and as he watched, a long cavalcade of powerful Gomangani emerged from the forest and entered the enclosure. Swung in hides between two poles, this party was carrying rough-hewn blocks of granite, four men to a block. Two or three Bolgani accompanied the long line of carriers, which was preceded and followed by a detachment of black warriors, armed with battle-axes and spears. The demeanor and attitude of the black porters, as well as of the Bolgani, suggested to the ape-man nothing more nor less than a caravan of donkeys, plodding their stupid way at the behest of their drivers. If one lagged he was prodded with the point of a spear or struck with its haft. There was no greater brutality shown than in the ordinary handling of beasts of burden the world around, nor in the demeanor of the blacks was there any more indication of objection or revolt than you see depicted upon the faces of a long line of burden-bearing mules; to all intents and purposes they were dumb, driven cattle. Slowly they filed through the gateway and disappeared from sight.

A few moments later another party came out of the forest and passed into the palace grounds. This consisted of fully fifty armed Bolgani and twice as many black warriors with spears and axes. Entirely surrounded by these armed creatures were four brawny porters, carrying a small litter, upon which was fastened an ornate chest about two feet wide by four feet long, with a depth of approximately two feet. The chest itself was of some dark, weather-worn wood, and was reinforced by bands and corners of what appeared to be virgin gold in which were set many diamonds. What the chest contained Tarzan could not, of course, conceive, but

that it was considered of great value was evidenced by the
precautions for safety with which it had been surrounded.
The chest was borne directly into the huge, ivy-covered tower
at the northeast corner of the palace, the entrance to which,
Tarzan now first observed, was secured by doors as large
and heavy as the east gate itself.

At the first opportunity that he could seize to accomplish it
undiscovered, Tarzan swung across the jungle trail and
continued through the trees to that one in which he had left
the body of the Bolgani. Throwing this across his shoulder
he returned to a point close above the trail near the east
gate, and seizing upon a moment when there was a lull in the
traffic he hurled the body as close to the portal as possible.

"Now," thought the ape-man, "let them guess who slew
their fellow if they can."

Making his way toward the southeast, Tarzan approached
the mountains which lie back of the Valley of the Palace of
Diamonds. He had often to make detours to avoid native
villages and to keep out of sight of the numerous parties of
Bolgani that seemed to be moving in all directions through
the forest. Late in the afternoon he came out of the hills into
full view of the mountains beyond—rough, granite hills they
were, whose precipitous peaks rose far above the timber line.
Directly before him a well-marked trail led into a canyon,
which he could see wound far upward toward the summit.
This, then, would be as good a place to commence his investigations as another. And so, seeing that the coast was clear,
the ape-man descended from the trees, and taking advantage of the underbrush bordering the trail, made his way
silently, yet swiftly, into the hills. For the most part he was
compelled to worm his way through thickets, for the trail was
in constant use by Gomangani and Bolgani, parties passing
up it empty-handed and, returning, bearing blocks of granite.
As he advanced more deeply into the hills the heavy underbrush gave way to a lighter growth of scrub, through which
he could pass with far greater ease though with considerable
more risk of discovery. However, the instinct of the beast
that dominated Tarzan's jungle craft permitted him to find
cover where another would have been in full view of every
enemy. Half way up the mountain the trail passed through
a narrow gorge, not more than twenty feet wide and eroded
from solid granite cliffs. Here there was no concealment
whatsoever, and the ape-man realized that to enter it would
mean almost immediate discovery. Glancing about, he saw
that by making a slight detour he could reach the summit of the gorge, where, amid tumbled, granite boulders and

stunted trees and shrubs, he knew that he could find
sufficient concealment, and perhaps a plainer view of the
trail beyond.

Nor was he mistaken, for, when he had reached a vantage
point far above the trail, he saw ahead an open pocket in
the mountain, the cliffs surrounding which were honeycombed
with numerous openings, which, it seemed to Tarzan, could
be naught else than the mouths of tunnels. Rough wooden
ladders reached to some of them, closer to the base of the
cliffs, while from others knotted ropes dangled to the ground
below. Out of these tunnels emerged men carrying little
sacks of earth, which they dumped in a common pile beside
a rivulet which ran through the gorge. Here other blacks,
supervised by Bolgani, were engaged in washing the dirt,
but what they hoped to find or what they did find, Tarzan
could not guess.

Along one side of the rocky basin many other blacks were
engaged in quarrying the granite from the cliffs, which had
been cut away through similar operations into a series of
terraces running from the floor of the basin to the summit of
the cliff. Here naked blacks toiled with primitive tools under
the supervision of savage Bolgani. The activities of the
quarrymen were obvious enough, but what the others were
bringing from the mouths of the tunnels Tarzan could not be
positive, though the natural assumption was that it was gold.
Where, then, did they obtain their diamonds? Certainly not
from these solid granite cliffs.

A few minutes' observation convinced Tarzan that the
trail he had followed from the forest ended in this little cul-
de-sac, and so he sought a way upward and around it, in
search of a pass across the range.

The balance of that day and nearly all the next he devoted to his efforts in this direction, only in the end to be
forced to admit that there was no egress from the valley upon
this side. To points far above the timber line he made his
way, but there, always, he came face to face with sheer,
perpendicular cliffs of granite towering high above him,
upon the face of which not even the ape-man could find
foothold. Along the southern and eastern sides of the basin
he carried his investigation, but with similar disappointing re-
sults, and then at last he turned his steps back toward the
forest with the intention of seeking a way out through the
valley of Opar with La, after darkness had fallen.

The sun had just risen when Tarzan arrived at the native
village in which he had left La, and no sooner did his eyes
rest upon it than he became apprehensive that something

was amiss, for not only was the gate wide open but there was no sign of life within the palisade, nor was there any movement of the swinging huts that would indicate that they were occupied. Always wary of ambush, Tarzan reconnoitered carefully before descending into the village. To his trained observation it became evident that the village had been deserted for at least twenty-four hours. Running to the hut in which La had been hidden he hastily ascended the rope and examined the interior—it was vacant, nor was there any sign of the High Priestess. Descending to the ground, the ape-man started to make a thorough investigation of the village in search of clews to the fate of its inhabitants and of La. He had examined the interiors of several huts when his keen eyes noted a slight movement of one of the swinging, cage-like habitations some distance from him. Quickly he crossed the intervening space, and as he approached the hut he saw that no rope trailed from its doorway. Halting beneath, Tarzan raised his face to the aperture, through which nothing but the roof of the hut was visible.

"Gomangani," he cried, "it is I, Tarzan of the Apes. Come to the opening and tell me what has become of your fellows and of my mate, whom I left here under the protection of your warriors."

There was no answer, and again Tarzan called, for he was positive that someone was hiding in the hut.

"Come down," he called again, "or I will come up after you."

Still there was no reply. A grim smile touched the ape-man's lips as he drew his hunting knife from its sheath and placed it between his teeth, and then, with a cat-like spring, leaped for the opening, and catching its sides, drew his body up into the interior of the hut.

If he had expected opposition, he met with none, nor in the dimly lighted interior could he at first distinguish any presence, though, when his eyes became accustomed to the semi-darkness, he descried a bundle of leaves and grasses lying against the opposite wall of the structure. Crossing to these he tore them aside revealing the huddled form of a terrified woman. Seizing her by a shoulder he drew her to a sitting position.

"What has happened?" he demanded. "Where are the villagers? Where is my mate?"

"Do not kill me! Do not kill me!" she cried. "It was not I. It was not my fault."

"I do not intend to kill you," replied Tarzan. "Tell me the truth and you shall be safe."

"The Bolgani have taken them away," cried the woman. "They came when the sun was low upon the day that you arrived, and they were very angry, for they had found the body of their fellow outside the gate of the Palace of Diamonds. They knew that he had come here to our village, and no one had seen him alive since he had departed from the palace. They came, then, and threatened and tortured our people, until at last the warriors told them all. I hid. I do not know why they did not find me. But at last they went away, taking all the others with them; taking your mate, too. They will never come back."

"You think that the Bolgani will kill them?" asked Tarzan.

"Yes," she replied, "they kill all who displease them."

Alone, now, and relieved of the responsibility of La, Tarzan might easily make his way by night through the valley of Opar and to safety beyond the barrier. But perhaps such a thought never entered his head. Gratitude and loyalty were marked characteristics of the ape-man. La had saved him from the fanaticism and intrigue of her people. She had saved him at a cost of all that was most dear to her, power and position, peace and safety. She had jeopardized her life for him, and became an exile from her own country. The mere fact then that the Bolgani had taken her with the possible intention of slaying her, was not sufficient for the ape-man. He must know whether or not she lived, and if she lived he must devote his every energy to winning her release and her eventual escape from the dangers of this valley.

Tarzan spent the day reconnoitering outside the palace grounds, seeking an opportunity of gaining entrance without detection, but this he found impossible inasmuch as there was never a moment that there were not Gomangani or Bolgani in the outer garden. But with the approach of darkness the great east gate was closed, and the inmates of the huts and palace withdrew within their walls, leaving not even a single sentinel without—a fact that indicated clearly that the Bolgani had no reason to apprehend an attack. The subjugation of the Gomangani, then, was apparently complete, and so the towering wall surrounding their palace, which was more than sufficient to protect them from the inroads of lions, was but the reminder of an ancient day when a once-powerful, but now vanished, enemy threatened their peace and safety.

When darkness had finally settled Tarzan approached the gate, and throwing the noose of his grass rope over one of the carved lions that capped the gate posts, ascended quickly to the summit of the wall, from where he dropped lightly into the garden below. To insure an avenue for quick escape in the event that he found La, he unlatched the heavy gates and swung them open. Then he crept stealthily toward the ivy-covered east tower, which he had chosen after a day of investigation as offering easiest ingress to the palace. The success of his plan hinged largely upon the age and strength of the ivy which grew almost to the summit of the tower, and, to his immense relief, he found that it would easily support his weight.

Far above the ground, near the summit of the tower, he had seen from the trees surrounding the palace an open window, which, unlike the balance of those in this part of the palace, was without bars. Dim lights shone from several of the tower windows, as from those of other parts of the palace. Avoiding these lighted apertures, Tarzan ascended quickly, though carefully, toward the unbarred window above, and as he reached it and cautiously raised his eyes above the level of the sill, he was delighted to find that it opened into an unlighted chamber, the interior of which, however, was so shrouded in darkness that he could discern nothing within. Drawing himself carefully to the level of the sill he crept quietly into the apartment beyond. Groping through the blackness, he cautiously made the rounds of the room, which he found to contain a carved bedstead of peculiar design, a table, and a couple of benches. Upon the bedstead were stuffs of woven material, thrown over the softly tanned pelts of antelopes and leopards.

Opposite the window through which he had entered was a closed door. This he opened slowly and silently, until, through a tiny aperture he could look out upon a dimly lighted corridor or circular hallway, in the center of which was an opening about four feet in diameter, passing through which and disappearing beyond a similar opening in the ceiling directly above was a straight pole with short crosspieces fastened to it at intervals of about a foot—quite evidently the primitve staircase which gave communication between the various floors of the tower. Three upright columns, set at equal intervals about the circumference of the circular opening in the center of the floor helped to support the ceiling above. Around the outside of this circular hallway there were other doors, similar to that opening into the apartment in which he was.

Hearing no noise and seeing no evidence of another than himself, Tarzan opened the door and stepped into the hallway. His nostrils were now assailed strongly by the same heavy fragrance of incense that had first greeted him upon his approach to the palace several days before. In the interior of the tower, however, it was much more powerful, practically obliterating all other odors, and placing upon the ape-man an almost prohibitive handicap in his search for La. In fact as he viewed the doors upon this single stage of the tower, he was filled with consternation at the prospect of the well-nigh impossible task that confronted him. To search this great tower alone, without any assistance whatever from his keen sense of scent, seemed impossible of accomplishment, if he were to take even the most ordinary precautions against detection.

The ape-man's self-confidence was in no measure blundering egotism. Knowing his limitations, he knew that he would have little or no chance against even a few Bolgani were he to be discovered within their palace, where all was familiar to them and strange to him. Behind him was the open window, and the silent jungle night, and freedom. Ahead danger, predestined failure; and, quite likely, death. Which would he choose? For a moment he stood in silent thought, and then, raising his head and squaring his great shoulders, he shook his black locks defiantly and stepped boldly toward the nearest door. Room after room he had investigated until he had made the entire circle of the landing, but in so far as La or any clew to her were concerned his search was fruitless. He found quaint furniture and rugs and tapestries, and ornaments of gold and diamonds, and in one dimly lighted chamber he came upon a sleeping Bolgani, but so silent were the movements of the ape-man that the sleeper slept on undisturbed, even though Tarzan passed entirely around his bed, which was set in the center of the chamber, and investigated a curtained alcove beyond.

Having completed the rounds of this floor, Tarzan determined to work upward first and then, returning, investigate the lower stages later. Pursuant to this plan, therefore, he ascended the strange stairway. Three landings he passed before he reached the upper floor of the tower. Circling each floor was a ring of doors, all of which were closed, while dimly lighting each landing were feebly burning cressets—shallow, golden bowls—containing what appeared to be tallow, in which floated a tow-like wick.

Upon the upper landing there were but three doors, all of which were closed. The ceiling of this hallway was the dome-like roof of the tower, in the center of which was another circular opening, through which the stairway protruded into the darkness of the night above.

As Tarzan opened the door nearest him it creaked

THE GOLDEN INGOTS 101

upon its hinges, giving forth the first audible sound that had
resulted from his investigations up to this point The interior
of the apartment before him was unlighted, and as Tarzan
stood there in the entrance in statuesque silence for a few
seconds following the creaking of the hinge, he was suddenly
aware of movement—of the faintest shadow of a sound—behind him. Wheeling quickly he saw the figure of a man standing in an open doorway upon the opposite site of the landing.

12

The Golden Ingots

ESTEBAN MIRANDA had played the rôle of Tarzan of
the Apes with the Warizi as his audience for less than
twenty-four hours when he began to realize that, even
with the lee-way that his supposedly injured brain gave him,
it was going to be a very difficult thing to carry on the
deception indefinitely. In the first place Usula did not seem
at all pleased at the idea of merely taking the gold away
from the intruders and then running from them. Nor did his
fellow warriors seem any more enthusiastic over the plan
than he. As a matter of fact they could not conceive that any
number of bumps upon the head could render their Tarzan
of the Apes a coward, and to run away from these west
coast blacks and a handful of inexperienced whites seemed
nothing less than cowardly.

Following all this, there had occurred in the afternoon
that which finally decided the Spaniard that he was building
for himself anything other than a bed of roses, and that the
sooner he found an excuse for quitting the company of the
Waziri the greater would be his life expectancy.

They were passing through rather open jungle at the time.
The brush was not particularly heavy and the trees were at
considerable distances apart, when suddenly, without warning, a rhinoceros charged them. To the consternation of the
Waziri, Tarzan of the Apes turned and fled for the nearest
tree the instant his eyes alighted upon the charging Buto.
In his haste Esteban tripped and fell, and when at last he

reached the tree instead of leaping agilely into the lower branches, he attempted to shin up the huge bole as a schoolboy shins up a telegraph pole, only to slip and fall back again to the ground.

In the meantime Buto, who charges either by scent or hearing, rather than by eyesight, his powers of which are extremely poor, had been distracted from his original direction by one of the Waziri, and after missing the fellow had gone blundering on to disappear in the underbrush beyond.

When Esteban finally arose and discovered that the rhinoceros was gone, he saw surrounding him a semi-circle of huge blacks, upon whose faces were written expressions of pity and sorrow, not unmingled, in some instances, with a tinge of contempt. The Spaniard saw that he had been terrified into a practically irreparable blunder, yet he seized despairingly upon the only excuse he could conjure up.

"My poor head," he cried, pressing both palms to his temples.

"The blow was upon your *head*, Bwana," said Usula, "and your faithful Waziri thought that it was the *heart* of their master that knew no fear."

Esteban made no reply, and in silence they resumed their march. In silence they continued until they made camp before dark upon the bank of the river just above a waterfall. During the afternoon Esteban had evolved a plan of escape from his dilemma, and no sooner had he made camp than he ordered the Waziri to bury the treasure.

"We shall leave it here," he said, "and tomorrow we shall set forth in search of the thieves, for I have decided to punish them. They must be taught that they may not come into the jungle of Tarzan with impunity. It was only the injury to my head that prevented me from slaying them immediately I discovered their perfidy."

This attitude pleased the Waziri better. They commenced to see a ray of hope. Once again was Tarzan of the Apes becoming Tarzan. And so it was that with lighter hearts and a new cheerfulness they set forth the next morning in search of the camp of the Englishmen, and by shrewd guessing on Usula's part they cut across the jungle to intercept the probable march of the Europeans to such advantage that they came upon them just as they were making camp that night. Long before they reached them they smelled the smoke of their fires and heard the songs and chatter of the west coast carriers.

Then it was that Esteban gathered the Waziri about him. "My children," he said, addressing Usula in English, "these strangers have come here to wrong Tarzan. To Tarzan, then, belongs the vengeance. Go, therefore, and leave me to punish my enemies alone and in my own way. Return home, leave the gold where it is, for it will be a long time before I shall need it."

The Waziri were disappointed, for this new plan did not at all accord with their desires, which contemplated a cheerful massacre of the west coast blacks. But as yet the man before them was Tarzan, their big Bwana, to whom they had never failed in implicit obedience. For a few moments following Esteban's declaration of his intention, they stood in silence shifting uneasily, and then at last they commenced to speak to one another in Waziri. What they said the Spaniard did not know, but evidently they were urging something upon Usula, who presently turned toward him.

"Oh, Bwana," cried the black. "How can we return home to the Lady Jane and tell her that we left you injured and alone to face the rifles of the white men and their askari? Do not ask us to do it, Bwana. If you were yourself we should not fear for your safety, but since the injury to your head you have not been the same, and we fear to leave you alone in the jungle. Let us, then, your faithful Waziri, punish these people, after which we will take you home in safety, where you may be cured of the evils that have fallen upon you."

The Spaniard laughed. "I am entirely recovered," he said, "and I am in no more danger alone than I would be with you," which he knew, even better than they, was but a mild statement of the facts. "You will obey my wishes," he continued sternly. "Go back at once the way that we have come. After you have gone at least two miles you may make camp for the night, and in the morning start out again for home. Make no noise, I do not want them to know that I am here. Do not worry about me. I am all right, and I shall probably overtake you before you reach home. Go!"

Sorrowfully the Waziri turned back upon the trail they had just covered and a moment later the last of them disappeared from the sight of the Spaniard.

With a sigh of relief Esteban Miranda turned toward the camp of his own people. Fearing that to surprise them suddenly might invite a volley of shots from the askari he whistled, and then called aloud as he approached.

"It is Tarzan!" cried the first of the blacks who saw him. "Now indeed shall we all be killed."

Esteban saw the growing excitement among the carriers

and askari—he saw the latter seize their rifles and that they were fingering the triggers nervously.

"It is I, Esteban Miranda," he called aloud. "Flora! Flora, tell those fools to lay aside thier rifles."

The whites, too, were standing watching him, and at the sound of his voice Flora turned toward the blacks. "It is all right," she said, "that is not Tarzan. Lay aside your rifles."

Esteban entered the camp, smiling. "Here I am," he said.

"We thought that you were dead," said Kraski. "Some of these fellows said that Tarzan said that he had killed you."

"He captured me," said Esteban, "but as you see he did not kill me. I thought that he was going to, but he did not, and finally he turned me loose in the jungle. He may have thought that I could not survive and that he would accomplish his end just as surely without having my blood upon his hands."

" 'E must have knowed you," said Peebles. "You'd die, all right, if you were left alone very long in the jungle—you'd starve to death."

Esteban made no reply to the sally but turned toward Flora. "Are you not glad to see me, Flora?" he asked.

The girl shrugged her shoulders. "What is the difference?" she asked. "Our expedition is a failure. Some of them think you were largely to blame." She nodded her head in the general direction of the other whites.

The Spaniard scowled. None of them cared very much to see him. He did not care about the others, but he had hoped that Flora would show some enthusiasm about his return. Well, if she had known what he had in his mind, she might have been happier to see him, and only too glad to show some kind of affection. But she did not know. She did not know that Esteban Miranda had hidden the golden ingots where he might go another day and get them. It had been his intention to persuade her to desert the others, and then, later, the two would return and recover the treasure, but now he was piqued and offended—none of them would have a shilling of it—he would wait until they left Africa and then he would return and take it all for himself. The only fly in the ointment was the thought that the Waziri knew the location of the treasure, and that, sooner or later, they would return with Tarzan and get it. This weak spot in his calculations must be strengthened, and to strengthen it he must have assistance which would mean sharing his secret with another, but whom?

Outwardly oblivious of the sullen glances of his companions he took his place among them. It was evident to him that they were far from being glad to see him, but just why he did not know, for he had not heard of the plan that Kraski and Owaza had hatched to steal the loot of the ivory raiders, and that their main objection to his presence was the fear that they would be compelled to share the loot with him. It was Kraski who first voiced the thought that was in the minds of all but Esteban.

"Miranda," he said, "it is the consensus of opinion that you and Bluber are largely responsible for the failure of our venture. We are not finding fault. I just mention it as a fact. But since you have been away we have struck upon a plan to take something out of Africa that will partially recompense us for the loss of the gold. We have worked the thing all out carefully and made our plans. We don't need you to carry them out. We have no objection to your coming along with us, if you want to, for company, but we want to have it understood from the beginning that you are not to share in anything that we get out of this."

The Spaniard smiled and waved a gesture of unconcern. "It is perfectly all right," he said. "I shall ask for nothing. I would not wish to take anything from any of you." And he grinned inwardly as he thought of the more than quarter of a million pounds in gold which he would one day take out of Africa for himself, alone.

At this unexpected attitude of acquiescence upon Esteban's part the others were greatly relieved, and immediately the entire atmosphere of constraint was removed.

"You're a good fellow, Esteban," said Peebles. "I've been sayin' right along that you'd want to do the right thing, and I want to say that I'm mighty glad to see you back here safe an' sound. I felt terrible when I 'eard you was croaked, that I did."

"Yes," said Bluber, "John he feel so bad he cry himself to sleep every night, ain't it, John?"

"Don't try to start nothin', Bluber," growled Peebles, glaring at the fat man.

"I vasn't commencing to start nodding," replied Adolph, seeing that the big Englishman was angry; "of course ve vere all sorry dat ve t'ought Esteban was killed und ve is all glad dat he is back."

"And that he don't want any of the swag," added Throck.

"Don't worry," said Esteban, "If I get back to London I'll be happy enough—I've had enough of Africa to last me all the rest of my life."

Before he could get to sleep that night, the Spaniard spent a wakeful hour or two trying to evolve a plan whereby he might secure the gold absolutely to himself, without fear of its being removed by the Waziri later. He knew that he could easily find the spot where he had buried it and remove it to another close by, provided that he could return immediately over the trail along which Usula had led them that day, and he could do this alone, insuring that no one but himself would know the new location of the hiding place of the gold, but he was equally positive that he could never again return later from the coast and find where he had hidden it. This meant that he must share his secret with another —one familiar with the country who could find the spot again at any time and from any direction. But who was there whom he might trust! In his mind he went carefully over the entire personnel of their safari, and continually his mind reverted to a single individual—Owaza. He had no confidence in the wily old scoundrel's integrity, but there was no other who suited his purpose as well, and finally he was forced to the conclusion that he must share his secret with this black, and depend upon avarice rather than honor for his protection. He could repay the fellow well—make him rich beyond his wildest dreams, and this the Spaniard could well afford to do in view of the tremendous fortune at stake. And so he fell asleep dreaming of what gold, to the value of over a quarter of a million pounds sterling, would accomplish in the gay capitals of the world.

The following morning while they were breakfasting Esteban mentioned casually that he had passed a large herd of antelope not far from their camp the previous day, and suggested that he take four or five men and do a little hunting, joining the balance of the party at camp that night. No one raised any objection, possibly for the reason that they assumed that the more he hunted and the further from the safari he went the greater the chances of his being killed, a contingency that none of them would have regretted, since at heart they had neither liking nor trust for him.

"I will take Owaza," he said. "He is the cleverest hunter of them all, and five or six men of his choosing." But later, when he approached Owaza, the black interposed objections to the hunt.

"We have plenty of meat for two days," he said. "Let us go on as fast as we can, away from the land of the Waziri and Tarzan. I can find plenty of game anywhere between here and the coast. March for two days, and then I will hunt with you."

"Listen," said Esteban, in a whisper. "It is more than antelope that I would hunt. I cannot tell you here in camp, but when we have left the others I will explain. It will pay you better to come with me today than all the ivory you can hope to get from the raiders." Owaza cocked an attentive ear and scratched his woolly head.

"It is a good day to hunt, Bwana," he said. "I will come with you and bring five boys."

After Owaza had planned the march for the main party and arranged for the camping place for the night, so that he and the Spaniard could find them again, the hunting party set out upon the trail that Usula had followed from the buried treasure the preceding day. They had not gone far before Owaza discovered the fresh spoor of the Waziri.

"Many men passed here late yesterday," he said to Esteban, eyeing the Spaniard quizzically.

"I saw nothing of them," replied the latter. "They must have come this way after I passed."

"They came almost to our camp, and then they turned about and went away again," said Owaza. "Listen, Bwana, I carry a rifle and you shall march ahead of me. If these tracks were made by your people, and you are leading me into ambush, you shall be the first to die."

"Listen, Owaza," said Esteban, "we are far enough from camp now so that I may tell you all. These tracks were made by the Waziri of Tarzan of the Apes, who buried the gold for me a day's march from here. I have sent them home, and I wish you to go back with me and move the gold to another hiding place. After these others have gotten their ivory and returned to England, you and I will come back and get the gold, and then, indeed, shall you be well rewarded."

"Who are you, then?" asked Owaza. "Often I have doubted that you are Tarzan of the Apes. The day that we left the camp outside of Opar one of my men told me that you had been poisoned by your own people and left in the camp. He said that he saw it with his own eyes—your body lying hidden behind some bushes—and yet you were with us upon the march that day. I thought that he lied to me, but I saw the consternation in his face when he saw you, and so I have often wondered if there were two Tarzans of the Apes."

"I am not Tarzan of the Apes," said Esteban. "It was Tarzan of the Apes who was poisoned in our camp by the others. But they only gave him something that would put him to sleep for a long time, possibly with the hope that he would be killed by wild animals before he awoke. Whether or not he still lives we do not know. Therefore you have nothing to fear from the Waziri or Tarzan on my account,

Owaza, for I want to keep out of their way even more than you."

The black nodded. "Perhaps you speak the truth," he said, but still he walked behind, with his rifle always ready in his hand.

They went warily, for fear of overtaking the Waziri, but shortly after passing the spot where the latter had camped they saw that they had taken another route and that there was no danger of coming in contact with them.

When they had reached a point within about a mile of the spot where the gold had been buried, Esteban told Owaza to have his boys remain there while they went ahead alone to effect the transfer of the ingots.

"The fewer who know of this," he said to the black, "the safer we shall be."

"The Bwana speaks words of wisdom," replied the wily black.

Esteban found the spot near the waterfall without difficulty, and upon questioning Owaza he discovered that the latter knew the location perfectly, and would have no difficulty in coming directly to it again from the coast. They transferred the gold but a short distance, concealing it in a heavy thicket near the edge of the river, knowing that it would be as safe from discovery there as though they had transported it a hundred miles, for the chances were extremely slight that the Waziri or anyone else who should learn of its original hiding place would imagine that anyone would go to the trouble of removing it but a matter of a hundred yards.

When they had finished Owaza looked at the sun.

"We will never reach camp tonight," he said, "and we will have to travel fast to overtake them even tomorrow."

"I did not expect to," replied Esteban, "but could not tell them that. If we never find them again I shall be satisfied." Owaza grinned. In his crafty mind an idea was formed.

"Why," he thought, "risk death in a battle with the Arab ivory raiders on the chance of securing a few tusks, when all this gold awaits only transportation to the coast to be ours?"

13

A Strange, Flat Tower

TARZAN turning, discovered the man standing behind him on the top level of the ivy-covered east tower of the Palace of Diamonds. His knife leaped from its sheath at the touch of his quick fingers. But almost simultaneously his hand dropped to his side, and he stood contemplating the other, with an expression of incredulity upon his face that but reflected a similar emotion registered upon the countenance of the stranger. For what Tarzan saw was no Bolgani, nor a Gomangani, but a white man, bald and old and shriveled, with a long, white beard—a white man, naked but for barbaric ornaments of gold spangles and diamonds.

"God!" exclaimed the strange apparition.

Tarzan eyed the other quizzically. That single English word opened up such tremendous possibilities for conjecture as baffled the mind of the ape-man.

"What are you? Who are you?" continued the old man, but this time in the dialect of the great apes.

"You used an English word a moment ago," said Tarzan. "Do you speak that language?" Tarzan himself spoke in English.

"Ah, dear God!" cried the old man, "that I should have lived to hear that sweet tongue again." And he, too, now spoke in English, halting English, as might one who was long unaccustomed to voicing the language.

"Who are you?" asked Tarzan, "and what are you doing here?"

"It is the same question that I asked you," replied the old man. "Do not be afraid to answer me. You are evidently an Englishman, and you have nothing to fear from me."

"I am here after a woman, captured by the Bolgani," replied Tarzan.

The other nodded. "Yes," he said, "I know. She is here."

"Is she safe?" asked Tarzan.

"She has not been harmed. She will be safe until tomorrow or the next day," replied the old man. "But who are you, and how did you find your way here from the outer world?"

"I am Tarzan of the Apes," replied the ape-man. "I came into this valley looking for a way out of the valley of Opar where the life of my companion was in danger. And you?"

"I am an old man," replied the other, "and I have been here ever since I was a boy. I was a stowaway on the ship that brought Stanley to Africa after the establishment of the station on Stanley Pool, and I came into the interior with him. I went out from camp to hunt, alone, one day. I lost my way and later was captured by unfriendly natives. They took me farther into the interior to their village from which I finally escaped, but so utterly confused and lost that I had no idea what direction to take to find a trail to the coast. I wandered thus for months, until finally, upon an accursed day I found an entrance to this valley. I do not know why they did not put me to death at once, but they did not, and later they discovered that my knowledge could be turned to advantage to them. Since then I have helped them in their quarrying and mining and in their diamond cutting. I have given them iron drills with hardened points and drills tipped with diamonds. Now I am practically one of them, but always in my heart has been the hope that some day I might escape from the valley—a hopeless hope, though, I may assure you."

"There is no way out?" asked Tarzan.

"There is a way, but it is always guarded."

"Where is it?" queried Tarzan.

"It is a continuation of one of the mine tunnels, passing entirely through the mountain to the valley beyond. The mines have been worked by the ancestors of this race for an almost incalculable length of time. The mountains are honeycombed with their shafts and tunnels. Back of the gold-bearing quartz lies an enormous deposit of altered peridotite, which contains diamonds, in the search for which it evidently became necessary to extend one of the shafts to the opposite side of the mountain, possibly for purposes of ventilation. This tunnel and the trail leading down into Opar are the only means of ingress to the valley. From time immemorial they have kept the tunnel guarded, more particularly, I imagine, to prevent the escape of slaves than to thwart the inroads of an enemy, since they believe that there is no fear of the latter emergency. The trail to Opar they do not guard, because they no longer fear the Oparians, and know quite well that none of their Gomangani slaves would dare enter the valley of the sunworshipers. For the same reason, then, that the slaves cannot escape, we, too, must remain prisoners here forever."

"How is the tunnel guarded?" asked Tarzan.

"Two Bolgani and a dozen or more Gomangani warriors are always upon duty there," replied the old man.

"The Gomangani would like to escape?"

"They have tried it many times in the past, I am told," replied the old man, "though never since I have lived here, and always they were caught and tortured. And all their race was punished and worked the harder because of these attempts upon the part of a few."

"They are numerous—the Gomangani?"

"There are probably five thousand of them in the valley," replied the old man.

"And how may Bolgani?" the ape-man asked.

"Between ten and eleven hundred."

"Five to one," murmured Tarzan, "and yet they are afraid to attempt to escape."

"But you must remember," said the old man, "that the Bolgani are the dominant and intelligent race—the others are intellectually little above the beasts of the forest."

"Yet they are men," Tarzan reminded him.

"In figure only," replied the old man. "They cannot band together as men do. They have not as yet reached the community plane of evolution. It is true that families reside in a single village, but that idea, together with their weapons, was given to them by the Bolgani that they might not be entirely exterminated by the lions and panthers. Formerly, I am told, each individual Gomangani, when he became old enough to hunt for himself, constructed a hut apart from others and took up his solitary life, there being at that time no slightest semblance of family life. Then the Bolgani taught them how to build palisaded villages and compelled the men and women to remain in them and rear their children to maturity, after which the children were required to remain in the village, so that now some of the communities can claim as many as forty or fifty people. But the death rate is high among them, and they cannot multiply as rapidly as people living under normal conditions of peace and security. The brutalities of the Bolgani kill many; the carnivora take a considerable toll."

"Five to one, and still they remain in slavery—what cowards they must be," said the ape-man.

"On the contrary, they are far from cowardly," replied the old man. "They will face a lion with the utmost bravery. But for so many ages have they been subservient to the will of the Bolgani, that it has become a fixed habit in them—as the fear of God is inherent in us, so is the fear of the Bolgani inherent in the minds of the Gomangani from birth."

"It is interesting," said Tarzan. "But tell me now where the woman is of whom I have come in search."

"She is your mate?" asked the old man.

"No," replied Tarzan. "I told the Gomangani that she was, so that they would protect her. She is La, queen of Opar, High Priestess of the Flaming God."

The old man looked his incredulity. "Impossible!" he cried. "It cannot be that the queen of Opar has risked her life by coming to the home of her hereditary enemies."

"She was forced to it," replied Tarzan, "her life being threatened by a part of her people because she had refused to sacrifice me to their god."

"If the Bolgani knew this there would be great rejoicing," replied the old man.

"Tell me where she is," demanded Tarzan. "She preserved me from her people, and I must save her from whatever fate the Bolgani contemplate for her."

"It is hopeless," said the old man. "I can tell you where she is, but you cannot rescue her."

"I can try," replied the ape-man.

"But you will fail and die."

"If what you tell me is true, that there is absolutely no chance of my escaping from the valley, I might as well die," replied the ape-man. "However, I do not agree with you."

The old man shrugged. "You do not know the Bolgani," he said.

"Tell me where the woman is," said Tarzan.

"Look," replied the old man, motioning Tarzan to follow him into his apartment, and approaching a window which faced toward the west, he pointed towards a strange flat tower which rose above the roof of the main building near the west end of the palace. "She is probably somewhere in the interior of that tower," said the old man to Tarzan, "but as far as you are concerned, she might as well be at the north pole."

Tarzan stood in silence for a moment, his keen eyes taking in every salient detail of the prospect before him. He saw the strange, flat-topped tower, which it seemed to him might be reached from the roof of the main building. He saw, too, branches of the ancient trees that sometimes topped the roof itself, and except for the dim light shining through some of the palace windows he saw no signs of life. He turned suddenly upon the old man.

"I do not know you," he said, "but I believe I may trust you, since after all blood ties are strong, and we are the only men of our race in this valley. You might gain something in favor by betraying me, but I cannot believe that you will do it."

"Do not fear," said the old man, "I hate them. If I could help you I would, but I know that there is no hope of success for whatever plan you may have in mind—the woman will never be rescued; you will never leave the Valley of the Palace of Diamonds—you will never leave the palace itself unless the Bolgani wish it."

The ape-man grinned. "You have been here so long," he said, "that you are beginning to assume the attitude of mind that keeps the Gomangani in perpetual slavery. If you want to escape, come with me. We may not succeed, but at least you will have a better chance if you try than as if you remained forever in this tower."

The old man shook his head. "No," he said, "it is hopeless. If escape had been possible I should have been away from here long ago."

"Good-bye then," said Tarzan, and swinging out of the window he clambered toward the roof below, along the stout stem of the old ivy.

The old man watched him for a moment until he saw him make his way carefully across the roof toward the flat-topped tower where he hoped to find and liberate La. Then the old fellow turned and hurried rapidly down the crude stairway that rose ladder-like to the center of the tower.

Tarzan made his way across the uneven roof of the main building, clambering up the sides of its higher elevations and dropping again to its lower levels as he covered a considerable distance between the east tower and that flat-topped structure of peculiar design in which La was supposed to be incarcerated. His progress was slow, for he moved with the caution of a beast of prey, stopping often in dense shadows to listen.

When at last he reached the tower, he found that it had many openings letting upon the roof—openings which were closed only with hangings of the heavy tapestried stuff which he had seen in the tower. Drawing one of these slightly aside he looked within upon a large chamber, bare of furnishings, from the center of which there protruded through a

circular aperture the top of a stairway similar to that he had
ascended in the east tower. There was no one in sight within
the chamber, and Tarzan crossed immediately to the stairway. Peering cautiously into the opening Tarzan saw that the
stairway descended for a great distance, passing many floors.
How far it went he could not judge, except it seemed likely
that it pierced subterranean chambers beneath the palace.
Sounds of life came up to him through the shaft, and odors,
too, but the latter largely nullified, in so far as the scent
impressions which they offered Tarzan were concerned,
by the heavy incense which pervaded the entire palace.

It was this perfume that was to prove the ape-man's undoing, for otherwise his keen nostrils would have detected the
scent of a near-by Gomangani. The fellow lay behind one of
the hangings at an aperture in the tower wall. He had been
lying in such a position that he had seen Tarzan enter the
chamber, and he was watching him now as the ape-man stood
looking down the shaft of the stairway. The eyes of the
black had at first gone wide in terror at sight of this strange
apparition, the like of which he had never seen before. Had
the creature been of sufficient intelligence to harbor superstition, he would have thought Tarzan a god descended from
above. But being of too low an order to possess any imagination whatsoever, he merely knew that he saw a strange
creature, and that all strange creatures must be enemies, he
was convinced. His duty was to apprise his masters of this
presence in the palace, but he did not dare to move until
the apparition had reached a sufficient distance from him to
insure that the movements of the Gomangani would not be
noticed by the intruder—he did not care to call attention
to himself, for he had found that the more one effaced one-
self in the presence of the Bolgani, the less one was likely to
suffer. For a long time the stranger peered down the shaft
of the stairway, and for a long time the Gomangani lay
quietly watching him. But at last the former descended the
stairs and passed out of sight of the watcher, who immediately leaped to his feet and scurried away across the roof
of the palace toward a large tower arising at its western end.

As Tarzan descended the ladder the fumes of the incense
became more and more annoying. Where otherwise he might
have investigated quickly by scent he was now compelled to
listen for every sound, and in many cases to investigate the
chambers opening upon the central corridor by entering them.
Where the doors were locked, he lay flat and listened close
to the aperture at their base. On several occasions he risked
calling La by name, but in no case did he receive any reply.

He had investigated four landings and was descending to the fifth when he saw standing in one of the doorways upon this level an evidently much excited and possibly terrified black. The fellow was of giant proportions and entirely unarmed. He stood looking at the ape-man with wide eyes as the latter jumped lightly from the stairway and stood facing him upon the same level.

"What do you want?" finally stammered the black. "Are you looking for the white she, your mate, whom the Bolgani took?"

"Yes," replied Tarzan. "What do you know of her?"

"I know where she is hidden," replied the black, "and if you will follow me I will lead you to her."

"Why do you offer to do this for me?" asked Tarzan, immediately suspicious. "Why is it that you do not go at once to your masters and tell them that I am here that they may send men to capture me?"

"I do not know the reason that I was sent to tell you this," replied the black. "The Bolgani sent me. I did not wish to come for I was afraid."

"Where did they tell you to lead me?" asked Tarzan.

"I am to lead you into a chamber, the door of which will be immediately bolted upon us. You will then be a prisoner."

"And you?" inquired Tarzan.

"I, too, shall be a prisoner with you. The Bolgani do not care what becomes of me. Perhaps you will kill me, but they do not care."

"If you lead me into a trap I shall kill you," replied Tarzan. "But if you lead me to the woman perhaps we shall all escape. You would like to escape, would you not?"

"I should like to escape, but I cannot."

"Have you ever tried?"

"No, I have not. Why should I try to do something that cannot be done?"

"If you lead me into the trap I shall surely kill you. If you lead me to the woman, you at least have the chance that I do to live. Which will you do?"

The black scratched his head in thought, the idea slowly filtering through his stupid mind. At last he spoke.

"You are very wise," he said. "I will lead you to the woman."

"Go ahead, then," said Tarzan, "and I will follow you." The black descended to the next level and opening the door entered a long, straight corridor. As the ape-man followed his guide be had leisure to reflect upon the means through which the Bolgani had learned of his presence in the tower, and the only conclusion he could arrive at was that the old man had betrayed him, since in so far as Tarzan was aware he alone knew that the ape-man was in the palace. The corridor along which the black was leading him was very dark, receiving a dim and inadequate illumination from the dimly lighted corridor they had just left, the door into which remained open behind them. Presently the black stopped, before a closed door.

"The woman is in there," said the black, pointing to the door.

"She is alone?" asked Tarzan.

"No," replied the black. "Look," and he opened the door, revealing a heavy hanging, which he gently separated, revealing to Tarzan the interior of the chamber beyond.

Seizing the black by the wrist, that he might not escape, Tarzan stepped forward and put his eyes to the aperture. Before him lay a large chamber, at one end of which was a raised dais, the base of which was of a dark, ornately carved wood. The central figure upon this dais was a huge, black-maned lion—the same that Tarzan had seen escorted through the gardens of the palace. His golden chains were now fastened to rings in the floor, while the four blacks stood in statuesque rigidity, two upon either side of the beast. Upon golden thrones behind the lion sat three magnificently ornamented Bolgani. At the foot of the steps leading to the stair stood La, between two Gomangani guards. Upon either side of a central aisle were carved benches facing the dais, and occupying the front section of these were some fifty Bolgani, among whom Tarzan almost immediately espied the little, old man that he had met in the tower, the sight of whom instantly crystallized the ape-man's conviction of the source of his betrayal.

The chamber was lighted by hundreds of cressets, burning a substance which gave forth both light and the heavy incense that had assailed Tarzan's nostrils since first he had entered the domain of the Bolgani. The long, cathedralesque windows upon one side of the apartment were thrown wide, admitting the soft air of the jungle summer night. Through them Tarzan could see the palace grounds and that this chamber was upon the same level as the terrace upon which the palace stood. Beyond those windows was an open gateway to the jungle and freedom, but interposed between him and the windows were fifty armed gorilla-men. Perhaps, then, strategy would be a better weapon than force with which to carve his way to freedom with La. Yet to the forefront of his mind was evidently a belief in the probability that in the end it would be force rather than strategy upon which he must depend. He turned to the black at his side.

"Would the Gomangani guarding the lion like to escape from the Bolgani?" he asked.

"The Gomangani would all escape if they could," replied the black.

"If it is necessary for me to enter the room, then," said Tarzan to the black, "will you accompany me and tell the other Gomangani that if they will fight for me I will take them out of the valley?"

"I will tell them, but they will not believe," replied the black.

"Tell them that they will die if they do not help me, then," said Tarzan.

"I will tell them."

As Tarzan turned his attention again to the chamber before him he saw that the Bolgani occupying the central golden throne was speaking.

"Nobles of Numa, King of Beasts, Emperor of All Created Things," he said in deep, growling tones, "Numa has heard the words that this she has spoken, and it is the will of Numa that she die. The Great Emperor is hungry. He, himself, will devour her here in the presence of his Nobles and the Imperial Council of Three. It is the will of Numa."

A growl of approval arose from the beast-like audience, while the great lion bared his hideous fangs and roared until the palace trembled, his wicked, yellow-green eyes fixed terribly upon the woman before him, evidencing the fact that these ceremonies were of sufficient frequency to have accustomed the lion to what he might expect as the logical termination of them.

"Day after tomorrow," continued the speaker, "the mate of of this creature, who is by this time safely imprisoned in the Tower of the Emperors, will be brought before Numa for judgment. Slaves," he cried suddenly in a loud voice, rising to his feet and glaring at the guards holding La, "drag the woman to your emperor."

Instantly the lion became frantic, lashing its tail and straining at its stout chains, roaring and snarling as it reared upon its hind feet and sought to leap upon La, who was now being forcibly conducted up the steps of the dais toward the bejeweled man-eater so impatiently awaiting her.

She did not cry out in terror, but she sought to twist herself free from the detaining hands of the powerful Gomangani—all futilely, however.

They had reached the last step, and were about to push

La into the claws of the lion, when they were arrested by a loud cry from one side of the chamber—a cry that halted the Gomangani and brought the assembled Bolgani to their feet in astonishment and anger, for the sight that met their eyes was well-qualified to arouse the latter within them. Leaping into the room with raised spear was the almost naked white man of whom they had heard, but whom none of them had as yet seen. And so quick was he that in the very instant of entry—even before they could rise to their feet—he had launched his spear.

14

The Chamber of Horrors

A BLACK-MANED lion moved through the jungle night. With majestic unconcern for all other created things he took his lordly way through the primeval forest. He was not hunting, for he made no efforts toward stealth, nor, on the other hand, did he utter any vocal sound. He moved swiftly, though sometimes stopping with uplifted nose to scent the air and to listen. And thus at last he came to a high wall, along the face of which he sniffed, until the wall was broken by a half-opened gateway, through which he passed into the enclosure.

Before him loomed a great building, and presently as he stood watching it and listening, there broke from the interior the thunderous roar of an angry lion.

He of the black mane cocked his head upon one side and moved stealthily forward.

At the very instant that La was about to be thrust into the clutches of Numa, Tarzan of the Apes leaped into the apartment with a loud cry that brought to momentary pause the Gomangani that were dragging her to her doom, and in that brief instant of respite which the ape-man knew would follow his interruption the swift spear was launched. To the rage and consternation of the Bolgani they saw it bury itself in the heart of their Emperor—the great, blackmaned lion.

At Tarzan's side stood the Gomangani whom he had terrified into service, and as Tarzan rushed forward toward La the black accompanied him, crying to his fellows that if they would help this stranger they might be free and escape from the Bolgani forever.

"You have permitted the great Emperor to be slain," he cried to the poor Gomangani who guarded Numa. "For this the Bolgani will kill you. Help to save the strange Tarmangani and his mate and you have at least a chance for life and freedom. And you," he added, addressing the two who had been guarding La, "they will hold you responsible also—your only hope lies with us."

Tarzan had reached La's side and was dragging her up the steps of the dais where he hoped that he might make a momentary stand against the fifty Bolgani who were now rushing forward from their seats toward him.

"Slay the three who sit upon the dais," cried Tarzan to the Gomangani, who were now evidently hesitating as to which side they would cast their lot with. "Slay them if you wish your freedom! Slay them if you wish to live!"

The authoritative tones of his voice, the magnetic appeal of his personality, his natural leadership won them to him for the brief instant that was necessary to turn them upon the hated authority that the three Bolgani upon the dais represented, and as they drove their spears into the shaggy black bodies of their masters they became then and forever the creatures of Tarzan of the Apes, for there could be no future hope for them in the land of the Bolgani.

With one arm around La's waist the ape-man carried her to the summit of the dais, where he seized his spear and drew it from the body of the dead lion. Then, turning about, and facing the advancing Bolgani, he placed one foot upon the carcass of his kill and raised his voice in the terrifying victory cry of the apes of Kerchak.

Before him the Bolgani paused, behind him the Gomangani quailed in terror.

"Stop!" cried Tarzan, raising a palm toward the Bolgani. "Listen! I am Tarzan of the Apes. I sought no quarrel with your people. I but look for a passage through your country to my own. Let me go my way in peace with this woman, taking these Gomangani with me."

For answer a chorus of savage growls arose from the Bolgani as they started forward again toward the dais. From their ranks there suddenly leaped the old man of the east tower, who ran swiftly toward Tarzan.

"Ah, traitor," cried the ape-man, "you would be the

first, then, to taste the wrath of Tarzan?" He spoke in English and the old man replied in the same tongue.

"Traitor?" he exclaimed in surprise.

"Yes, traitor," thundered Tarzan. "Did you not hurry here to tell the Bolgani that I was in the palace, that they might send the Gomangani to lure me to a trap?"

"I did nothing of the kind," replied the other. "I came here to place myself near the white woman, with the thought that I might be of service to her or you if I were needed. I come now, Englishman, to stand at your side and die at your side, for die you shall, as sure as there is a God in heaven. Nothing can save you now from the wrath of the Bolgani whose Emperor you have killed."

"Come, then," cried Tarzan, "and prove your loyalty. It were better to die now than to live in slavery forever."

The six Gomangani had ranged themselves, three upon either side of Tarzan and La, while the seventh, who had entered the chamber with Tarzan unarmed, was taking weapons from the body of one of the three Bolgani who had been slain upon the dais.

Before this array of force so new to them, the Bolgani paused at the foot of the steps leading to the dais. But only for a moment they paused, for there were but nine against fifty, and as they surged up the steps, Tarzan and his Gomangani met them with battle ax, and spear, and bludgeon. For a moment they pressed them back, but the numbers against them were too great, and once again a wave swept up that seemed likely to overwhelm them, when there broke upon the ears of the contestants a frightful roar, which, coming from almost at their sides, brought a sudden, momentary cessation of the battle.

Turning their eyes in the direction of the sound they saw a huge, black-maned lion standing upon the floor of the apartment, just within one of the windows. For an instant he stood like a statue of golden bronze, and then again the building trembled to the reverberations of his mighty roar.

Towering above them all Tarzan of the Apes looked down from the dais upon the great beast below them, and then in quick elation he raised his voice above the growlings of the Bolgani.

"Jad-bal-ja," he cried, and pointing toward the Bolgani, "Kill! Kill!"

Scarcely had the words been uttered ere the huge monster, a veritable devil incarnate, was upon the hairy gorilla-men. And simultaneously there occurred to the mind of the ape-man a daring plan of salvation for himself and the others who were dependent upon him.

"Quick," he cried to the Gomangani, "fall upon the Bolgani. Here at last is the true Numa, King of Beasts, and ruler of all creation. He slays his enemies but he will protect Tarzan of the Apes and the Gomangani, who are his friends."

Seeing their hated masters falling back before the terrific onslaughts of the lion, the Gomangani rushed in with battle axes and clubs, while Tarzan, casting aside his spear, took his place among them with drawn knife, and, keeping close to Jad-bal-ja, directed the lion from one victim to another, lest he fall by mistake upon the Gomangani or the little, old, white man, or even La herself. Twenty of the Bolgani lay dead upon the floor before the balance managed to escape from the chamber, and then Tarzan, turning to Jad-bal-ja, called him to heel.

"Go!" he said, turning toward the Gomangani, "and drag the body of the false Numa from the dias. Remove it from the room, for the true Emperor has come to claim his throne."

The old man and La were eyeing Tarzan and the lion in amazement.

"Who are you," asked the former, "that you can work such miracles with a savage beast of the jungle? Who are you, and what do you intend to do?"

"Wait and see," said Tarzan with a grim smile. "I think that we shall all be safe now, and that the Gomangani may live in comfort for a long time hereafter."

When the blacks had removed the carcass of the lion from the dias and thrown it from one of the windows of the chamber, Tarzan sent Jad-bal-ja to sit in the place upon the dais that had formerly been occupied by the lion, Numa.

"There," he said, turning to the Gomangani, "you see the true Emperor, who does not have to be chained to his throne. Three of you will go to the huts of your people behind the palace and summon them to the throne room, that they, too, may see what has transpired. Hurry, that we may have many warriors here before the Bolgani return in force."

Filled with an excitement which almost shook their dull minds into a semblance of intelligence three of the Gomangani hastened to do Tarzan's bidding, while the others stood gazing at Tarzan with expressions of such awe that might only be engendered by the sight of deity. La came then and stood beside Tarzan, looking up into his face with eyes that reflected a reverence fully as deep as that held by the blacks.

"I have not thanked you, Tarzan of the Apes," she said,

"for what you have risked and done for me. I know that you must have come here in search of me, to save me from these creatures, and I know that it was not love that impelled you to this heroic and well-nigh hopeless act. That you have succeeded thus far is little short of miraculous, but I, in the legends of whose people are recounted the exploits of the Bolgani, know that there can be no hope of eventual escape for us all, and so I beseech that you go at once and make good your escape alone, if possible, for you alone of us have any possible chance of escape."

"I do not agree with you that we have no chance to escape, La," replied the ape-man. "It seems to me that now we not only have every reason to believe that we are practically assured of escape, but that we may insure also to these poor Gomangani freedom from slavery and from the tyranny of the Bolgani. But this is not all. With this I shall not be satisfied. Not only must these people who show no hospitality to strangers be punished, but your own disloyal priests as well. To this latter end I intend to march out of the Valley of the Palace of Diamonds, down upon the city of Opar with a force of Gomangani sufficient to compel Cadj to relinquish the power he has usurped and replace you upon the throne of Opar. Nothing less than this shall satisfy me, and nothing less than this shall I accomplish before I leave."

"You are a brave man," said the old man, "and you have succeeded beyond what I thought could be possible, but La is right, you do not know the ferocity or the resources of the Bolgani, or the power which they wield over the Gomangani. Could you raise from the stupid minds of the blacks the incubus of fear that rests so heavily upon them you might win over a sufficient number to make good your escape from the valley, but that, I fear, is beyond even you. Our only hope, therefore, is to escape from the palace while they are momentarily disorganized, and trust to fleetness and to luck to carry us beyond the limits of the valley before we are apprehended."

"See," cried La, pointing; "even now it is too late—they return."

Tarzan looked in the direction that she indicated and saw through the open doorway at the far end of the chamber a large number of gorilla-men approaching. His eyes moved swiftly to the windows in the other wall. "But wait," he said, "behold another factor in the equation!"

The others looked toward the windows which opened upon the terrace, and they saw beyond them what appeared to be a crowd of several hundred blacks running rapidly toward the windows. The other blacks upon the dais cried out excitedly: "They come! They come! We shall be free, and no longer shall the Bolgani be able to make us work until we drop from exhaustion, or beat us, or torture us, or feed us to Numa."

As the first of the Bolgani reached the doorway leading into the chamber, the Gomangani commenced to pour through the several windows in the opposite wall. They were led by the three who had been sent to fetch them, and to such good effect had these carried their message that the blacks already seemed like a new people, so transfigured were they by the thought of immediate freedom. At sight of them the leader of the Bolgani cried aloud for them to seize the intruders upon the dais, but his answer was a spear hurled by the nearest black, and as he lunged forward, dead, the battle was on.

The Bolgani in the palace greatly outnumbered the blacks, but the latter had the advantage of holding the interior of the throne room in sufficient numbers to prevent the entry of many Bolgani simultaneously. Tarzan, immediately he recognized the temper of the blacks, called Jad-bal-ja to follow him, and, descending from the dais, he took command of the Gomangani. At each opening he placed sufficient men to guard it, and at the center of the room he held the balance in reserve. Then he called the old man into consultation.

"The gate in the east wall is open," he said. "I left it so when I entered. Would it be possible for twenty or thirty blacks to reach it in safety and, entering the forest, carry word to the villagers of what is transpiring here in the palace, and prevail upon them to send all of their warriors immediately to complete the work of emancipation that we have begun?"

"It is an excellent plan," replied the old man. "The Bolgani are not upon that side of the palace between us and the gate, and if it may ever be accomplished, now is the time. I will pick your men for you. They must be head-men, whose words will carry some weight with the villagers outside the palace walls."

"Good!" exclaimed Tarzan. "Select them immediately; tell them what we want and urge upon them the necessity for haste."

One by one the old man chose thirty warriors, whose duty he carefully explained to each. They were delighted with the plan and assured Tarzan that in less than an hour the first of the reinforcements would come.

"As you leave the enclosure," said the ape-man, "destroy

the lock if you can, so that the Bolgani may not lock it again and bar out our reinforcements. Carry also the word that the first who come are to remain outside the wall until a sufficient number have arrived to make entry into the palace grounds reasonably safe—at least as many as are within this room now."

The blacks signified their understanding, and a moment later passed out of the room through one of the windows and disappeared into the darkness of the night beyond.

Shortly after the blacks had left the Bolgani made a determined rush upon the Gomangani guarding the main entrance to the throne room, with the result that a score or more of the gorilla-men succeeded in cutting their way into the room. At this first indication of reversal the blacks showed signs of faltering, the fear of the Bolgani that was inherent in them showing in their wavering attitude and seeming reluctance to force a counter attack. As Tarzan leaped forward to assist in checking the rush of the Bolgani into the throne room he called to Jad-bal-ja, and as the great lion leaped from the dais the ape-man, pointing to the nearest Bolgani, cried: "Kill! Kill!"

Straight for the throat of the nearest leaped Jad-bal-ja. The great jaws closed upon the snarling face of the frightened gorilla-man but once, and then, at the command of his master the golden lion dropped the carcass after a single shake and leaped upon another. Three had died thus in quick succession when the balance of the Bolgani turned to flee this chamber of horrors; but the Gomangani, their confidence restored by the ease with which this fierce ally brought death and terror to the tyrants, interposed themselves between the Bolgani and the doorway, shutting off their retreat.

"Hold them! Hold them!" cried Tarzan. "Do not kill them!" And then to the Bolgani: "Surrender and you will not be harmed!"

Jad-bal-ja clung close to the side of his master, glaring and growling at the Bolgani, and casting an occasional beseeching look at the ape-man which said plainer than words, "Send me among them."

Fifteen of the Bolgani who had entered the room survived. For a moment they hesitated, and then one of them threw his weapons upon the floor. Immediately the others followed suit.

Tarzan turned toward Jad-bal-ja. "Back!" he said, pointing toward the dais, and as the lion wheeled and slunk away toward the platform, Tarzan turned again toward the Bolgani.

"Let one of your number go," he said, "and announce to your fellows that I demand their immediate surrender."

The Bolgani whispered among themselves for a few moments and finally one of them announced that he would go and see the others. After he had left the room the old man approached Tarzan.

"They will never surrender," he said. "Look out for treachery."

"It is all right," said Tarzan. "I am expecting that, but I am gaining time, and that is what we need most. If there were a place near where I might confine these others I should feel better, for it would cut down our antagonists by at least that many."

"There is a room there," said the old man, pointing toward one of the doorways in the throne room, "where you can confine them—there are many such rooms in the Tower of the Emperors."

"Good," said Tarzan, and a moment later, following his instructions the Bolgani were safely locked in a room adjoining the throne room. In the corridors without they could hear the main body of the gorilla-men in argument. It was evident that they were discussing the message sent to them by Tarzan. Fifteen minutes passed, and finally thirty, with no word from the Bolgani and no resumption of hostilities, and then there came to the main entrance of the throne room the fellow whom Tarzan had despatched with his demand for surrender.

"Well," asked the ape-man, "what is their answer?"

"They will not surrender," replied the Bolgani, "but they will permit you to leave the valley provided that you will release those whom you have taken prisoner and harm no others."

The ape-man shook his head. "That will not do," he replied. "I hold the power to crush the Bolgani of the Valley of Diamonds. Look," and he pointed toward Jad-bal-ja, "here is the true Numa. The creature you had upon your throne was but a wild beast, but this is Numa, King of Beasts, Emperor of All Created Things. Look at him. Must he be held in leash by golden chains like some prisoner or slave? No! He is indeed an Emperor. But there is one yet greater than he, one from whom he takes commands. And that one is I, Tarzan of the Apes. Anger me and you shall feel not only the wrath of Numa, but the wrath of Tarzan as well. The Gomangani are my people, the Bolgani shall be my slaves. Go and tell your fellows that, and that if they would live at all they had best come soon and sue for mercy. Go!"

When the messenger had again departed Tarzan looked at the old man, who was eyeing him with an expression which might have denoted either awe or reverence, were it not for the vaguest hint of a twinkle in the corners of the eyes. The ape-man breathed a deep sigh of relief. "That will give us at least another half hour," he said.

"We shall need it, and more, too," replied the old man, "though, at that, you have accomplished more than I had thought possible, for at least you have put a doubt in the minds of the Bolgani, who never before have had cause to question their own power."

Presently from the outer corridors the sounds of argument and discussion gave place to that of movement among the Bolgani. A company, comprising some fifty of the gorilla-men, took post directly outside the main entrance of the throne room where they stood in silence, their weapons ready, as though for the purpose of disputing any effort upon the part of the inmates of the room to escape. Beyond them the balance of the gorilla-men could be seen moving away and disappearing through doorways and corridors leading from the main hallway of the palace. The Gomangani, together with La and the old man, watched impatiently for the coming of the black reinforcements, while Tarzan sat upon the edge of the dais half-reclining, with an arm about the neck of Jad-bal-ja.

"They are up to something," said the old man. "We must watch carefully against a surprise. If the blacks would but come now, while the doorway is held by only fifty, we should overcome them easily, and have, I do verily believe, some slight chance of escaping from the palace grounds."

"Your long residence here," said Tarzan, "has filled you with the same senseless fear of the Bolgani that the Gomangani hold. From the attitude of mind which you hold toward them one would think them some manner of supermen—they are only beasts, my friend, and if we remain loyal to our cause we shall overcome them."

"Beasts they may be," replied the old man, "but they are beasts with the brains of men—their cunning and their cruelty are diabolical."

A long silence ensued, broken only by the nervous whisperings of the Gomangani, whose morale, it was evident, was slowly disintegrating under the nervous strain of the enforced wait, and the failure of their fellows of the forest to come quickly to their aid. To this was added the demoralizing effect of speculation upon what the Bolgani were planning or what plan they already were putting into effect. The very silence of the gorilla-men was more terrible than the din of actual assault. La was the first of the whites to break the silence.

"If thirty of the Gomangani could leave the palace so easily, why might not we leave also?" she asked.

"There were two reasons," replied Tarzan. "One was that should we have left simultaneously the Bolgani, greatly outnumbering us as they did, could have harassed us and detained us for a sufficient length of time to have permitted their messengers to reach the villagers ahead of us, with the result that in a short time we should have been surrounded by thousands of hostile warriors. The second reason is that I desire to punish the creatures, so that in future a stranger may be safe in the Valley of the Palace of Diamonds." He paused. "And now I shall give you a third reason why we may not seek to escape at this moment." He pointed toward the windows overlooking the terrace. "Look," he said, "the terrace and the gardens are filled with Bolgani. Whatever their plan I think its success depends upon our attempt to escape from this room through the windows, for, unless I am mistaken, the Bolgani upon the terrace and in the gardens are making an attempt to hide themselves from us."

The old man walked to a part of the room from which he could see the greater part of the terrace and gardens upon which the windows of the throne room looked.

"You are right," he said when he returned to the apeman's side; "the Bolgani are all massed outside these windows with the exception of those who guard the entrance, and possibly some others at the doorways at other portions of the throne room. That, however, we must determine." He walked quickly to the opposite side of the chamber and drew back the hangings before one of the apertures, disclosing beyond a small band of Bolgani. They stood there motionless, not making any effort to seize or harm him. To another exit, and another, he went, and beyond each discovered to the occupants of the chamber the same silent gorilla guardians. He made the circle of the room, passing over the dais behind the three thrones, and then he came back to Tarzan and La.

"It is as I suspected," he said, "we are entirely surrounded. Unless help comes soon we are lost."

"But their force is divided," Tarzan reminded him.

"Even so, it is sufficient to account for us," replied the old man.

"Perhaps you are right," said Tarzan, "but at least we shall have a bully fight."

"What is that!" exclaimed La, and simultaneously, attracted

by the same noise, the inmates of the throne room raised their
eyes to the ceiling above them, where they saw that traps
had been lifted from a dozen openings, revealing the scowling faces of several score of gorilla-men.

"What are they up to now!" exclaimed Tarzan, and as
though in answer to the query the Bolgani above began
hurling bundles of burning, oil-soaked rags, tied in goat skins,
into the throne room, which immediately commenced to fill
it with a thick, suffocating smoke, accompanied by the
stench of burning hide and hair.

15

The Map of Blood

AFTER Esteban and Owaza had buried the gold they returned to the spot where they had left their five boys,
and proceeding with them to the river made camp for
the night. Here they discussed their plans, deciding to abandon
the balance of the party to reach the coast as best they
might, while they returned to another section of the coast
where they could recruit sufficient porters to carry out the
gold.

"Instead of going way back to the coast for porters,"
asked Esteban, "why could we not just as well recruit them
from the nearest village?"

"Such men would not go with us way to the coast," replied
Owaza. "They are not porters. At best they would but carry
our gold to the next village."

"Why not that, then?" inquired the Spaniard. "And at
the next village we could employ porters to carry us on still
farther, until we could employ other men to continue on with
us."

Owaza shook his head. "It is a good plan, Bwana, but
we cannot do it, because we have nothing with which to pay
our porters."

Esteban scratched his head. "You are right," he said, "but
it would save us that damnable trip to the coast and return."
They sat for some moments in silence, thinking. "I have it!"

at last exclaimed the Spaniard. "Even if we had the porters now we could not go directly to the coast for fear of meeting Flora Hawkes's party—we must let them get out of Africa before we take the gold to the coast. Two months will be none too long to wait, for they are going to have a devil of a time getting to the coast at all with that bunch of mutinous porters. While we are waiting, therefore, let us take one of the ingots of gold to the nearest point at which we can dispose of it for trade goods. Then we can return and hire porters to carry it from village to village."

"The Bwana speaks words of wisdom," replied Owaza. "It is not as far to the nearest trading post as it is back to the coast, and thus we shall not only save time, but also many long, hard marches."

"In the morning, then, we shall return and unearth one of the ingots, but we must be sure that none of your men accompanies us, for no one must know until it is absolutely necessary where the gold is buried. When we return for it, of course, then others must know, too, but inasmuch as we shall be with it constantly thereafter there will be little danger of its being taken from us."

And so upon the following morning the Spaniard and Owaza returned to the buried treasure, where they unearthed a single ingot.

Before he left the spot the Spaniard drew upon the inner surface of the leopard skin that he wore across his shoulder an accurate map of the location of the treasure, making the drawing with a sharpened stick, dipped in the blood of a small rodent he had killed for the purpose. From Owaza he obtained the native names of the river and of such landmarks as were visible from the spot at which the treasure was buried, together with as explicit directions as possible for reaching the place from the coast. This information, too, he wrote below the map, and when he had finished he felt much relieved from the fear that should aught befall Owaza he might never be able to locate the gold.

When Jane Clayton reached the coast to take passage for London she found awaiting her a wire stating that her father was entirely out of danger, and that there was no necessity for her coming to him. She, therefore, after a few days of rest, turned her face again toward home, and commenced to retrace the steps of the long, hot, weary journey that she had just completed. When, finally, she arrived at the bungalow she learned, to her consternation, that Tarzan of the Apes had not yet returned from his expedition to the city of Opar after the gold from the treasure vaults. She found Korak, evidently much exercised, but unwilling to voice a doubt as to the ability of his father to care for himself. She learned of the escape of the golden lion with regret, for she knew that Tarzan had become much attached to the noble beast.

It was the second day after her return that the Waziri who had accompanied Tarzan returned without him. Then, indeed, was her heart filled with fear for her lord and master. She questioned the men carefully, and when she learned from them that Tarzan had suffered another accident that had again affected his memory, she immediately announced that she would set out on the following day in search of him, commanding the Waziri who had just returned to accompany her.

Korak attempted to dissuade her, but failing in that insisted upon accompanying her.

"We must not all be away at once," she said. "You remain here, my son. If I fail I shall return and let you go."

"I cannot let you go alone, Mother," replied Korak.

"I am not alone when the Waziri are with me," she laughed. "And you know perfectly well, boy, that I am as safe anywhere in the heart of Africa with them as I am here at the ranch."

"Yes, yes, I suppose so," he replied, "but I wish I might go, or that Meriem were here."

"Yes, I, too, wish that Meriem were here," replied Lady Greystoke. "However, do not worry. You know that my jungle-craft, while not equal to that of Tarzan or Korak, is by no means a poor asset, and that, surrounded by the loyalty and bravery of the Waziri, I shall be safe."

"I suppose you are right," replied Korak, "but I do not like to see you go without me."

And so, notwithstanding his objections, Jane Clayton set out the next morning with fifty Waziri warriors in search of her savage mate.

When Esteban and Owaza had not returned to camp as they had promised, the other members of the party were at first inclined to anger, which was later replaced by concern, not so much for the safety of the Spaniard but for fear that Owaza might have met with an accident and would not return to take them in safety to the coast, for of all the blacks he alone seemed competent to handle the surly and mutinous carriers. The negroes scouted the idea that Owaza had become lost and were more inclined to the opinion that he and

Esteban had deliberately deserted them. Luvini, who acted as head-man in Owaza's absence, had a theory of his own.

"Owaza and the Bwana have gone after the ivory raiders alone. By trickery they may accomplish as much as we could have accomplished by force, and there will only be two among whom to divide the ivory."

"But how may two men overcome a band of raiders?" inquired Flora, skeptically.

"You do not know Owaza," answered Luvini. "If he can gain the ears of their slaves he will win them over, and when the Arabs see that he who accompanies Owaza and who fights at the head of the mutinous slaves is Tarzan of the Apes, they will flee in terror."

"I believe he is right," muttered Kraski, "it sounds just like the Spaniard," and then suddenly he turned upon Luvini. "Can you lead us to the raiders' camp?" he demanded.

"Yes," replied the negro.

"Good," exclaimed Kraski; "and now, Flora, what do you think of this plan? Let us send a swift runner to the raiders, warning them against Owaza and the Spaniard, and telling them that the latter is not Tarzan of the Apes, but an impostor. We can ask them to capture and hold the two until we come, and after we arrive we can make such further plans as the circumstances permit. Very possibly we can carry out our original design after we have once entered their camp as friends."

"Yes, that sounds good," replied Flora, "and it is certainly crooked enough—just like you, yourself."

The Russian blushed. " 'Birds of a feather'—" he quoted.

The girl shrugged her shoulders indifferently, but Bluber, who, with Peebles and Throck, had been silent listeners to the conversation, blustered.

"Vot do you mean birds vit fedders?" he demanded. "Who vas a crook? I tell you, Master Carl Kraski, I am an honest man, dot is von t'ing dot no man don't say about Adolph Bluber, he is a crook."

"O shut up," snapped Kraski, "if there's anything in it you'll be for it—if there's no risk. These fellows stole the ivory themselves, and killed a lot of people, probably, to do it. In addition they have taken slaves, which we will free."

"O vell," said Bluber, "if it is fair und eqvitable, vy, all right, but just remember, Mister Kraski, dot I am an honest man."

"Blime!" exclaimed Throck, "we're all honest; I've never seen such a downy bunch of parsons in all me life."

"Sure we're honest," roared John Peebles, "and anyone

'at says we ain't gets 'is bally 'ead knocked off, and 'ere we are, 'n that's that."

The girl smiled wearily. "You can always tell honest men," she said. "They go around telling the world how honest they are. But never mind that; the thing now is to decide whether we want to follow Kraski's suggestion or not. It's something we've got all pretty well to agree upon before we undertake it. There are five of us. Let's leave it to a vote. Do we, or don't we?"

"Will the men accompany us?" asked Kraski, turning to Luvini.

"If they are promised a share of the ivory they will," replied the black.

"How many are in favor of Carl's plan?" asked Flora.

They were unanimously for it, and so it was decided that they would undertake the venture, and a half hour later a runner was despatched on the trail to the raiders' camp with a message for the raider chief. Shortly after, the party broke camp and took up its march in the same direction.

A week later, when they reached the camp of the raiders they found that their messenger had arrived safely and that they were expected. Esteban and Owaza had not put in an appearance nor had anything been seen or heard of them in the vicinity. The result was that the Arabs were inclined to be suspicious and surly, fearing that the message brought to them had been but a ruse to permit this considerable body of whites and armed blacks to enter their stockade in safety.

Jane Clayton and her Waziri moving rapidly, picked up the spoor of Flora Hawkes's safari at the camp where the Waziri had last seen Esteban, whom they still thought to have been Tarzan of the Apes. Following the plainly marked trail, and moving much more rapidly than the Hawkes safari, Jane and the Waziri made camp within a mile of the ivory raiders only about a week after the Hawkes party had arrived and where they still remained, waiting either for the coming of Owaza and Esteban, or for a propitious moment in which they could launch their traitorous assault upon the Arabs. In the meantime, Luvini and some of the other blacks had succeeded in secretly spreading the propaganda of revolt among the slaves of the Arabs. Though he reported his progress daily to Flora Hawkes, he did not report the steady growth and development of a little private plan of his own, which contemplated, in addition to the revolt of the slaves, and the slaying of the Arabs, the murder of all the whites in the camp, with the exception of Flora Hawkes, whom Luvini wished to preserve either for himself or for sale to some black sultan of the north. It was Luvini's shrewd plan first to slay the Arabs, with the assistance of the whites, and then to fall upon the whites and slay them, after their body servants had stolen their weapons from them.

That Luvini would have been able to carry out his plan with ease there is little doubt, had it not been for the loyalty and affection of a young black boy attached to Flora Hawkes for her personal service.

The young white woman, notwithstanding the length to which she would go in the satisfaction of her greed and avarice, was a kind and indulgent mistress. The kindnesses she had shown this ignorant little black boy were presently to return her dividends far beyond her investment.

Luvini had been to her upon a certain afternoon to advise her that all was ready, and that the revolt of the slaves and the murder of the Arabs should take place that evening, immediately after dark. The cupidity of the whites had long been aroused by the store of ivory possessed by the raiders, with the result that all were more than eager for the final step in the conspiracy that would put them in possession of considerable wealth.

It was just before the evening meal that the little negro boy crept into Flora Hawkes's tent. He was very wide-eyed, and terribly frightened.

"What is the matter?" she demanded.

"S-sh!" he cautioned. "Do not let them hear you speak to me, but put your ear close to me while I tell you in a low voice what Luvini is planning."

The girl bent her head close to the lips of the little black. "You have been kind to me," he whispered, "and now that Luvini would harm you I have come to tell you."

"What do you mean?" exclaimed Flora, in a low voice.

"I mean that Luvini, after the Arabs are killed, has given orders that the black boys kill all the white men and take you prisoner. He intends either to keep you for himself or to sell you in the north for a great sum of money."

"But how do you know all this?" demanded the girl.

"All the blacks in camp know it," replied the boy. "I was to have stolen your rifle and your pistol, as each of the boys will steal the weapons of his white master."

The girl sprang to her feet. "I'll teach that traitor a lesson," she cried, seizing her pistol and striding toward the flap of the tent.

The boy seized her about the knees and held her. "No! no!" he cried. "Do not do it. Do not say anything. It will only mean that they will kill the white men sooner and take you prisoner just the same. Every black boy in the camp is against you. Luvini has promised that the ivory shall be divided equally among them all. They are ready now, and if you should threaten Luvini, or if in any other way they should learn that you were aware of the plot, they would fall upon you immediately."

"What do you expect me to do then?" she asked.

"There is but one hope, and that is in flight. You and the white men must escape into the jungle. Not even I may accompany you."

The girl stood looking at the little boy in silence for a moment, and then finally she said, "Very well, I will do as you say. You have saved my life. Perhaps I may never be able to repay you, and perhaps, again, I may. Go, now, before suspicion alights upon you."

The black withdrew from the tent, crawling beneath the back wall to avoid being seen by any of his fellows who were in the center of the camp from which the front of the tent was in plain view. Immediately he was gone Flora walked casually into the open and went to Kraski's tent, which the Russian occupied in common with Bluber. She found the two men and in low whispers apprised them of what the black had told her. Kraski then called Peebles and Throck, it being decided that they should give no outward sign of holding any suspicion that aught was wrong. The Englishmen were for jumping in upon the blacks and annihilating them, but Flora Hawkes dissuaded them from any such rash act by pointing out how greatly they were outnumbered by the natives, and how hopeless it would be to attempt to overpower them.

Bluber, with his usual cunning and shrewdness which inclined always to double dealing where there was the slightest possibility for it, suggested that they secretly advise the Arabs of what they had learned, and joining forces with them take up as strong a position in the camp as possible and commence to fire into the blacks without waiting for their attack.

Again Flora Hawkes vetoed the suggestion. "It will not do," she said, "for the Arabs are at heart as much our enemies as the blacks. If we were successful in subduing the latter it would be but a question of minutes before the Arabs knew every detail of the plot that we had laid against them, after which our lives would not be worth *that*," and she snapped her fingers.

"I guess Flora is right, as usual," growled Peebles, "but what in 'ell are we goin' to do wanderin' around in this 'ere jungle without nobody to hunt for us, or cook for us, or

carry things for us, or find our way for us, that's wot I'd like
to know, and 'ere we are, 'n that's that."

"I guess there ain't nothin' else to do," said Throck; "but
blime if I likes to run away."

There came then to the ears of the whites, rumbling from
the far distance in the jungle, the roar of a lion.

"*Ach, weh!*" cried Bluber. "Ve go out all alone in dot
jungle? *Mein Gott!* I just as soon stay here und get killed
like a vite man."

"They won't kill you like a white man," said Kraski.
"They'll torture you if you stay."

Bluber wrung his hands, and the sweat of fear rolled down
his oily face. "*Ach!* vy did I done it? vy did I done it?" he
wailed. "Vy didn't I stay home in London vere I belong?"

"Shut up!" snapped Flora. "Don't you know that if you do
anything to arouse the suspicion of these fellows they will
be on us at once? There is only one thing for us to do and
that is to wait until they precipitate the attack upon the
Arabs. We will still have our weapons, for they do not plan
to steal them from us until after the Arabs are killed. In the
confusion of the fight, we must make our escape into the
jungle, and after that—God knows—and God help us."

"Yes," blubbered Bluber, who was in a blue funk,
"*Gott* help us!"

A moment later Luvini came to them. "All is ready,
Bwanas," he said. "As soon as the evening meal has been
eaten, be in readiness. You will hear a shot, that will be
the signal. Then open fire upon the Arabs."

"Good," said Kraski; "we have just been talking about
it and we have decided that we will take our stand near the
gate to prevent their escape."

"It is well," said Luvini, "but you must remain here." He
was addressing Flora. "It would not be safe for you to be
where there is to be fighting. Remain here in your tent,
and we will confine the fighting to the other side of the village
and possibly to the gate, if any of them makes a break for
escape."

"All right," said Flora, "I will remain here where it is
safe."

Satisfied that things could not have worked into his hands
to better advantage the black left them, and presently the
entire camp was occupied with the evening meal. There was
an atmosphere of restraint, and high, nervous tension throughout the entire camp that must have been noticeable, even to
the Arabs, though they, alone of the entire company, were
ignorant as to its cause. Bluber was so terrified that he could

not eat, but sat white and trembling with his eyes roving wildly about the camp—first to the blacks, then to the Arabs, and then to the gate, the distance to which he must have measured a hundred times as he sat there waiting for the shot that was to be the signal for the massacre that was to send him out into the jungle to be, he surely thought, the immediate prey of the first hunting lion that passed.

Peebles and Throck ate their meal stolidly, much to Bluber's disgust. Kraski, being of a highly nervous temperament, ate but little, but he showed no signs of fear. Nor did Flora Hawkes, though at heart she realized the hopelessness of their situation.

Darkness had fallen. Some of the blacks and Arabs were still eating, when suddenly the silence was shattered by the sharp staccato report of a rifle. An Arab sank silently to the earth. Kraski rose and grasped Flora by the arm. "Come!" he cried.

Followed by Peebles and Throck, and preceded by Bluber, to whose feet fright had lent wings, they hurried toward the gate of the palisade.

By now the air was filled with the hoarse cries of fighting men and the report of rifles. The Arabs, who had numbered but about a dozen, were putting up a game fight, and being far better marksmen than the blacks, the issue of the battle was still in doubt when Kraski opened the gate and the five whites fled into the darkness of the jungle.

The outcome of the fight within the camp could not have been other than it was, for so greatly did the blacks outnumber the Arabs, that eventually, notwithstanding their poor marksmanship, they succeeded in shooting down the last of the nomads of the north. Then it was that Luvini turned his attention to the other whites only to discover that they had fled the village. The black realized two things instantly. One was that someone had betrayed him, and the other, that the whites could not have gone far in the short time since they had left the camp.

Calling his warriors about him he explained to them what had happened, and impressing upon them that the whites, if permitted to escape, would eventually return with reinforcements to punish the blacks, he aroused his followers, who now numbered over two hundred warriors, to the necessity of setting out immediately upon the trail of the fugitives and overtaking them before they could carry word even to a neighboring village, the nearest of which was not more than a day's march distant.

16

The Diamond Hoard

A S THE primitive smoke bombs filled the throne room of the Tower of the Emperors with their suffocating fumes, the Gomangani clustered about Tarzan begging him to save them, for they, too, had seen the massed Bolgani before every entrance and the great body of them that awaited in the gardens and upon the terrace without.

"Wait a minute," said Tarzan, "until the smoke is thick enough to hide our movements from the Bolgani, and then we will rush the windows overlooking the terrace, for they are nearer the east gate than any other exit, and thus some of us will have a better chance for escape."

"I have a better plan," said the old man. "When the smoke conceals us, follow me. There is one exit that is unguarded, probably because they do not dream that we would use it. When I passed over the dais behind the throne I took occasion to note that there were no Bolgani guarding it."

"Where does it lead?" asked Tarzan.

"Into the basement of the Tower of Diamonds—the tower in which I discovered you. That portion of the palace is nearest to the east gate, and if we can reach it before they suspect our purpose there will be little doubt that we can reach the forest at least."

"Splendid!" ejaculated the ape-man. "It will not be long now before the smoke hides us from the Bolgani."

In fact it was so thick by this time that the occupants of the throne room were finding difficulty in breathing. Many of them were coughing and choking and the eyes of all were watering from the effects of the acrid smoke. And yet they were not entirely hidden from the observation of the watchers all about them.

137

"I don't know how much more of this we can stand," said Tarzan. "I have about all I care for, now."

"It *is* thickening up a bit," said the old man. "Just a moment more and I think we can make it unseen."

"I can stand it no longer," cried La. "I am suffocating and I am half-blinded."

"Very well," said the old man; "I doubt if they can see us now. It is pretty thick. Come, follow me"; and he led the way up the steps of the dais and through an aperture behind the thrones—a small opening hidden by hangings. The old man went first, and then La, followed by Tarzan and Jad-bal-ja, who had about reached the limit of his endurance and patience, so that it had been with difficulty that Tarzan had restrained him, and who now was voicing his anger in deep growls which might have apprised the Bolgani of their avenue of escape. Behind Tarzan and the lion crowded the coughing Gomangani; but because Jad-bal-ja was just in front of them they did not crowd as closely upon the party ahead of them as they probably would have done otherwise.

The aperture opened into a dark corridor which led down a flight of rough steps to a lower level, and then straight through utter darkness for the rather considerable distance which separated the Tower of Diamonds from the Tower of the Emperors. So great was their relief at escaping the dense smoke of the throne room that none of the party minded the darkness of the corridor, but followed patiently the lead of the old man who had explained that the first stairs down which they had passed were the only obstacles to be encountered in the tunnel.

At the corridor's end the old man halted before a heavy door, which after considerable difficulty he managed to open.

"Wait a moment," he said, "until I find a cresset and make a light."

They heard him moving about beyond the doorway for a moment and then a dim light flared, and presently the wick in a cresset flickered. In the dim rays Tarzan saw before them a large rectangular chamber, the great size of which was only partially suggested in the wavering light of the cresset.

"Get them all in," said the old man, "and close the door"; and when that had been done he called to Tarzan. "Come!" he said. "Before we leave this chamber I want to show you such a sight as no other human eyes have ever rested upon."

He led him to the far side of the chamber where, in the light of the cresset, Tarzan saw tier after tier of shelves, upon which were stacked small sacks made of skins. The old man set the cresset upon one of the shelves and taking a sack opened it and spilled a portion of the contents into the palm of his hand. "Diamonds," he said. "Each of these packages weighs five pounds and each contains diamonds. They have been accumulating them for countless ages, for they mine far more than they can use themselves. In their legends is the belief that some day the Atlantians will return and they can sell the diamonds to them. And so they continue to mine them and store them as though there was a constant and ready market for them. Here, take one of the bags with you," he said. He handed one to Tarzan and another to La.

"I do not believe that we shall ever leave the valley alive, but we might"; and he took a third bag for himself.

From the diamond vault the old man led them up a primitive ladder to the floor above, and quickly to the main entrance of the Tower. Only two heavy doors, bolted upon the inside, now lay between them and the terrace, a short distance beyond which the east gate swung open. The old man was about to open the doors when Tarzan stopped him.

"Wait a moment," he said, "until the rest of the Gomangani come. It takes them some time to ascend the ladder. When they are all here behind us, swing the doors open, and you and La, with this ten or a dozen Gomangani that are immediately around us, make a break for the gate. The rest of us will bring up the rear and hold the Bolgani off in case they attack us. Get ready," he added a moment later, "I think they are all up."

Carefully Tarzan explained to the Gomangani the plan he had in mind, and then, turning to the old man, he commanded "Now!" The bolt slipped, the doors swung open, and simultaneously the entire party started at a run toward the east gate.

The Bolgani, who were still massed about the throne room, were not aware that their victims had eluded them until Tarzan, bringing up the rear with Jad-bal-ja was passing through the east gate. Then the Bolgani discovered him, and immediately set up a hue and cry that brought several hundred of them on a mad run in pursuit.

"Here they come," cried Tarzan to the others, "make a run of it—straight down the valley toward Opar, La."

"And you?" demanded the young woman.

"I shall remain a moment with the Gomangani, and attempt to punish these fellows."

La stopped in her tracks. "I shall not go a step without you, Tarzan of the Apes," she said. "Too great already are the risks you have taken for me. No; I shall not go without you."

The ape-man shrugged. "As you will," he said. "Here they come."

With great difficulty he rallied a portion of the Gomangani who, once through the gate, seemed imbued but with a single purpose, and that to put as much distance between the Palace of Diamonds and themselves as possible. Perhaps fifty warriors rallied to his call, and with these he stood in the gateway toward which several hundred Bolgani were now charging.

The old man came and touched Tarzan on the arm. "You had better fly," he said. "The Gomangani will break and run at the first assault."

"We will gain nothing by flying," said Tarzan, "for we should only lose what we have gained with the Gomangani, and then we should have the whole valley about us like hornets."

He had scarcely finished speaking when one of the Gomangani cried: "Look! Look! They come"; and pointed along the trail into the forest.

"And just in time, too," remarked Tarzan, as he saw the first of a swarm of Gomangani pouring out of the forest toward the east gate. "Come!" he cried to the advancing blacks, "the Bolgani are upon us. Come, and avenge your wrongs!" Then he turned, and calling to the blacks around him, leaped forward to meet the onrushing gorilla-men. Behind them wave after wave of Gomangani rolled through the east gate of the Palace of Diamonds, carrying everything before them to break at last like surf upon the wavering wall of Bolgani that was being relentlessly hurled back against the palace walls.

The shouting and the fighting and the blood worked Jad-bal-ja into such a frenzy of excitement that Tarzan with difficulty restrained him from springing upon friend and foe alike, with the result that it required so much of the ape-man's time to hold in leash his ferocious ally that he was able to take but little part in the battle, yet he saw that it was going his way, and that, but for the occurrence of some untoward event, the complete defeat of the Bolgani was assured.

Nor were his deductions erroneous. So frantic were the Gomangani with the blood-lust of revenge and so enthused by the first fruits of victory, that they went fully as mad as Jad-bal-ja himself. They neither gave nor asked quarter, and the fighting ended only when they could find no more Bolgani to slay.

The fighting over, Tarzan, with La and the old man, returned to the throne room, from which the fumes of the smoke bombs had now disappeared. To them they summoned the head-man of each village, and when they had assembled before the dais, above which stood the three whites, with the great, black-maned lion Jad-bal-ja, Tarzan addressed them.

"Gomangani of the Valley of the Palace of Diamonds," he said, "you have this night won your freedom from the tyrannical masters that have oppressed you since far beyond the time the oldest of you may remember. For so many countless ages have you been oppressed that there has never developed among you a leader capable of ruling you wisely and justly. Therefore you must select a ruler from another race than your own."

"You! You!" cried voice after voice as the head-men clamored to make Tarzan of the Apes their king.

"No," cried the ape-man, holding up his hand for silence, "but there is one here who has lived long among you, and who knows your habits and your customs, your hopes and your needs better than any other. If he will stay with you and rule you he will, I am sure, make you a good king," and Tarzan pointed to the old man.

The old man looked at Tarzan in bewilderment. "But I want to go away from here," he said; "I want to get back into the world of civilization, from which I have been buried all these years."

"You do not know what you are talking about," replied the ape-man. "You have been gone very long. You will find no friends left back there from whence you came. You will find deceit, and hypocrisy, and greed, and avarice, and cruelty. You will find that no one will be interested in you and that you will be interested in no one there. I, Tarzan of the Apes, have left my jungle and gone to the cities built by men, but always I have been disgusted and been glad to return to my jungle—to the noble beasts that are honest in their loves and in their hates—to the freedom and genuineness of nature.

"If you return you will be disappointed, and you will realize that you have thrown away an opportunity of accomplishing a work well worth your while. These poor creatures need you. I cannot remain to guide them out of darkness, but you may, and you may so mold them that they will be an industrious, virtuous, and kindly people, not untrained, however, in the arts of warfare, for when we have that which is good, there will always be those who are envious and who, if they are more powerful than we, will attempt to come and take what we have by force. Therefore, you must train your people to protect their country and their rights, and to protect them they must have the ability and the knowledge to fight successfully, and the weapons wherewith to wage their wars."

"You speak the truth, Tarzan of the Apes," replied the old man. "There is nothing for me in that other world, so, if the Gomangani wish me to be their chief I will remain here."

The head-men, when he questioned them, assured Tarzan that if they could not have him for chief they would be very glad to have the old man, whom they all knew, either by sight or reputation, as one who had never perpetrated any cruelties upon the Gomangani.

The few surviving Bolgani who had taken refuge in various parts of the palace were sought out and brought to the throne room. Here they were given the option of remaining in the valley as slaves, or leaving the country entirely. The Gomangani would have fallen upon them and slain them, but that their new king would not permit.

"But where shall we go if we leave the Valley of the Palace of Diamonds?" asked one of the Bolgani. "Beyond the city of Opar we know not what exists, and in Opar may we find only enemies."

Tarzan sat eyeing them quizzically, and in silence. For a long time he did not speak, while several of the Gomangani head-men, and others of the Bolgani, made suggestions for the future of the gorilla-men. Finally the ape-man arose and nodded toward the Bolgani.

"There are about a hundred of you," he said. "You are powerful creatures and should be ferocious fighters. Beside me sits La, the High Priestess and queen of Opar. A wicked priest, usurping her power, has driven her from her throne, but to-morrow we march upon Opar with the bravest Gomangani of the Valley of the Palace of Diamonds, and there we punish Cadj, the High Priest, who has proven a traitor to his queen; and La, once more, ascends the throne of Opar. But where the seeds of treason have once been broadcast the plant may spring up at any time and where least expected. It will be long, therefore, before La of Opar may have full confidence in the loyalty of her people—a fact which offers you an opportunity and a country. Accompany us, therefore, to Opar, and fight with us to replace La upon her throne, and then, when the fighting is over, remain there as La's bodyguard to protect her, not only from enemies without, but from enemies within."

The Bolgani discussed the matter for several minutes, and then one of them came to Tarzan. "We will do as you suggest," he said.

"And you will be loyal to La?" asked the ape-man.

"A Bolgani is never a traitor," replied the gorilla-man.

"Good!" exclaimed Tarzan, "and you, La, are you satisfied with this arrangement?"

"I accept them in my service," replied she.

Early the next morning Tarzan and La set out with three thousand Gomangani and a hundred Bolgani to punish the traitorous Cadj. There was little or no attempt at strategy or deception. They simply marched down through the Valley of the Palace of Diamonds, descended the rocky ravine into the valley of Opar, and made straight for the rear of the palace of La.

A little gray monkey, sitting among the vines and creepers upon the top of the temple walls, saw them coming. He cocked his head, first upon one side and then upon the other, and became so interested and excited that for a moment he forgot to scratch his belly—an occupation he had been assiduously pursuing for some time. The closer the column approached the more excited became Manu, the monkey, and when he realized vaguely the great numbers of the Gomangani he was fairly beside himself, but the last straw that sent him scampering madly back to the palace of Opar was the sight of the Bolgani—the ogres of his little world.

Cadj was in the courtyard of the inner temple, where at sunrise he had performed a sacrifice to the Flaming God. With Cadj were a number of the lesser priests, and Oah and her priestesses. That there was dissension among them was evident by the scowling faces fully as much as by the words which Oah directed at Cadj.

"Once again have you gone too far, Cadj," she cried bitterly. "Only may the High Priestess of the Flaming God perform the act of sacrifice. Yet again and again do you persist in defiling the sacred knife with your unworthy hand."

"Silence, woman," growled the High Priest. "I am Cadj, King of Opar, High Priest of the Flaming God. You are what you are only because of the favor of Cadj. Try not my patience too far or you shall indeed know the feel of the sacred knife." There could be no mistaking the sinister menace in his words. Several of those about him could ill conceal the shocked surprise they felt at his sacrilegious attitude toward their High Priestess. However little they

thought of Oah, the fact remained that she had been ele-
vated to the highest place among them, and those that believed that La was dead, as Cadj had taken great pains to
lead them all to believe, gave in full to Oah the reverence
which her high office entitled her to.

"Have a care, Cadj," warned one of the older priests.
"There is a limit beyond which not even you may pass."

"You dare threaten me?" cried Cadj, the maniacal fury
of fanaticism gleaming in his eyes. "You dare threaten *me*,
Cadj, the High Priest of the Flaming God?" And as he spoke
he leaped toward the offending man, the sacrificial knife
raised menacingly above his head, and just at that moment
a little gray monkey came chattering and screaming through
an embrasure in the wall overlooking the court of the temple.

"The Bolgani! The Bolgani!" he shrieked. "They come!
They come!"

Cadj stopped and wheeled toward Manu, the hand that
held the knife dropping at his side. "You saw them, Manu?"
he asked. "You are speaking the truth? If this is another of
your tricks you will not live to play another joke upon Cadj."

"I speak the truth," chattered the little monkey. "I saw
them with my own eyes."

"How many of them are there?" asked Cadj. "And how
near to Opar have they come?"

"They are as many as the leaves upon the trees," replied
Manu, "and they are already close to the temple wall—the
Bolgani and the Gomangani, they come as the grasses that
grow in the ravines where it is cool and damp."

Cadj turned and raised his face toward the sun, and throwing back his head gave voice to a long-drawn scream that
ended in a piercing shriek. Three times he voiced the hideous
cry, and then with a command to the others in the court to
follow him he started at a brisk trot toward the palace proper.
As Cadj directed his steps toward the ancient avenue, upon
which the palace of Opar faced, there issued from every
corridor and doorway groups of the knurled and hairy men
of Opar, armed with their heavy bludgeons and their knives.
Screaming and chattering in the trees above them were a score
or more of little gray monkeys.

"Not here," they cried, "not here," and pointed toward the
south side of the city.

Like an undisciplined mob the horde of priests and warriors
reentered the palace at Cadj's heels, and retraced their
steps toward the opposite side of the edifice. Here they
scrambled to the summit of the lofty wall which guards the
palace, just as Tarzan's forces came to a halt outside.

"Rocks! Rocks!" screamed Cadj, and in answer to his commands the women in the courtyard below commenced to gather the loose fragments of stone that had crumbled from the wall and from the palace, and to toss them up to the warriors above.

"Go away!" screamed Cadj to the army outside his gates. "Go away! I am Cadj, High Priest of the Flaming God, and this is his temple. Defile not the temple of the Flaming God or you shall know his wrath."

Tarzan stepped forward a little ahead of the others, and raised his hand for silence.

"La, your High Priestess and your queen, is here," he cried to the Oparians upon the wall. "Cadj is a traitor and an impostor. Open your gates and receive your queen. Give up the traitors to justice, and no harm will befall you; but refuse La entry to her city and we shall take by force and with bloodshed that which belongs to La rightfully."

As he ceased speaking La stepped to his side that all her people might see her, and immediately there were scattering cries for La and a voice or two raised against Cadj. Evidently realizing that it would not take much to turn the scale against him, Cadj shrieked to his men to attack, and simultaneously launched a stone at Tarzan. Only the wondrous agility that he possessed saved the ape-man, and the missile passed by, and striking a Gomangani over the heart, felled him. Instantly a shower of missiles fell upon them, and then Tarzan called to his followers to charge. Roaring and growling, the Bolgani and the Gomangani leaped forward to the attack. Cat-like they ran up the rough wall in the face of the menacing bludgeons above. Tarzan, who had chosen Cadj as his objective, was among the first to reach the summit. A hairy, crooked warrior struck at him with a bludgeon, and hanging to the summit of the wall with one hand, Tarzan caught the weapon in the other and wrested it from his assailant. At the same time he saw Cadj turn and disappear into the courtyard beyond. Then Tarzan drew himself to the top where he was immediately engaged by two other warriors of Opar. With the weapon he had wrested from their fellow he knocked them to right and left, so great an advantage his great height and strength gave him over them, and then, remembering only that Cadj, who was the ring-leader of the revolt against La, must not be permitted to escape Tarzan leaped to the pavement below just as the High Priest disappeared through an archway at the opposite end of the courtyard.

Some priests and priestesses sought to impede his progress. Seizing one of the former by the ankles he swung the body in circles about him, clearing his own pathway as he ran for the opposite end of the courtyard, and there he halted and wheeled and putting all the strength of his great muscles into the effort, he swung the body of the priest once more and hurled it back into the faces of his pursuers.

Without waiting to note the effect of his act he turned again and continued in pursuit of Cadj. The fellow kept always just ahead of him, because Cadj knew his way through the labyrinthian mazes of the palace and temple and courtyards better than Tarzan. That the trail was leading toward the inner courts of the temple Tarzan was convinced. There Cadj would find easy ingress to the pits beneath the palace and a hiding place from which it would be difficult to dislodge him, so numerous and winding were the dark subterranean tunnels. And so Tarzan put forth every effort to reach the sacrificial court in time to prevent Cadj from gaining the comparative safety of the underground passages; but as he finally leaped through the doorway into the court, a noose, cunningly laid, closed about one of his ankles and he was hurled heavily to the ground. Almost instantly a number of the crooked little men of Opar leaped upon him, where he lay, half-stunned by the fall, and before he had fully regained his faculties they had trussed him securely.

Only about half conscious, he felt them raise him from the ground and carry him, and presently he was deposited upon a cold stone surface. Then it was that full consciousness returned to him, and he realized that he lay outstretched once more upon the sacrificial altar of the inner court of the Temple of the Flaming God and above him stood Cadj, the High Priest, his cruel face contorted in a grimace of hate and the anticipation of revenge long deferred.

"At last!" gloated the creature of hate. "This time, Tarzan of the Apes, you shall know the fury not of the Flaming God, but of Cadj, the man; nor shall there be any wait nor any interference."

He swung the sacrificial knife high above his head. Beyond the point of the knife Tarzan of the Apes saw the summit of the courtyard wall, and just surmounting it the head and shoulders of a mighty, black-maned lion.

"Jad-bal-ja!" he cried. "Kill! Kill!"

Cadj hesitated, his knife poised on high. He saw the direction of the ape-man's eyes and followed them, and in that instant the golden lion leaped to the pavement, and with two mighty bounds was upon the High Priest of Opar. The knife clattered to the floor and the great jaws closed upon the horrid face.

The lesser priests who had seized Tarzan, and who had remained to witness his death at the hands of Cadj, had fled screaming from the court the instant that the golden lion had leaped upon their master, and now Tarzan and Jad-bal-ja and the corpse of Cadj were the sole occupants of the sacrificial courtyard of the temple.

"Come, Jad-bal-ja," commanded Tarzan; "let no one harm Tarzan of the Apes."

An hour later the victorious forces of La were over-running the ancient palace and temples of Opar. The priests and warriors who had not been killed had quickly surrendered and acknowledged La as their queen and High Priestess, and now at La's command the city was being searched for Tarzan and Cadj. It was thus that La herself, leading a searching party, entered the sacrificial courtyard.

The sight that met her eyes brought her to a sudden halt, for there, bound upon the altar, lay Tarzan of the Apes, and standing above him, his snarling face and gleaming eyes glaring directly at her was Jad-bal-ja, the golden lion.

"Tarzan!" shrieked La, taking a step toward the altar. "Cadj has had his way at last. God of my fathers have pity on me—Tarzan is dead."

"No," cried the ape-man; "far from dead. Come and release me. I am only bound, but had it not been for Jad-bal-ja I had been dead beneath your sacrificial knife."

"Thank God," cried La, and started to approach the altar, but paused before the menacing attitude of the growling lion.

"Down!" cried Tarzan, "let her approach"; and Jad-bal-ja lay down beside his master and stretched his whiskered chin across the ape-man's breast.

La came then, and picking up the sacrificial knife, cut the bonds that held the lord of the jungle captive, and then she saw beyond the altar the corpse of Cadj.

"Your worst enemy is dead," said Tarzan, "and for his death you may thank Jad-bal-ja, as I thank him for my life. You should rule now in peace and happiness and in friendship with the people of the Valley of the Palace of Diamonds."

That night Tarzan and the Bolgani and the head-men of the Gomangani, and the priests and priestesses of Opar, sat in the great banquet hall of the Palace of Opar, as the guests of La, the queen, and ate from the golden platters of the ancient Atlantians—platters that had been fashioned on a continent that exists today only in the legends of antiquity. And the following morning Tarzan and Jad-bal-ja set forth upon their return journey to the land of the Waziri and home.

17

The Torture of Fire

F LORA HAWKES and her four confederates, pursued by
Luvini and his two hundred warriors, stumbled through
the darkness of the jungle night. They had no objective,
for, guided entirely as they had been by the blacks, they
knew not where they were and were completely lost. The
sole idea dominating the mind of each was to put as much
distance between themselves and the camp of the ivory raiders as possible, for no matter what the outcome of the battle
there might have been, their fate would be the same should
the victorious party capture them. They had stumbled on for
perhaps half an hour when, during a momentary rest, they
heard plainly behind them the sound of pursuit, and again
they plunged on in their aimless flight of terror.

Presently, to their surprise, they discerned the glow of a
light ahead. What could it be? Had they made a complete circle, and was this again the camp they had been fleeing? They
pushed on to reconnoiter, until at last they saw before them
the outlines of a camp surrounded by a thorn boma, in the
center of which was burning a small camp-fire. About the
fire were congregated half-a-hundred black warriors, and
as the fugitives crept closer they saw among the blacks a
figure standing out clearly in the light of the camp-fire—a
white woman—and behind them rose louder and louder the
sound of pursuit.

From the gestures and gesticulations of the blacks around
the camp-fire it was evident that they were discussing the
sounds of the battle they had recently heard in the direction
of the raiders' camp, for they often pointed in that direction,
and now the woman raised her hand for silence and they all
listened, and it was evident that they, too, heard the coming

148

of the warriors who were pursuing Flora Hawkes and her confederates.

"There is a white woman there," said Flora to the others. "We do not know who she is, but she is our only hope, for those who are pursuing us will overtake us quickly. Perhaps this woman will protect us. Come, I am going to find out"; and without waiting for an answer she walked boldly toward the boma.

They had come but a short distance when the keen eyes of the Waziri discovered them, and instantly the boma wall was ringed with bristling spears.

"Stop!" cried one of the warriors. "We are the Waziri of Tarzan. Who are you?"

"I am an Englishwoman," called Flora in reply. "I and my companions are lost in the jungle. We have been betrayed by our safari—our head-man is pursuing us now with warriors. There are but five of us and we ask your protection."

"Let them come," said Jane to the Waziri.

As Flora Hawkes and the four men entered the boma beneath the scrutiny of Jane Clayton and the Waziri, another pair of eyes watched from the foliage of the great tree that overhung the camp upon the opposite side—gray eyes to which a strange light came as they recognized the girl and her companions.

As the newcomers approached Lady Greystoke the latter gave an exclamation of surprise. "Flora!" she exclaimed, in astonishment. "Flora Hawkes, what in the world are you doing here?"

The girl, startled too, came to a full stop. "Lady Greystoke!" she ejaculated.

"I do not understand," continued Lady Greystoke. "I did not know that you were in Africa."

For a moment the glib Flora was overcome by consternation, but presently her native wit came to her assistance. "I am here with Mr. Bluber and his friends," she said, "who came to make scientific researches, and brought me along because I had been to Africa with you and Lord Greystoke, and knew something of the manners and customs of the country, and now our boys have turned against us and unless you can help us we are lost."

"Are they west coast boys?" asked Jane.

"Yes," replied Flora.

"I think my Waziri can handle them. How many of them are there?"

"About two hundred," said Kraski.

Lady Greystoke shook her head. "The odds are pretty

heavy," she commented, and then she called to Usula, who was in charge. "There are two hundred west coast boys coming after these people," she said; "we shall have to fight to defend them."

"We are Waziri," replied Usula, simply, and a moment later the van of Luvini's forces broke into view at the outer rim of the camp-fire's reach.

At sight of the glistening warriors ready to receive them the west coast boys halted. Luvini, taking in the inferior numbers of the enemy at a glance, stepped forward a few paces ahead of his men and commenced to shout taunts and insults, demanding the return of the whites to him. He accompanied his words with fantastic and grotesque steps, at the same time waving his rifle and shaking his fist. Presently his followers took up the refrain until the whole band of two hundred was shrieking and yelling and threatening, the while they leaped up and down as they worked themselves into a frenzy of excitement that would impart to them the courage necessary for the initiating of a charge.

The Waziri, behind the boma wall, schooled and disciplined by Tarzan of the Apes, had long since discarded the fantastic overture to battle so dear to the hearts of other warlike tribes and, instead, stood stolid and grim awaiting the coming of the foe.

"They have a number of rifles," commented Lady Greystoke; "that looks rather bad for us."

"There are not over half-a-dozen who can hit anything with their rifles," said Kraski.

"You men are all armed. Take your places among my Waziri. Warn your men to go away and leave us alone. Do not fire until they attack, but at the first overt act, commence firing, and keep it up—there is nothing that so discourages a west coast black as the rifle fire of white men. Flora and I will remain at the back of the camp, near that large tree." She spoke authoritatively, as one who is accustomed to command and knows whereof she speaks. The men obeyed her; even Bluber, though he trembled pitiably as he moved forward to take his place in the front ranks among the Waziri.

Their movements, in the light of the camp-fire, were all plainly discernible to Luvini, and also to that other who watched from the foliage of the tree beneath which Jane Clayton and Flora Hawkes took refuge. Luvini had not come to fight. He had come to capture Flora Hawkes. He turned to his men. "There are only fifty of them," he said. "We can kill them easily, but we did not come to make war. We came to get the white girl back again. Stay here and make a great show against those sons of jackals. Keep them always looking at you. Advance a little and then fall back again, and while you are thus keeping their attention attracted in this direction I will take fifty men and go to the rear of their camp and get the white girl, and when I have her I will send word to you and immediately you can return to the village, where, behind the palisade, we shall be safe against attack."

Now this plan well suited the west coast blacks, who had no stomach for the battle looming so imminent, and so they danced and yelled and menaced more vociferously than before, for they felt they were doing it all with perfect impunity, since presently they should retire, after a bloodless victory, to the safety of their palisade.

As Luvini, making a detour, crept through the concealment of the dense jungles to the rear of the camp while the din of the west coast blacks arose to almost deafening proportions, there dropped suddenly to the ground before the two white women from the tree above them, the figure of a white giant, naked except for loin cloth and leopard skin—his godlike contour picked out by the flickering light of the beast fire.

"John!" exclaimed Lady Greystoke. "Thank God it is you."

"S-s-sh!" cautioned the white giant, placing a forefinger to his lips, and then suddenly he wheeled upon Flora Hawkes. "It is you I want," he cried, and seizing the girl he threw her lightly across his shoulders, and before Lady Greystoke could interfere—before she half-realized what had occurred—he had lightly leaped the protecting boma in the rear of the camp and disappeared into the jungle beyond.

For a moment Jane Clayton stood reeling as one stunned by an unexpected blow, and then, with a stifled moan, she sank sobbing to the ground, her face buried in her arms.

It was thus that Luvini and his warriors found her as they crept stealthily over the boma and into the camp in the rear of the defenders upon the opposite side of the beast fire. They had come for a white woman and they had found one, and roughly dragging her to her feet, smothering her cries with rough and filthy palms, they bore her out into the jungle toward the palisaded village of the ivory raiders.

Ten minutes later the white men and the Waziri saw the west coast blacks retire slowly into the jungle, still yelling and threatening, as though bent on the total annihilation of their enemies—the battle was over without a shot fired or a spear hurled.

"Blime," said Throck, "what was all the bloomin' fuss

about anyhow? I thought they was goin' to eat us up, an' the blighters never done nothin' but yell, an' 'ere we are, 'n that's that."

Bluber swelled out his chest. "It takes more as a bunch of natives to bluff Adolph Bluber," he said pompously.

Kraski looked after the departing blacks, and then, scratching his head, turned back toward the camp-fire. "I can't understand it," he said, and then, suddenly, "Where are Flora and Lady Greystoke?"

It was then that they discovered that the two women were missing.

The Waziri were frantic. They called the name of their mistress aloud, but there was no reply. "Come!" cried Usula, "we, the Waziri, shall fight, after all," and running to the boma he leaped it, and, followed by his fifty blacks, set out in pursuit of the west coast boys.

It was but a moment or two before they overtook them, and that which ensued resembled more a rout than a battle. Fleeing in terror toward their palisade with the Waziri at their heels the west coast blacks threw away their rifles that they might run the faster, but Luvini and his party had had sufficient start so that they were able to reach the village and gain the safety of the palisade before pursued and pursuers reached it. Once inside the gate the defenders made a stand, for they realized that if the Waziri entered they should all be massacred, and so they fought as a cornered rat will fight, with the result that they managed to hold off the attackers until they could close and bar the gate. Built as it had been as a defense against far greater numbers the village was easy to defend, for there were less than fifty Waziri now, and nearly two hundred fighting men within the village to defend it against them.

Realizing the futility of blind attack Usula withdrew his forces a short distance from the palisade, and there they squatted, their fierce, scowling faces glaring at the gateway while Usula pondered schemes for outwitting the enemy, which he realized he could not overcome by force alone.

"It is only Lady Greystoke that we want," he said; "vengeance can wait until another day."

"But we do not even know that she is within the village," reminded one of his men.

"Where else could she be, then?" asked Usula. "It is true that you may be right—she may not be within the village, but that I intend to find out. I have a plan. See; the wind is from the opposite side of the village. Ten of you will accompany me, the others will advance again before the gate and make much noise, and pretend that you are about to attack. After awhile the gate will open and they will come out. That I promise you. I will try to be here before that happens, but if I am not, divide into two parties and stand upon either side of the gateway and let the west coast blacks escape; we do not care for them. Watch only for Lady Greystoke, and when you see her take her away from those who guard her. Do you understand?" His companions nodded. "Then come," he said, and selecting ten men disappeared into the jungle.

Luvini had carried Jane Clayton to a hut not far from the gateway to the village. Here he had bound her securely and tied her to a stake, still believing that she was Flora Hawkes, and then he had left her to hurry back toward the gate that he might take command of his forces in defense of the village.

So rapidly had the events of the past hour transpired that Jane Clayton was still half dazed from the series of shocks that she had been called upon to endure. Dwarfing to nothingness the menace of her present position was the remembrance that her Tarzan had deserted her in her hour of need, and carried off into the jungle another woman. Not even the remembrance of what Usula had told her concerning the accident that Tarzan had sustained, and which had supposedly again affected his memory, could reconcile her to the brutality of his desertion, and now she lay, face down, in the filth of the Arab hut, sobbing as she had not for many years.

As she lay there torn by grief, Usula and his ten crept stealthily and silently around the outside of the palisade to the rear of the village. Here they found great quantities of dead brush left from the clearing which the Arabs had made when constructing their village. This they brought and piled along the palisade, close against it, until nearly three-quarters of the palisade upon that side of the village was banked high with it. Finding that it was difficult to prosecute their work in silence, Usula despatched one of his men to the main body upon the opposite side of the village, with instructions that they were to keep up a continuous din of shouting to drown the sound of the operations of their fellows. The plan worked to perfection, yet even though it permitted Usula and his companions to labor with redoubled efforts, it was more than an hour before the brush pile was disposed to his satisfaction.

Luvini, from an aperture in the palisade, watched the main body of the Waziri who were now revealed by the rising of the moon, and finally he came to the conclusion that they did not intend to attack that night, and therefore he might relax his watchfulness and utilize the time in another and more agreeable manner. Instructing the bulk of his warriors to remain near the gate and ever upon the alert, with orders that he be summoned the moment that the Waziri showed any change in attitude, Luvini repaired to the hut in which he had left Lady Greystoke.

The black was a huge fellow, with low, receding forehead and prognathous jaw. As he entered the hut with a lighted torch which he stuck in the floor, his bloodshot eyes gazed greedily at the still form of the woman lying prone before him. He licked his thick lips and, coming closer, reached out and touched her. Jane Clayton looked up, and recoiling in revulsion shrunk away. At sight of the woman's face the black looked his surprise.

"Who are you?" he demanded in the pidgin English of the coast.

"I am Lady Greystoke, wife of Tarzan of the Apes," replied Jane Clayton. "If you are wise you will release me at once."

Surprise and terror showed in the eyes of Luvini, and another emotion as well, but which would dominate the muddy brain it was difficult, then, to tell. For a long time he sat gazing at her, and slowly the greedy, gloating expression upon his face dominated and expunged the fear that had at first been written there, and in the change Jane Clayton read her doom.

With fumbling fingers Luvini untied the knots of the bonds that held Jane Clayton's wrists and ankles. She felt his hot breath upon her and saw his bloodshot eyes and the red tongue that momentarily licked the thick lips. The instant that she felt the last thong with which she was tied fall away she leaped to her feet and sprang for the entrance to the hut, but a great hand reached forth and seized her, and as Luvini dragged her back toward him, she wheeled like a mad tigress and struck repeatedly at his grinning, ugly face. By brute force, ruthless and indomitable, he beat down her weak resistance and slowly and surely dragged her closer to him. Oblivious to aught else, deaf to the cries of the Waziri before the gate and to the sudden new commotion that arose in the village, the two struggled on, the woman, from the first, foredoomed to defeat.

Against the rear palisade Usula had already put burning torches to his brush pile at half-a-dozen different places. The flames, fanned by a gentle jungle breeze, had leaped almost immediately into a roaring conflagration, before which the dry wood of the palisade crumbled in a shower of ruddy sparks which the wind carried to the thatched roofs of the huts beyond, until in an incredibly short period of time the village was a roaring inferno of flames. And even as Usula had predicted the gate swung open and the west coast blacks swarmed forth in terror toward the jungle. Upon either side of the gateway the Waziri stood, looking for their mistress, but though they waited and watched in silence until no more came from the gateway of the village, and until the interior of the palisade was a seething hell of fire, they saw nothing of her.

Long after they were convinced that no human being could remain alive in the village they still waited and hoped; but at last Usula gave up the useless vigil.

"She was never there," he said, "and now we must pursue the blacks and capture some of them, from whom we may learn the whereabouts of Lady Greystoke."

It was daylight before they came upon a small band of stragglers, who were in camp a few miles toward the west. These they quickly surrounded, winning their immediate surrender by promises of immunity in the event that they would answer truthfully the questions that Usula should propound.

"Where is Luvini?" demanded Usula, who had learned the name of the leader of the west coast boys from the Europeans the evening before.

"We do not know; we have not seen him since we left the village," replied one of the blacks. "We were some of the slaves of the Arabs, and when we escaped the palisade last night we ran away from the others, for we thought that we should be safer alone than with Luvini, who is even crueller than the Arabs."

"Did you see the white women that he brought to the camp last night?" demanded Usula.

"He brought but one white woman," replied the other.

"What did he do with her? Where is she now?" asked Usula.

"I do not know. When he brought her he bound her hand and foot and put her in the hut which he occupied near the village gate. We have not seen her since."

Usula turned and looked at his companions. A great fear was in his eyes, a fear that was reflected in the countenances of the others.

"Come!" he said, "we shall return to the village. And you will go with us," he added, addressing the west coast blacks, "and if you have lied to us—" he made a significant movement with his forefinger across his throat.

"We have not lied to you," replied the others.

Quickly they retraced their steps toward the ruins of the

Arab village, nothing of which was left save a few piles of smouldering embers.

"Where was the hut in which the white woman was confined?" demanded Usula, as they entered the smoking ruins.

"Here," said one of the blacks, and walked quickly a few paces beyond what had been the village gateway. Suddenly he halted and pointed at something which lay upon the ground.

"There," he said, "is the white woman you seek."

Usula and the others pressed forward. Rage and grief contended for mastery of them as they beheld, lying before them, the charred remnants of a human body.

"It is she," said Usula, turning away to hide his grief as the tears rolled down his ebon cheeks. The other Waziri were equally affected, for they all had loved the mate of the big Bwana.

"Perhaps it is not she," suggested one of them; "perhaps it is another."

"We can tell quickly," cried a third. "If her rings are among the ashes it is indeed she," and he knelt and searched for the rings which Lady Greystoke habitually wore.

Usula shook his head despairingly. "It is she," he said, "there is the very stake to which she was fastened"—he pointed to the blackened stub of a stake close beside the body—"and as for the rings, even if they are not there it will mean nothing, for Luvini would have taken them away from her as soon as he captured her. There was time for everyone else to leave the village except she, who was bound and could not leave—no, it cannot be another."

The Waziri scooped a shallow grave and reverently deposited the ashes there, marking the spot with a little cairn of stones.

18

The Spoor of Revenge

AS TARZAN of the Apes, adapting his speed to that of Jad-bal-ja, made his comparatively slow way toward home, he reviewed with varying emotions the experiences of the past week. While he had been unsuccessful in raiding the treasure vaults of Opar, the sack of diamonds which he carried compensated several-fold for this miscarriage of his plans. His only concern now was for the safety of his Waziri, and, perhaps, a troublesome desire to seek out the whites who had drugged him and mete out to them the punishment they deserved. In view, however, of his greater desire to return home he decided to make no effort at apprehending them for the time being at least.

Hunting together, feeding together, and sleeping together, the man and the great lion trod the savage jungle trails toward home. Yesterday they had shared the meat of Bara, the deer, today they feasted upon the carcass of Horta, the boar, and between them there was little chance that either would go hungry.

They had come within a day's march of the bungalow when Tarzan discovered the spoor of a considerable body of warriors. As some men devour the latest stock-market quotations as though their very existence depended upon an accurate knowledge of them, so Tarzan of the Apes devoured every scrap of information that the jungle held for him, for, in truth, an accurate knowledge of all that this information could impart to him had been during his lifetime a *sine qua non* to his existence. So now he carefully examined the spoor that lay before him, several days old though it was and partially obliterated by the passage of beasts since it had been made, but yet legible enough to the keen eyes and nostrils of the ape-man. His partial indifference suddenly gave way to keen interest, for among the footprints of the great warriors he saw now and again the smaller one of a white woman —a loved footprint that he knew as well as you know your mother's face.

"The Waziri returned and told her that I was missing," he soliloquized, "and now she has set out with them to search for me." He turned to the lion. "Well, Jad-bal-ja, once again we turn away from home—but no, where she is is home."

The direction that the trail led rather mystified Tarzan of the Apes, as it was not along the direct route toward Opar, but in a rather more southerly direction. On the sixth day his keen ears caught the sound of approaching men, and presently there was wafted to his nostrils the spoor of blacks. Sending Jad-bal-ja into a thicket to hide, Tarzan took to the trees and moved rapidly in the direction of the approaching negroes. As the distance between them lessened the scent became stronger, until, even before he saw them, Tarzan knew that they were Waziri, but the one effluvium that would have filled his soul with happiness was lacking.

It was a surprised Usula who, at the head of the sad and dejected Waziri, came at the turning of the trail suddenly face to face with his master.

"Tarzan of the Apes!" cried Usula. "Is it indeed you?"

"It is none other," replied the ape-man, "but where is Lady Greystoke?"

"Ah, master, how can we tell you!" cried Usula.

"You do not mean—" cried Tarzan. "It cannot be. Nothing could happen to her while she was guarded by my Waziri!"

The warriors hung their heads in shame and sorrow. "We offer our lives for hers," said Usula, simply. He threw down his spear and shield and, stretching his arms wide apart, bared his great breast to Tarzan. "Strike, Bwana," he said.

The ape-man turned away with bowed head. Presently he looked at Usula again. "Tell me how it happened," he said, "and forget your foolish speech as I have forgotten the suggestion which prompted it."

Briefly Usula narrated the events which had led up to the death of Jane, and when he was done Tarzan of the Apes spoke but three words, voicing a question which was typical of him.

"Where is Luvini?" he asked.

"Ah, that we do not know," replied Usula.

"But I shall know," said Tarzan of the Apes. "Go upon your way, my children, back to your huts, and your women and your children, and when next you see Tarzan of the Apes you will know that Luvini is dead."

They begged permission to accompany him, but he would not listen to them.

"You are needed at home at this time of year," he said. "Already have you been gone too long from the herds and fields. Return, then, and carry word to Korak, but tell him that it is my wish that he, too, remains at home—if I fail, then may he come and take up my unfinished work if he wishes to do so." As he ceased speaking he turned back in the direction from which he had come, and whistled once a single, low, long-drawn note, and a moment later Jad-bal-ja, the golden lion, bounded into view along the jungle trail.

"The golden lion!" cried Usula. "When he escaped from Keewazi it was to search for his beloved Bwana."

Tarzan nodded. "He followed many marches to a strange country until he found me," he said, and then he bid the Waziri good-bye and bent his steps once more away from home in search of Luvini and revenge.

John Peebles, wedged in the crotch of a large tree, greeted the coming dawn with weary eyes. Near him was Dick Throck, similarly braced in another crotch, while Kraski, more intelligent and therefore possessing more inventive genius, had rigged a small platform of branches across two parallel boughs, upon which he lay in comparative comfort. Ten feet above him Bluber swung, half exhausted and wholly terrified, to a smaller branch, supported in something that approximated safety by a fork of the branch to which he clung.

"Gord," groaned Peebles, "hi'll let the bloody lions 'ave me before hi'll spend another such a night as this, an' 'ere we are, 'n that's that!"

"And blime, too," said Throck, "hi sleeps on the ground hafter this, lions or no lions."

"If the combined intelligence of the three of you was equal to that of a walrus," remarked Kraski, "we might have slept in comparative safety and comfort last night on the ground."

"Hey there, Bluber, *Mister* Kraski is spikin' to yer," called Peebles in fine sarcasm, accenting the Mister.

"*Ach, weh!* I don't care vat nobody says," moaned Bluber.

" 'E wants us to build a 'ouse for 'im hevery night," continued Peebles, "while 'e stands abaht and tells us bloomin' well 'ow to do it, and 'im, bein' a fine gentleman, don't do no work."

"Why should I do any work with my hands when you two big beasts haven't got anything else to work with?" asked Kraski. "You would all have starved by this time if I hadn't found food for you. And you'll be lion meat in the end, or die of exhaustion if you don't listen to me—not that it would be much loss."

The others paid no attention to his last sally. As a matter of fact they had all been quarreling so much for such a long time that they really paid little attention to one another. With the exception of Peebles and Throck they all hated one another cordially, and only clung together because they were afraid to separate. Slowly Peebles lowered his bulk to the ground. Throck followed him, and then came Kraski, and then, finally, Bluber, who stood for a moment in silence, looking down at his disreputable clothing.

"*Mein Gott!*" he exclaimed at last. "Look at me! Dis suit, vat it cost me twenty guineas, look at it. Ruined. Ruined. It vouldn't bring vun penny in der pound."

"The hell with your clothes!" exclaimed Kraski. "Here we are, lost, half starved, constantly menaced by wild animals, and maybe, for all we know, by cannibals, with Flora missing in the jungle, and you can stand there and talk about your 'tventy guinea' suit. You make me tired, Bluber. But come on, we might as well be moving."

"Which way?" asked Throck.

"Why, to the west, of course," replied Kraski. "The coast is there, and there is nothing else for us to do but try to reach it."

"We can't reach it by goin' east," roared Peebles, "an' 'ere we are, 'n that's that."

"Who said we could?" demanded Kraski.

"Well, we was travelin' east all day yesterday," said Peebles. "I knew all the time that there was somethin' wrong, and I just got it figured out."

Throck looked at his partner in stupid surprise. "What do you mean?" he growled. "What makes you think we was travelin' east?"

"It's easy enough," replied Peebles, "and I can prove it to you. Because this party here knows so much more than the rest of us we've been travelin' straight toward the interior ever since the natives deserted us." He nodded toward the Russian, who stood with his hands on his hips, eyeing the other quizzically.

"If you think I'm taking you in the wrong direction, Peebles," said Kraski, "you just turn around and go the other way; but I'm going to keep on the way we've been going, which is the right way."

"It ain't the right way," retorted Peebles, "and I'll show yer. Listen here. When you travel west the sun is at your left side, isn't it—that is, all durin' the middle of the day. Well, ever since we've been travelin' without the natives the sun has been on our right. I thought all the time there was somethin' wrong, but I could never figure it out until just now. It's plain as the face on your nose. We've been travelin' due east right along."

"Blime," cried Throck, "that we have, due east, and this blighter thinks as 'ow 'e knows it all."

"Ach!" groaned Bluber, "und ve got to valk it all back again yet, once more?"

Kraski laughed and turned away to resume the march in the direction he had chosen. "You fellows go on your own way if you want to," he said, "and while you're traveling, just ponder the fact that you're south of the equator and that therefore the sun is always in the north, which, however, doesn't change its old-fashioned habit of setting in the west."

Bluber was the first to grasp the truth of Kraski's statement.

"Come on, boys," he said, "Carl vas right," and he turned and followed the Russian.

Peebles stood scratching his head, entirely baffled by the puzzling problem, which Throck, also, was pondering deeply. Presently the latter turned after Bluber and Kraski. "Come on, John," he said to Peebles, "hi don't hunderstand it, but hi guess they're right. They are headin' right toward where the sun set last night, and that sure must be west."

His theory tottering, Peebles followed Throck, though he remained unconvinced.

The four men, hungry and footsore, had dragged their weary way along the jungle trail toward the west for several hours in vain search for game. Unschooled in jungle craft they blundered on. There might have been on every hand fierce carnivore or savage warriors, but so dull are the perceptive faculties of civilized man, the most blatant foe might have stalked them unperceived.

And so it was that shortly after noon, as they were crossing a small clearing, the zip of an arrow that barely missed Bluber's head, brought them to a sudden, terrified halt. With a shrill scream of terror Adolph crumpled to the ground. Kraski threw his rifle to his shoulder and fired.

"There!" he cried, "behind those bushes," and then another arrow, from another direction, pierced his forearm. Peebles and Throck, beefy and cumbersome, got into action with less celerity than the Russian, but, like him, they showed no indication of fear.

"Down," cried Kraski, suiting the action to the word. "Lie down and let them have it."

Scarcely had the three men dropped among the long grass when a score of pigmy hunters came into the open, and a volley of arrows whizzed above the prone men, while from a nearby tree two steel-gray eyes looked down upon the ambush.

Bluber lay upon his belly with his face buried in his arms, his useless rifle lying at his side, but Kraski, Peebles, and Throck, fighting for their lives, pumped lead into the band of yelling pigmies.

Kraski and Peebles each dropped a native with his rifle and then the foe withdrew into the concealing safety of the surrounding jungle. For a moment there was a cessation of hostilities. Utter silence reigned, and then a voice broke the quiet from the verdure of a nearby forest giant.

"Do not fire until I tell you to," it said, in English, "and I will save you."

Bluber raised his head. "Come qvick! Come qvick!" he

cried, "ve vill not shoot. Safe me, safe me, und I giff you
five pounds."

From the tree from which the voice had issued there came
a single, low, long-drawn, whistled note, and then silence
for a time.

The pigmies, momentarily surprised by the mysterious voice
emanating from the foliage of a tree, ceased their activities,
but presently, hearing nothing to arouse their fear, they
emerged from the cover of the bushes and launched another
volley of arrows toward the four men lying among the grasses
in the clearing. Simultaneously the figure of a giant white
leaped from the lower branches of a patriarch of the jungle,
as a great black-maned lion sprang from the thicket below.

"Ach!" shrieked Bluber, and again buried his face in his
arms.

For an instant the pigmies stood terrified, and then their
leader cried: "It is Tarzan!" and turned and fled into the
jungle.

"Yes, it is Tarzan—Tarzan of the Apes," cried Lord Greystoke. "It is Tarzan and the golden lion," but he spoke in
the dialect of the pigmies, and the whites understood no word
of what he said. Then he turned to them. "The Gomangani
have gone," he said; "get up."

The four men crawled to their feet. "Who are you, and
what are you doing here?" demanded Tarzan of the Apes.
"But I do not need to ask who you are. You are the men
who drugged me, and left me helpless in your camp, a prey
to the first passing lion or savage native."

Bluber stumbled forward, rubbing his palms together and
cringing and smiling. "Ach, nein! Mr. Tarzan, ve did not
know you. Neffer vould ve did vat ve done, had ve known it
vas Tarzan of der Apes. Safe me! Ten pounds—twenty
pounds—anyt'ing. Name your own price. Safe me, und it is
yours."

Tarzan ignored Bluber and turned toward the others. "I
am looking for one of your men," he said; "a black named
Luvini. He killed my wife. Where is he?"

"We know nothing of that," said Kraski. "Luvini betrayed
us and deserted us. Your wife and another white woman
were in our camp at the time. None of us knows what became
of them. They were behind us when we took our post to
defend the camp from our men and the slaves of the Arabs.
Your Waziri were there. After the enemy had withdrawn
we found that the two women had disappeared. We do not
know what became of them. We are looking for them now."

"My Waziri told me as much," said Tarzan, "but have you seen aught of Luvini since?"

"No, we have not," replied Kraski.

"What are you doing here?" demanded Tarzan.

"We came with Mr. Bluber on a scientific expedition," replied the Russian. "We have had a great deal of trouble. Our head-men, askari, and porters have mutinied and deserted. We are absolutely alone and helpless."

"*Ja, Ja!*" cried Bluber. "Safe us! Safe us! But keep dat lion avay. He makes me nerfous."

"He will not hurt you—unless I tell him to," said Tarzan.

"Den please don't tell him to," cried Bluber.

"Where do you want to go?" asked Tarzan.

"We are trying to get back to the coast," replied Kraski, "and from there to London."

"Come with me," said Tarzan, "possibly I can help you. You do not deserve it, but I cannot see white men perish here in the jungle."

They followed him toward the west, and that night they made camp beside a small jungle stream.

It was difficult for the four Londoners to accustom themselves to the presence of the great lion, and Bluber was in a state of palpable terror.

As they squatted around the fire after the evening meal, which Tarzan had provided, Kraski suggested that they set to and build some sort of a shelter against the wild beasts.

"It will not be necessary," said Tarzan. "Jad-bal-ja will guard you. He will sleep here beside Tarzan of the Apes, and what one of us does not hear the other will."

Bluber sighed. *"Mein Gott!"* he cried. "I should giff ten pounds for vun night's sleep."

"You may have it tonight for less than that," replied Tarzan, "for nothing shall befall you while Jad-bal-ja and I are here."

"Vell, den I t'ink I say good night," said Bluber, and moving a few paces away from the fire he curled up and was soon asleep. Throck and Peebles followed suit, and shortly after Kraski, too.

As the Russian lay, half dozing, his eyes partially open, he saw the ape-man rise from the squatting position he had maintained before the fire, and turn toward a nearby tree. As he did so something fell from beneath his loin cloth—a little sack made of hides—a little sack, bulging with its contents.

Kraski, thoroughly awakened now, watched it as the ape-man moved off a short distance, accompanied by Jad-bal-ja, and lay down to sleep.

The great lion curled beside the prostrate man, and presently the Russian was assured that both slept. Immediately he commenced crawling, stealthily and slowly toward the little package lying beside the fire. With each forward move that he made he paused and looked at the recumbent figures of the two ferocious beasts before him, but both slept on peacefully. At last the Russian could reach out and grasp the sack, and drawing it toward him he stuffed it quickly inside his shirt. Then he turned and crawled slowly and carefully back to his place beyond the fire. There, lying with his head upon one arm as though in profound slumber, he felt carefully of the sack with the fingers of his left hand.

"They feel like pebbles," he muttered to himself, "and doubtless that is what they are, for the barbaric ornamentation of this savage barbarian who is a peer of England. It does not seem possible that this wild beast has sat in the House of Lords."

Noiselessly Kraski undid the knot which held the mouth of the sack closed, and a moment later he let a portion of the contents trickle forth into his open palm.

"My God!" he cried, "diamonds!"

Greedily he poured them all out and gloated over them—great scintillating stones of the first water—five pounds of pure, white diamonds, representing so fabulous a fortune that the very contemplation of it staggered the Russian.

"My God!" he repeated, "the wealth of Crœsus in my own hand."

Quickly he gathered up the stones and replaced them in the sack, always with one eye upon Tarzan and Jad-bal-ja; but neither stirred, and presently he had returned them all to the pouch and slipped the package inside his shirt.

"Tomorrow," he muttered, "tomorrow—would to God that I had the nerve to attempt it tonight."

In the middle of the following morning Tarzan, with the four Londoners, approached a good sized, stockaded village, containing many huts. He was received not only graciously, but with the deference due an emperor.

The whites were awed by the attitude of the black chief and his warriors as Tarzan was conducted into their presence.

After the usual ceremony had been gone through, Tarzan turned and waved his hand toward the four Europeans. "These are my friends," he said to the black chief, "and they wish to reach the coast in safety. Send with them, then, sufficient warriors to feed and guard them during the journey. It is I, Tarzan of the Apes, who requests this favor."

"Tarzan of the Apes, the great chief, Lord of the Jungle, has but to command," replied the black.

"Good!" exclaimed Tarzan, "feed them well and treat them well. I have other business to attend to and may not remain."

"Their bellies shall be filled, and they shall reach the coast unscratched," replied the chief.

Without a word of farewell, without even a sign that he realized their existence, Tarzan of the Apes passed from the sight of the four Europeans, while at his heels paced Jad-bal-ja, the golden lion.

19

A Barbed Shaft Kills

K RASKI spent a sleepless night. He could not help but realize that sooner or later Tarzan would discover the loss of his pouch of diamonds, and that he would return and demand an accounting of the four Londoners he had befriended. And so it was that as the first streak of dawn lighted the eastern horizon, the Russian arose from his pallet of dried grasses within the hut that had been assigned him and Bluber by the chief, and crept stealthily out into the village street.

"God!" he muttered to himself. "There is only one chance in a thousand that I can reach the coast alone, but this," and he pressed his hand over the bag of diamonds that lay within his shirt—"but this, this is worth every effort, even to the sacrifice of life—the fortune of a thousand kings—my God, what could I not do with it in London, and Paris, and New York!"

Stealthily he slunk from the village, and presently the verdure of the jungle beyond closed about Carl Kraski, the Russian, as he disappeared forever from the lives of his companions.

Bluber was the first to discover the absence of Kraski, for, although there was no love between the two, they had been thrown together owing to the friendship of Peebles and Throck.

"Have you seen Carl dis morning?" he asked Peebles as the three men gathered around the pot containing the unsavory stew that had been brought to them for their breakfast.

"No," said Peebles. "He must be asleep yet."

"He is not in der hut," replied Bluber. "He vas not dere ven I woke up."

"He can take care of himself," growled Throck, resuming his breakfast. "You'll likely find him with some of the ladies," and he grinned in appreciation of his little joke on Kraski's well-known weakness.

They had finished their breakfast and were attempting to communicate with some of the warriors, in an effort to learn when the chief proposed that they should set forth for the coast, and still Kraski had not made an appearance. By this time Bluber was considerably concerned, not at all for Kraski's safety, but for his own, since, if something could happen to Kraski in this friendly village in the still watches of the night, a similar fate might overtake him, and when he made this suggestion to the others it gave them food for thought, too, so that there were three rather apprehensive men who sought an audience with the chief.

By means of signs and pidgin English, and distorted native dialect, a word or two of which each of the three understood, they managed to covey to the chief the information that Kraski had disappeared, and they wanted to know what had become of him.

The chief was, of course, as much puzzled as they, and immediately instituted a thorough search of the village, with the result that it was soon found that Kraski was not within the palisade, and shortly afterward footprints were discovered leading through the village gateway into the jungle.

"*Mein Gott!*" exclaimed Bluber, "he vent out dere, und he vent alone, in der middle of der night. He must have been crazy."

"Gord!" cried Throck, "what did he want to do that for?"

"You ain't missed nothin', have you?" asked Pebbles of the other two. " 'E might 'ave stolen somethin'."

"*Ach, weh!* Vot have ve got to steal?" cried Bluber. "Our guns, our ammunition—dey are here beside us. He did not take them. Beside dose ve have nothing of value except my tventy guinea suit."

"But what did 'e do it for?" demanded Peebles.

" 'E must 'ave been walkin' in 'is bloomin' sleep," said Throck. And that was as near to an explanation of Kraski's mysterious disappearance as the three could reach. And hour later they set out toward the coast under the protection of a company of the chief's warriors.

Kraski, his rifle slung over his shoulder, moved doggedly along the jungle trail, a heavy automatic pistol grasped in his right hand. His ears were constantly strained for the first intimation of pursuit as well as for whatever other dangers might lurk before or upon either side. Alone in the mysterious jungle he was experiencing a nightmare of terror, and with each mile that he traveled the value of the diamonds became less and less by comparison with the frightful ordeal that he realized he must pass through before he could hope to reach the coast.

One Histah, the snake, swinging from a low-hung branch across the trail, barred his way, and the man dared not fire at him for fear of attracting the attention of possible pursuers to his position. He was forced, therefore, to make a detour through the tangled mass of underbrush which grew closely upon either side of the narrow trail. When he reached it again, beyond the snake, his clothing was more torn and tattered than before, and his flesh was scratched and cut and bleeding from the innumerable thorns past which he had been compelled to force his way. He was soaked with perspiration and panting from exhaustion, and his clothing was filled with ants whose vicious attacks upon his flesh rendered him half mad with pain.

Once again in the clear he tore his clothing from him and sought frantically to rid himself of the torturing pests.

So thick were the myriad ants upon his clothing that he dared not attempt to reclaim it. Only the sack of diamonds, his ammunition and his weapons did he snatch from the ravening horde whose numbers were rapidly increasing, apparently by millions, as they sought again to lay hold upon him and devour him.

Shaking the bulk of the ants from the articles he had retrieved, Kraski dashed madly along the trail as naked as the day he was born, and when, a half hour later, stumbling and at last falling exhausted, he lay panting upon the damp jungle earth, he realized the utter futility of his mad attempt to reach the coast alone, even more fully than he ever could have under any other circumstances, since there is nothing that so paralyzes the courage and self-confidence of a civilized man as to be deprived of his clothing.

However scant the protection that might have been afforded by the torn and tattered garments he had discarded, he could not have felt more helpless had he lost his weapons and ammunition instead, for to such an extent are we the creatures of habit and environment. It was, therefore, a terrified Kraski, already foredoomed to failure, who crawled fearfully along the jungle trail.

That night, hungry and cold, he slept in the crotch of a tree while the hunting carnivore roared, and coughed, and growled through the blackness of the jungle about him. Shivering with terror he started momentarily to fearful wakefulness, and when, from exhaustion, he would doze again it was not to rest but to dream of horrors that a sudden roar would merge into reality. Thus the long hours of a frightful night dragged out their tedious length, until it seemed that dawn would never come. But come it did, and once again he took up his stumbling way toward the west.

Reduced by fear and fatigue and pain to a state bordering upon half consciousness, he blundered on, with each passing hour becoming perceptibly weaker, for he had been without food or water since he had deserted his companions more than thirty hours before.

Noon was approaching. Kraski was moving but slowly now with frequent rests, and it was during one of these that there came to his numbed sensibilities an insistent suggestion of the voices of human beings not far distant. Quickly he shook himself and attempted to concentrate his waning faculties. He listened intently, and presently with a renewal of strength he arose to his feet.

There was no doubt about it. He heard voices but a short distance away and they sounded not like the tones of natives, but rather those of Europeans. Yet he was still careful, and so he crawled cautiously forward, until at a turning of the trail he saw before him a clearing dotted with trees which bordered the banks of a muddy stream. Near the edge of the river was a small hut thatched with grasses and surrounded by a rude palisade protected by an outer boma of thorn bushes.

It was from the direction of the hut that the voices were coming, and now he clearly discerned a woman's voice raised in protest and in anger, and replying to it the deep voice of a man.

Slowly the eyes of Carl Kraski went wide in incredulity, not unmixed with terror, for the tones of the voice of the man he heard were the tones of the dead Esteban Miranda, and the voice of the woman was that of the missing Flora Hawkes, whom he had long since given up as dead also. But Carl Kraski was no great believer in the supernatural. Disembodied spirits need no huts or palisades, or bomas of thorns. The owners of those voices were as live—as material—as he.

He started forward toward the hut, his hatred of Esteban and his jealousy almost forgotten in the relief he felt in the realization that he was to again have the companionship of creatures of his own kind. He had moved, however, but a few steps from the edge of the jungle when the woman's voice came again to his ear, and with it the sudden realization of his nakedness. He paused in thought, looking about him, and presently he was busily engaged gathering the long, broad-leaved jungle grasses, from which he fabricated a rude but serviceable skirt, which he fastened about his waist with a twisted rope of the same material. Then with a feeling of renewed confidence he moved forward toward the hut. Fearing that they might not recognize him at first, and, taking him for an enemy, attack him, Kraski, before he reached the entrance to the palisade, called Esteban by name. Immediately the Spaniard came from the hut, followed by the girl. Had Kraski not heard his voice and recognized him by it, he would have thought him Tarzan of the Apes, so close was the remarkable resemblance.

For a moment the two stood looking at the strange apparition before them.

"Don't you know me?" asked Kraski. "I am Carl—Carl Kraski. You know me, Flora."

"Carl!" exclaimed the girl, and started to leap forward, but Esteban grasped her by the wrist and held her back.

"What are you doing here, Kraski?" asked the Spaniard in a surly tone.

"I am trying to make my way to the coast," replied the Russian. "I am nearly dead from starvation and exposure."

"The way to the coast is there," said the Spaniard, and pointed down the trail toward the west. "Keep moving, Karski, it is not healthy for you here."

"You mean to say that you will send me on without food or water?" demanded the Russian.

"There is water," said Esteban, pointing at the river, "and the jungle is full of food for one with sufficient courage and intelligence to gather it."

"You cannot send him away," cried the girl. "I did not think it possible that even you could be so cruel," and then, turning to the Russian, "O Carl," she cried "do not go. Save me! Save me from this beast!'

"Then stand aside," cried Kraski, and as the girl wrenched herself free from the grasp of Miranda the Russian leveled his automatic and fired point-blank at the Spaniard. The bullet missed its target; the empty shell jammed in the breach and as Kraski pulled the trigger again with no result he glanced at his weapon and, discovering its uselessness, hurled it from him with an oath. As he strove frantically to bring his rifle into action Esteban threw back his spear hand with the short, heavy spear that he had learned by now so well to use, and before the other could press the trigger of his rifle the barbed shaft tore through his chest and heart. Without a sound Carl Kraski sank dead at the foot of his enemy and his rival, while the woman both had loved, each in his own selfish or brutal way, sank sobbing to the ground in the last and deepest depths of despair.

Seeing that the other was dead, Esteban stepped forward and wrenched his spear from Kraski's body and also relieved his dead enemy of his ammunition and weapons. As he did so his eyes fell upon a little bag made of skins which Kraski had fastened to his waist by the grass rope he had recently fashioned to uphold his primitive skirt.

The Spaniard felt of the bag and tried to figure out the nature of its contents, coming to the conclusion that it was ammunition, but he did not examine it closely until he had carried the dead man's weapons into his hut, where he had also taken the girl, who crouched in a corner, sobbing.

"Poor Carl! Poor Carl!" she moaned, and then to the man facing her: "You beast!"

"Yes," he cried, with a laugh, "I am a beast. I am Tarzan of the Apes, and that dirty Russian dared to call me Esteban I am Tarzan! I am Tarzan of the Apes!" he repeated in a loud scream. "Who dares call me otherwise dies. I will show them. I will show them," he mumbled.

The girl looked at him with wide and flaming eyes and shuddered.

"Mad," she muttered. "Mad! My God—alone in the jungle with a maniac!" And, in truth, in one respect was Esteban Miranda mad—mad with the madness of the artist who lives the part he plays. And for so long, now, had Esteban Miranda played the part, and so really proficient had he become in his interpretation of the noble character, that he believed himself Tarzan, and in outward appearance he might have deceived the ape-man's best friend. But within that godlike form was the heart of a cur and the soul of a craven.

"He would have stolen Tarzan's mate," muttered Esteban. "Tarzan, Lord of the Jungle! Did you see how I slew him, with a single shaft? You could love a weakling, could you, when you could have the love of the great Tarzan!"

"I loathe you," said the girl. "You are indeed a beast. You are lower than the beasts."

"You are mine, though," said the Spaniard, "and you shall

never be another's—first I would kill you—but let us see
what the Russian had in his little bag of hides, it feels like
ammunition enough to kill a regiment," and he untied the
thongs that held the mouth of the bag closed and let some
of the contents spill out upon the floor of the hut. As the
sparkling stones rolled scintillant before their astonished eyes,
the girl gasped in incredulity.

"Holy Mary!" exclaimed the Spaniard, "they are diamonds."

"Hundreds of them," murmured the girl. "Where could he
have gotten them?"

"I do not know and I do not care," said Esteban. "They
are mine. They are all mine—I am rich, Flora. I am rich,
and if you are a good girl you shall share my wealth with me."

Flora Hawkes's eyes narrowed. Awakened within her breast
was the always-present greed that dominated her being, and
beside it, and equally as powerful now to dominate her, her
hatred for the Spaniard. Could he have known it, possession
of those gleaming baubles had crystallized at last in the mind
of the woman a determination she had long fostered to
slay the Spaniard while he slept. Heretofore she had been
afraid of being left alone in the jungle, but now the desire
to possess this great wealth overcame her terror.

Tarzan, ranging the jungle, picked up the trail of the
various bands of west coast boys and the fleeing slaves of the
dead Arabs, and overhauling each in turn he prosecuted his
search for Luvini, awing the blacks into truthfulness and
leaving them in a state of terror when he departed. Each
and every one, they told him the same story. There was
none who had seen Luvini since the night of the battle and
the fire, and each was positive that he must have escaped
with some other band.

So thoroughly occupied had the ape-man's mind been during the past few days with his sorrow and his search that
lesser considerations had gone neglected, with the result that
he had not noted that the bag containing the diamonds
was missing. In fact, he had practically forgotten the diamonds when, by the merest vagary of chance his mind happened to revert to them, and then it was that he suddenly
realized that they were missing, but when he had lost them,
or the circumstances surrounding the loss, he could not recall.

"Those rascally Europeans," he muttered to Jad-bal-ja,
"they must have taken them," and suddenly with the thought
the scarlet scar flamed brilliantly upon his forehead, as just
anger welled within him against the perfidy and ingratitude
of the men he had succored. "Come," he said to Jad-bal-ja,

"as we search for Luvini we shall search for these others also." And so it was that Peebles and Throck and Bluber had traveled but a short distance toward the coast when, during a noon-day halt, they were surprised to see the figure of the ape-man moving majestically toward them while, at his side, paced the great, black-maned lion.

Tarzan made no acknowledgment of their exuberant greeting, but came forward in silence to stand at last with folded arms before them. There was a grim, accusing expression upon his countenance that brought the chill of fear to Bluber's cowardly heart, and blanched the faces of the two hardened English pugs.

"What is it?" they chorused. "What is wrong? What has happened?"

"I have come for the bag of stones you took from me," said Tarzan simply.

Each of the three eyed his companion suspiciously.

"I do not understand vot you mean, Mr. Tarzan," purred Bluber, rubbing his palms together. "I am sure dere is some mistake, unless—" he cast a furtive and suspicious glance in the direction of Peebles and Throck.

"I don't know nothin' about no bag of stones," said Peebles, "but I will say as 'ow you can't trust the likes of you."

"I don't trust any of you," said Tarzan. "I will give you five seconds to hand over the bag of stones, and if you don't produce it in that time I shall have you thoroughly searched."

"Sure," cried Bluber, "search me, search me, by all means. Vy, Mr. Tarzan, I vouldn't take notting from you for notting."

"There's something wrong here," growled Throck. "I ain't got nothin' of yours and I'm sure these two haven't neither."

"Where is the other?" asked Tarzan.

"Oh, Kraski? He disappeared the same night you brought us to that village. We hain't seen him since—that's it; I got it now—we wondered why he left, and now I see it as plain as the face on me nose. It was him that stole that bag of stones. That's what he done. We've been tryin' to figure out ever since he left what he stole, and now I see it plain enough."

"Sure," exclaimed Peebles. "That's it, and 'ere we are, 'n that's that."

"Ve might have knowed it, ve might have knowed it," agreed Bluber.

"But nevertheless I'm going to have you all searched," said Tarzan, and when the head-man came and Tarzan had explained what he desired, the three whites were quickly stripped and searched. Even their few belongings were thoroughly gone through, but no bag of stones was revealed.

Without a word Tarzan turned back toward the jungle, and in another moment the blacks and the three Europeans saw the leafy sea of foliage swallow the ape-man and the golden lion.

"Gord help Kraski!" exclaimed Peebles.

"Wot do yer suppose he wants with a bag o' stones?" inquired Throck. " 'E must be a bit balmy, I'll say."

"Balmy nudding," exclaimed Bluber. "Dere is but vun kind of stones in Africa vot Kraski would steal and run off into der jungle alone mit—diamonds."

Peebles and Throck opened their eyes in surprise. "The damned Russian!" exclaimed the former. "He double-crossed us, that's what 'e did."

"He likely as not saved our lives, says hi," said Throck. "If this ape feller had found Kraski and the diamonds with us we'd of all suffered alike—you couldn't 'a' made 'im believe we didn't 'ave a 'and in it. And Kraski wouldn't 'a' done nothin' to help us out."

"I 'opes 'e catches the beggar!" exclaimed Peebles, fervently.

They were startled into silence a moment later by the sight of Tarzan returning to the camp, but he paid no attention to the whites, going instead directly to the head-man, with whom he conferred for several minutes. Then, once more, he turned and left.

Acting on information gained from the head-man, Tarzan struck off through the jungle in the general direction of the village where he had left the four whites in charge of the chief, and from which Kraski had later escaped alone. He moved rapidly, leaving Jad-bal-ja to follow behind, covering the distance to the village in a comparatively short time, since he moved almost in an air line through the trees, where there was no matted undergrowth to impede his progress.

Outside the village gate he took up Kraski's spoor, now almost obliterated, it is true, but still legible to the keen perceptive faculties of the ape-man. This he followed swiftly, since Kraski had clung tenaciously to the open trail that wound in a general westward direction.

The sun had dropped almost to the western tree-tops, when Tarzan came suddenly upon a clearing beside a sluggish stream, near the banks of which stood a small, rude hut, surrounded by a palisade and a thorn boma.

The ape-man paused and listened, sniffing the air with his sensitive nostrils, and then on noiseless feet he crossed the clearing toward the hut. In the grass outside the palisade lay the dead body of a white man, and a single glance told the ape-man that it was the fugitive whom he sought. Instantly he realized the futility of searching the corpse for the bag of diamonds, since it was a foregone conclusion that they were now in the possession of whoever had slain the Russian. A perfunctory examination revealed the fact that he was right in so far as the absence of the diamonds was concerned.

Both inside the hut and outside the palisade were indications of the recent presence of a man and woman, the spoor of the former tallying with that of the creature who had killed Gobu, the great ape, and hunted Bara, the deer, upon the preserves of the ape-man. But the woman—who was she? It was evident that she had been walking upon sore, tired feet, and that in lieu of shoes she wore bandages of cloth.

Tarzan followed the spoor of the man and the woman where it led from the hut into the jungle. As it progressed it became apparent that the woman had been lagging behind, and that she had commenced to limp more and more painfully. Her progress was very slow, and Tarzan could see that the man had not waited for her, but that he had been, in some places, a considerable distance ahead of her.

And so it was that Esteban had forged far ahead of Flora Hawkes, whose bruised and bleeding feet would scarce support her.

"Wait for me, Esteban," she had pleaded. "Do not desert me. Do not leave me alone here in this terrible jungle."

"Then keep up with me," growled the Spaniard. "Do you think that with this fortune in my possession I am going to wait here forever in the middle of the jungle for someone to come and take it away from me? No, I am going on to the coast as fast as I can. If you can keep up, well and good. If you cannot, that is your own lookout."

"But you could not desert me. Even you, Esteban, could not be such a beast after all that you have forced me to do for you."

The Spaniard laughed. "You are nothing more to me," he said, "than an old glove. With this," and he held the sack of diamonds before him, "I can purchase the finest gloves in the capitals of the world—new gloves," and he laughed grimly at his little joke.

"Esteban, Esteban," she cried, "come back, come back. I can go no farther. Do not leave me. Please come back and save me." But he only laughed at her, and as a turn of the trail shut him from her sight, she sank helpless and exhausted to the ground.

20

The Dead Return

T HAT night Esteban made his lonely camp beside a jungle trail that wound through the dry wash of an old river bed, along which a tiny rivulet still trickled, according to the Spaniard the water which he craved.

The obsession which possessed him that he was in truth Tarzan of the Apes, imparted to him a false courage, so that he could camp alone upon the ground without recourse to artificial protection of any kind, and fortune had favored him in this respect in that it had sent no prowling beasts of prey to find him upon those occasions that he had dared too much. During the period that Flora Hawkes had been with him he had built shelters for her, but now that he had deserted her and was again alone, he could not, in the rôle that he had assumed, consider so effeminate an act as the building of even a thorn boma for protection during the darkness of the night.

He did, however, build a fire, for he had made a kill and had not yet reached a point of primitive savagery which permitted him even to imagine that he enjoyed raw meat.

Having devoured what meat he wanted and filled himself at the little rivulet, Esteban came back and squatted before his fire, where he drew the pouch of diamonds from his loin cloth and, opening it, spilled a handful of the precious gems into his palm. The flickering firelight playing upon them sent scintillant gleams shooting into the dark of the surrounding jungle night as the Spaniard let a tiny stream of the sparkling stones trickle from one hand to the other, and in the pretty play of light the Spaniard saw visions of the future—power, luxury, beautiful women—all that great wealth might purchase for a man. With half closed eyes he dreamed of the ideal that he should search the world over to obtain

—the dream-woman for whom he had always searched—
the dream-woman he had never found, the fit companion
for such as Esteban Miranda imagined himself to be. Presently through the dark lashes that veiled his narrowed lids
the Spaniard seemed to see before him in the flickering
light of his campfire a vague materialization of the figure of
his dream—a woman's figure, clothed in flowing diaphanous
white which appeared to hover just above him at the outer
rim of his firelight at the summit of the ancient river bank.

It was strange how the vision persisted. Esteban closed
his eyes tightly, and then opened them ever so little, and
there, as it had been before he closed them, the vision remained. And then he opened his eyes wide, and still the figure of the woman in white floated above him.

Esteban Miranda went suddenly pale. "Mother of God!"
he cried. "It is Flora. She is dead and has come back to
haunt me."

With staring eyes he slowly rose to his feet to confront
the apparition, when in soft and gentle tones it spoke.

"Heart of my heart," it cried, "it is really you!"

Instantly Esteban realized that this was no disembodied
spirit, nor was it Flora—but who was it? Who was this vision
of beauty, alone in the savage African wilderness?

Very slowly now it was descending the embankment and
coming toward him. Esteban returned the diamonds to the
pouch and replaced it inside his loin cloth.

With outstretched arms the girl came toward him. "My
love, my love," she cried, "do not tell me that you do not
know me." She was close enough now for the Spaniard to see
her rapidly rising and falling breasts and her lips trembling
with love and passion. A sudden wave of hot desire swept
over him, so with outstretched arms he sprang forward to
meet her and crush her to his breast.

Tarzan, following the spoor of the man and the woman,
moved in a leisurely manner along the jungle trail, for he
realized that no haste was essential to overtake these two. Nor
was he at all surprised when he came suddenly upon the
huddled figure of a woman, lying in the center of the pathway. He knelt beside her and laid a hand upon her shoulder,
eliciting a startled scream.

"God!" she cried, "this is the end!"

"You are in no danger," said the ape-man. "I will not
harm you."

She turned her eyes and looked up at him. At first she
thought he was Esteban. "You have come back to save me,
Esteban?" she asked.

"Esteban!" he exclaimed. "I am not Esteban. That is not my name." And then she recognized him.

"Lord Greystoke!" she cried. "It is really you?"

"Yes," he said, "and who are you?"

"I am Flora Hawkes. I was Lady Greystoke's maid."

"I remember you," he said. "What are you doing here?"

"I am afraid to tell you," she said. "I am afraid of your anger."

"Tell me," he commanded. "You should know, Flora, that I do not harm women."

"We came to get gold from the vaults of Opar," she said. "But that you know."

"I know nothing of it," he replied. "Do you mean that you were with those Europeans who drugged me and left me in their camp?"

"Yes," she said, "we got the gold, but you came with your Waziri and took it from us."

"I came with no Waziri and took nothing from you," said Tarzan. "I do not understand you."

She raised her eyebrows in surprise, for she knew that Tarzan of the Apes did not lie.

"We became separated," she said, "after our men turned against us. Esteban stole me from the others, and then, after a while Kraski found us. He was the Russian. He came with a bagful of diamonds and then Esteban killed him and took the diamonds."

It was now Tarzan's turn to experience surprise.

"And Esteban is the man who is with you?" he asked.

"Yes," she said, "but he has deserted me. I could not walk farther on my sore feet. He has gone and left me here to die and he has taken the diamonds with him."

"We shall find him," said the ape-man. "Come."

"But I cannot walk," said the girl.

"That is a small matter," he said, and stooping lifted her to his shoulder.

Easily the ape-man bore the exhausted girl along the trail. "It is not far to water," he said, "and water is what you need. It will help revive you and give you strength, and perhaps I shall be able to find food for you soon."

"Why are you so good to me?" asked the girl.

"You are a woman. I could not leave you alone in the jungle to die, no matter what you may have done," replied the ape-man. And Flora Hawkes could only sob a broken plea for forgiveness for the wrong she had done him.

It grew quite dark, but still they moved along the silent

trail until presently Tarzan caught in the distance the re-
flection of firelight.

"I think we shall soon find your friend," he whispered.
"Make no noise."

A moment later his keen ears caught the sound of voices.
He halted and lowered the girl to her feet.

"If you cannot follow," he said, "wait here. I do not wish
him to escape. I will return for you. If you can follow on
slowly, do so." And then he left her and made his way cautiously forward toward the light and the voices. He heard
Flora Hawkes moving directly behind him. It was evident
that she could not bear the thought of being left alone again
in the dark jungle. Almost simultaneously Tarzan heard a
low whine a few paces to his right. "Jad-bal-ja," he whispered
in a low voice, "heel," and the great black-maned lion crept
close to him, and Flora Hawkes, stifling a scream, rushed to
his side and grasped his arms.

"Silence," he whispered; "Jad-bal-ja will not harm you."

An instant later the three came to the edge of the ancient
river bank, and through the tall grasses growing there looked
down upon the little camp beneath.

Tarzan, to his consternation, saw a counterpart of himself
standing before a little fire, while slowly approaching the
man, with outstretched arms, was a woman, draped in flowing white. He heard her words; soft words of love and en-
dearment, and at the sound of the voice and the scent spoor
that a vagrant wind carried suddenly to his nostrils, a strange
complex of emotion overwhelmed him—happiness, despair,
rage, love, and hate.

He saw the man at the fire step forward with open arms
to take the woman to his breast, and then Tarzan separated
the grasses and stepped to the very edge of the embankment,
his voice shattering the jungle with a single word.

"Jane!" he cried, and instantly the man and woman turned
and looked up at him, where his figure was dimly revealed
in the light of the campfire. At sight of him the man wheeled
and raced for the opposite side of the river, and then Tarzan
leaped to the bottom of the wash below and ran toward the
woman.

"Jane," he cried, "it is you, it is you!"

The woman showed her bewilderment. She looked first
at the retreating figure of the man she had been about to
embrace and then turned her eyes toward Tarzan. She drew
her fingers across her brow and looked back toward Esteban, but Esteban was no longer in sight. Then she took a
faltering step toward the ape-man.

"My God," she cried, "what does it mean? Who are you, and if you are Tarzan who was he?"

"I am Tarzan, Jane," said the ape-man.

She looked back and saw Flora Hawkes approaching. "Yes," she said, "you are Tarzan. I saw you when you ran off into the jungle with Flora Hawkes. I cannot understand, John. I could not believe that you, even had you suffered an accident to your head, could have done such a thing."

"I, run off into the jungle with Flora Hawkes?" he asked, in unfeigned surprise.

"I saw you," said Jane.

The ape-man turned toward Flora. "I do not understand it," he said.

"It was Esteban who ran off into the jungle with me, Lady Greystoke," said the girl. "It was Esteban who was about to deceive you again. This is indeed Lord Greystoke. The other was an impostor, who only just deserted me and left me to die in the jungle. Had not Lord Greystoke come when he did I should be dead by now."

Lady Greystoke took a faltering step toward her husband. "Ah, John," she said, "I knew it could not have been you. My heart told me, but my eyes deceived me. Quick," she cried, "that impostor must be captured. Hurry, John, before he escapes."

"Let him go," said the ape-man. "As much as I want him, as much as I want that which he has stolen from me, I will not leave you alone again in the jungle, Jane, even to catch him."

"But Jad-bal-ja," she cried. "What of him?"

"Ah," cried the ape-man, "I had forgotten," and turning to the lion he pointed toward the direction in which the Spaniard had escaped. "Fetch him, Jad-bal-ja," he cried; and, with a bound, the tawny beast was off upon the spoor of his quarry.

"He will kill him?" asked Flora Hawkes, shuddering. And yet at heart she was glad of the just fate that was overtaking the Spaniard.

"No, he will not kill him," said Tarzan of the Apes. "He may maul him a bit, but he will bring him back alive if it is possible." And then, as though the fate of the fugitive were already forgotten, he turned toward his mate.

"Jane," he said, "Usula told me that you were dead. He said that they found your burned body in the Arab village and that they buried it there. How is it, then, that you are here alive and unharmed? I have been searching the jungles for Luvini to avenge your death. Perhaps it is well that I did not find him."

"You would never have found him," replied Jane Clayton, "but I cannot understand why Usula should have told you that he had found my body and buried it."

"Some prisoners that he took," replied Tarzan, "told him that Luvini had taken you bound hand and foot into one of the Arab huts near the village gateway, and that there he had further secured you to a stake driven into the floor of the hut. After the village had been destroyed by fire Usula and the other Waziri returned to search for you with some of the prisoners they had taken who pointed out the location of the hut, where the charred remains of a human body were found beside a burned stake to which it had apparently been tied."

"Ah!" exclaimed the girl, "I see. Luvini did bind me hand and foot and tie me to the stake, but later he came back into the hut and removed the bonds. He attempted to attack me—how long we fought I do not know, but so engrossed were we in our struggle that neither one of us was aware of the burning of the village about us. As I persistently fought him off I caught a glimpse of a knife in his belt, and then I let him seize me and as his arms encircled me I grasped the knife and, drawing it from its sheath, plunged it into his back, below his left shoulder—that was the end. Luvini sank lifeless to the floor of the hut. Almost simultaneously the rear and roof of the structure burst into flames.

"I was almost naked, for he had torn nearly all my clothing from me in our struggles. Hanging upon the wall of the hut was this white burnoose, the property, doubtless, of one of the murdered Arabs. I seized it, and throwing it about me ran into the village street. The huts were now all aflame, and the last of the natives was disappearing through the gateway. To my right was a section of palisade that had not yet been attacked by the flames. To escape into the jungle by the gateway would have meant running into the arms of my enemies, and so, somehow, I managed to scale the palisade and and drop into the jungle unseen by any.

"I have had considerable difficulty eluding the various bands of blacks who escaped the village. A part of the time I have been hunting for the Waziri and the balance I have had to remain in hiding. I was resting in the crotch of a tree, about half a mile from here, when I saw the light of this man's fire, and when I came to investigate I was almost stunned by joy to discover that I had, as I imagined, stumbled upon my Tarzan."

"It was Luvini's body, then, and not yours that they buried," said Tarzan.

"Yes," said Jane, "and it was this man who just escaped whom I saw run off into the jungle with Flora, and not you, as I believed."

Flora Hawkes looked up suddenly. "And it must have been Esteban who came with the Waziri and stole the gold from us. He fooled our men and he must have fooled the Waziri, too."

"He might have fooled anyone if he could deceive me," said Jane Clayton. "I should have discovered the deception in a few minutes I have no doubt, but in the flickering light of the campfire, and influenced as I was by the great joy of seeing Lord Greystoke again, I believed quickly that which I wanted to believe."

The ape-man ran his fingers through his thick shock of hair in a characteristic gesture of meditation. "I cannot understand how he fooled Usula in broad daylight," he said with a shake of his head.

"I can," said Jane. "He told him that he had suffered an injury to his head which had caused him to lose his memory partially—an explanation which accounted for many lapses in the man's interpretation of your personality."

"He was a clever devil," commented the ape-man.

"He was a devil, all right," said Flora.

It was more than an hour later that the grasses at the river bank suddenly parted and Jad-bal-ja emerged silently into their presence. Grasped in his jaws was a torn and bloody leopard skin which he brought and laid at the feet of his master.

The ape-man picked the thing up and examined it, and then he scowled. "I believe Jad-bal-ja killed him after all," he said.

"He probably resisted," said Jane Clayton, "in which event Jad-bal-ja could do nothing else in self-defense but slay him."

"Do you suppose he ate him?" cried Flora Hawkes, drawing fearfully away from the beast.

"No," said Tarzan, "he has not had time. In the morning we will follow the spoor and find his body. I should like to have the diamonds again." And then he told Jane the strange story connected with his acquisition of the great wealth represented by the little bag of stones.

The following morning they set out in search of Esteban's corpse. The trail led through dense brush and thorns to the edge of the river farther down stream, and there it disappeared, and though the ape-man searched both sides of the river for a couple of miles above and below the point at which he had lost the spoor, he found no further sign of the Spaniard. There was blood along the tracks that Esteban had made and blood upon the grasses at the river's brim.

At last the ape-man returned to the two women. "That is the end of the man who would be Tarzan," he said.

"Do you think he is dead?" asked Jane.

"Yes, I am sure of it," said the ape-man. "From the blood I imagine that Jad-bal-ja mauled him, but that he managed to break away and get into the river. The fact that I can find no indication of his having reached the bank within a reasonable distance of this spot leads me to believe that he has been devoured by crocodiles."

Again Flora Hawkes shuddered. "He was a wicked man," she said, "but I would not wish even the wickedest such a fate as that."

The ape-man shrugged. "He brought it upon himself, and, doubtless, the world is better off without him."

"It was my fault," said Flora. "It was my wickedness that brought him and the others here. I told them of what I had heard of the gold in the treasure vaults of Opar—it was my idea to come here and steal it and to find a man who could impersonate Lord Greystoke. Because of my wickedness many men have died, and you, Lord Greystoke, and your lady, have almost met your death—I do not dare to ask for forgiveness."

Jane Clayton put her arm about the girl's shoulder. "Avarice has been the cause of many crimes since the world began," she said, "and when crime is invoked in its aid it assumes its most repulsive aspect and brings most often its own punishment, as you, Flora, may well testify. For my part I forgive you. I imagine that you have learned your lesson."

"You have paid a heavy price for your folly," said the ape-man. "You have been punished enough. We will take you to your friends who are on their way to the coast under escort of a friendly tribe. They cannot be far distant, for, from the condition of the men when I saw them, long marches are beyond their physical powers."

The girl dropped to her knees at his feet. "How can I thank you for your kindness?" she said. "But I would rather remain here in Africa with you and Lady Greystoke, and work for you and show by my loyalty that I can redeem the wrong I did you."

Tarzan glanced at his wife questioningly, and Jane Clayton signified her assent to the girl's request.

"Very well, then," said the ape-man, "you may remain with us, Flora."

"You will never regret it," said the girl. "I will work my fingers off for you."

The three, and Jad-bal-ja, had been three days upon the march toward home when Tarzan, who was in the lead, paused, and, raising his head, sniffed the jungle air. Then he turned to them with a smile. "My Waziri are disobedient," he said. "I sent them home and yet here they are, coming toward us, directly away from home."

A few minutes later they met the van of the Waziri, and great was the rejoicing of the blacks when they found both their master and mistress alive and unscathed.

"And now that we have found you," said Tarzan, after the greetings were over, and innumerable questions had been asked and answered, "tell me what you did with the gold that you took from the camp of the Europeans."

"We hid it, O Bwana, where you told us to hide it," replied Usula.

"I was not with you, Usula," said the ape-man. "It was another, who deceived Lady Greystoke even as he deceived you—a bad man—who impersonated Tarzan of the Apes so cleverly that it is no wonder that you were imposed upon."

"Then it was not you who told us that your head had been injured and that you could not remember the language of the Waziri?" demanded Usula.

"It was not I," said Tarzan, "for my head has not been injured, and I remember well the language of my children."

"Ah," cried Usula, "then it was not our Big Bwana who ran from Buto, the rhinoceros?"

Tarzan laughed. "Did the other run from Buto?"

"That he did," cried Usula; "he ran in great terror."

"I do not know that I blame him," said Tarzan, "for Buto is no pleasant playfellow."

"But our Big Bwana would not run from him," said Usula, proudly.

"Even if another than I hid the gold it was you who dug the hole. Lead me to the spot then, Usula."

The Waziri constructed rude yet comfortable litters for the two white women, though Jane Clayton laughed at the idea that it was necessary that she be carried and insisted upon walking beside her bearers more often than she rode. Flora Hawkes, however, weak and exhausted as she was, could not have proceeded far without being carried, and was glad of the presence of the brawny Waziri who bore her along the jungle trail so easily.

It was a happy company that marched in buoyant spirits toward the spot where the Waziri had cached the gold for Esteban. The blacks were overflowing with good nature because they had found their master and their mistress, while the relief and joy of Tarzan and Jane were too deep for expression.

When at last they came to the place beside the river where they had buried the gold the Waziri, singing and laughing, commenced to dig for the treasure, but presently their singing ceased and their laughter was replaced by expressions of puzzled concern.

For a while Tarzan watched them in silence and then a slow smile overspread his countenance. "You must have buried it deep, Usula," he said.

The black scratched his head. "No, not so deep as this, Bwana," he cried. "I cannot understand it. We should have found the gold before this."

"Are you sure you are looking in the right place?" asked Tarzan.

"This is the exact spot, Bwana," the black assured him, "but the gold is not here. Someone has removed it since we buried it."

"The Spaniard again," commented Tarzan. "He was a slick customer."

"But he could not have taken it alone," said Usula. "There were many ingots of it."

"No," said Tarzan, "he could not, and yet it is not here."

The Waziri and Tarzan searched carefully about the spot where the gold had been buried, but so clever had been the woodcraft of Owaza that he had obliterated even from the keen senses of the ape-man every vestige of the spoor that he and the Spaniard had made in carrying the gold from the old hiding place to the new.

"It is gone," said the ape-man, "but I shall see that it does not get out of Africa," and he despatched runners in various directions to notify the chiefs of the friendly tribes surrounding his domain to watch carefully every safari crossing their territory, and to let none pass who carried gold.

"That will stop them," he said after the runners had departed.

That night as they made their camp upon the trail toward home, the three whites were seated about a small fire with Jad-bal-ja lying just behind the ape-man, who was examining the leopard skin that the golden lion had retrieved in his pursuit of the Spaniard, when Tarzan turned to his wife.

"You were right, Jane," he said. "The treasure vaults of Opar are not for me. This time I have lost not only the gold but a fabulous fortune in diamonds as well, beside risking that greatest of all treasures—yourself."

"Let the gold and the diamonds go, John," she said; "we have one another, and Korak."

"And a bloody leopard skin," he supplemented, "with a mysterious map painted upon it in blood."

Jad-bal-ja sniffed the hide and licked his chops in—anticipation or retrospection—which?

21

An Escape and a Capture

A T SIGHT of the true Tarzan, Esteban Miranda turned and fled blindly into the jungle. His heart was cold with terror as he rushed on in blind fear. He had no objective in mind. He did not know in what direction he was going. His only thought—the thought which dominated him—was based solely upon a desire to put as much distance as possible between himself and the ape-man, and so he blundered on, forcing his way through dense thickets of thorns that tore and lacerated his flesh until at every step he left a trail of blood behind him.

At the river's edge the thorns reached out and seized again, as they had several times before, the precious leopard skin to which he clung with almost the same tenacity as he clung to life itself. But this time the thorns would not leave go their hold, and as he struggled to tear it away from them his eyes turned back in the direction from which he had come. He heard the sound of a great body moving rapidly through the thicket toward him, and an instant later saw the baleful glare of two gleaming, yellow-green spots of flame. With a stifled cry of terror the Spaniard relinquished his hold upon the leopard skin and, wheeling, dived into the river.

As the black waters closed above his head Jad-bal-ja came to the edge of the bank and looked down upon the widening circles which marked the spot of his quarry's disappearance, for Esteban, who was a strong swimmer, struck boldly for the opposite side of the stream, keeping himself well submerged.

For a moment the golden lion scanned the surface of the river, and then he turned and sniffed at the hide the Spaniard had been forced to leave behind, and grasping it in his jaws tore it from the thorns that held it and carried it back to lay it at the feet of his master.

Forced at last to come to the surface for air the Spaniard arose amid a mass of tangled foliage and branches. For a moment he thought that he was lost, so tightly held was he by the entangling boughs, but presently he forced his way upward, and as his head appeared above the surface of the water amidst the foliage he discovered that he had arisen directly beneath a fallen tree that was floating down the center of the stream. After considerable effort he managed to draw himself up to the boughs and find a place astride the great bole, and thus he floated down stream in comparative safety.

He breathed a deep sigh of relief as he realized with what comparative ease he had escaped the just vengeance of the ape-man. It is true that he bemoaned the loss of the hide which carried the map to the location of the hidden gold, but he still retained in his possession a far greater treasure, and as he thought of it his hands gloatingly fondled the bag of diamonds fastened to his loin cloth. Yet, even though he possessed this great fortune in diamonds, his avaricious mind constantly returned to the golden ingots by the waterfall.

"Owaza will get it," he muttered to himself. "I never trusted the black dog, and when he deserted me I knew well enough what his plans were."

All night long Esteban Miranda floated down stream upon the fallen tree, seeing no sign of life, until shortly after daybreak he passed a native village upon the shore.

It was the village of Obebe, the cannibal, and at sight of the strange figure of the white giant floating down the stream upon the bole of a tree, the young woman who espied him raised a great hue and cry until the population of the village lined the shore watching him pass.

"It is a strange god," cried one.

"It is the river devil," said the witch doctor. "He is a friend of mine. Now, indeed, shall we catch many fish if for each ten that you catch you give one to me."

"It is not the river devil," rumbled the deep voice of Obebe, the cannibal. "You are getting old," he said to the witch doctor, "and of late your medicine has been poor medicine, and now you tell me that Obebe's greatest enemy is the river devil. That is Tarzan of the Apes. Obebe knows him well." And in truth every cannibal chief in the vicinity knew Tarzan of the Apes well and feared and hated him, for relentless had been the ape-man's war against them.

"It is Tarzan of the Apes," repeated Obebe, "and he is in trouble. Perhaps it is our chance to capture him."

He called his warriors about him, and presently half a hundred brawny young bucks started at a jog trot down the trail that paralleled the river. For miles they followed the slowly moving tree which carried Esteban Miranda until at last at a bend in the river the tree was caught in the outer circle of a slow-moving eddy, which carried it beneath the overhanging limbs of the trees growing close to the river's edge.

Cramped and chilled and hungry as he was, Esteban was glad of the opportunity to desert his craft and gain the shore. And so, laboriously, he drew himself up among the branches of the tree that momentarily offered him a haven of retreat from the river, and crawling to its stem lowered himself to the ground beneath, unconscious of the fact that in the grasses around him squatted half a hundred cannibal warriors.

Leaning against the bole of the tree the Spaniard rested for a moment. He felt for the diamonds and found that they were safe.

"I am a lucky devil, after all," he said aloud, and almost simultaneously the fifty blacks arose about him and leaped upon him. So sudden was the attack, so overwhelming the force, that the Spaniard had no opportunity to defend himself against them, with the result that he was down and securely bound almost before he could realize what was happening to him.

"Ah, Tarzan of the Apes, I have you at last," gloated Obebe, the cannibal, but Esteban did not understand a word the man said, and so he could make no reply. He talked to Obebe in English, but that language the latter did not understand.

Of only one thing was Esteban certain; that he was a prisoner and that he was being taken back toward the interior. When they reached Obebe's village there was great rejoicing on the part of the women and the children and the warriors who had remained behind. But the witch doctor shook his head and made wry faces and dire prophecies.

"You have seized the river devil," he said. "We shall catch no more fish, and presently a great sickness will fall upon Obebe's people and they will all die like flies." But Obebe only laughed at the witch doctor for, being an old man and a great king, he had accumulated much wisdom and, with the acquisition of wisdom man is more inclined to be skeptical in matters of religion.

"You may laugh now, Obebe," said the witch doctor, "but later you will not laugh. Wait and see."

"When, with my own hands, I kill Tarzan of the Apes, then indeed shall I laugh," replied the chief, "and when I and my warriors have eaten his heart and his flesh, then, indeed, shall we no longer fear any of your devils."

"Wait," cried the witch doctor angrily, "and you shall see."

They took the Spaniard, securely bound, and threw him into a filthy hut, through the doorway of which he could see the women of the village preparing cooking fires and pots for the feast of the coming night. A cold sweat stood out upon the brow of Esteban Miranda as he watched these grewsome preparations, the significance of which he could not misinterpret, when coupled with the gestures and the glances that were directed toward the hut where he lay, by the inhabitants of the village.

The afternoon was almost spent and the Spaniard felt that he could count the hours of life remaining to him upon possibly two fingers of one hand, when there came from the direction of the river a series of piercing screams which shattered the quiet of the jungle, and brought the inhabitants of the village to startled attention, and an instant later sent them in a mad rush in the direction of the fear-laden shrieks. But they were too late and reached the river only just in time to see a woman dragged beneath the surface by a huge crocodile.

"Ah, Obebe, what did I tell you?" demanded the witch doctor, exultantly. "Already has the devil god commenced his revenge upon your people."

The ignorant villagers, steeped in superstition, looked fearfully from their witch doctor to their chief. Obebe scowled. "He is Tarzan of the Apes," he insisted.

"He is the river devil who has taken the shape of Tarzan of the Apes," insisted the witch doctor.

"We shall see," replied Obebe. "If he is the river devil he can escape our bonds. If he is Tarzan of the Apes he cannot. If he is the river devil he will not die a natural death, like men die, but will live on forever. If he is Tarzan of the Apes some day he will die. We will keep him, then, and see, and that will prove whether or not he is Tarzan of the Apes or the river devil."

"How?" asked the witch doctor.

"It is very simple," replied Obebe. "If some morning we find that he has escaped we will know that he is the river devil, and because we have not harmed him but have fed him well while he has been here in our village, he will befriend us and no harm will come of it. But if he does not escape we will know that he is Tarzan of the Apes, provided he dies a natural death. And so, if he does not escape, we shall keep him until he dies and then we shall know that he was, indeed, Tarzan of the Apes."

"But suppose he does not die?" asked the witch doctor, scratching his woolly head.

"Then," exclaimed Obebe triumphantly, "we will know that you are right, and that he was, indeed, the river devil."

Obebe went and ordered women to take food to the Spaniard while the witch doctor stood, where Obebe had left him, in the middle of the street, still scratching his head in thought.

And thus was Esteban Miranda, possessor of the most fabulous fortune in diamonds that the world had ever known, condemned to life imprisonment in the village of Obebe, the cannibal.

While he had been lying in the hut his traitorous confederate, Owaza, from the opposite bank of the river from the spot where he and Esteban had hidden the golden ingots, saw Tarzan and his Waziri come and search for the gold and go away again, and the following morning Owaza came with fifty men whom he had recruited from a neighboring village and dug up the gold and started with it toward the coast.

That night Owaza made camp just outside a tiny village of a minor chief, who was weak in warriors. The old fellow invited Owaza into his compound, and there he fed him and gave him native beer, while the chief's people circulated among Owaza's boys plying them with innumerable questions until at last the truth leaked out and the chief knew that Owaza's porters were carrying a great store of yellow gold.

When the chief learned this for certain he was much perturbed, but finally a smile crossed his face as he talked with the half-drunken Owaza.

"You have much gold with you," said the old chief, "and it is very heavy. It will be hard to get your boys to carry it all the way back to the coast."

"Yes," said Owaza, "but I shall pay them well."

"If they did not have to carry it so far from home you would not have to pay them so much, would you?" asked the chief.

"No," said Owaza, "but I cannot dispose of it this side of the coast."

"I know where you can dispose of it within two days' march," replied the old chief.

"Where?" demanded Owaza. "And who here in the interior will buy it?"

"There is a white man who will give you a little piece of paper for it and you can take that paper to the coast and get the full value of your gold."

"Who is this white man?" demanded Owaza, "and where is he?"

"He is a friend of mine," said the chief, "and if you wish

I will take you to him on the morrow, and you can bring with you all your gold and get the little piece of paper."

"Good," said Owaza, "and then I shall not have to pay the carriers but a very small amount."

The carriers were glad, indeed, to learn the next day that they were not to go all the way to the coast, for even the lure of payment was not sufficient to overcome their dislike to so long a journey, and their fear of being at so great a distance from home. They were very happy, therefore, as they set forth on a two days' march toward the northeast. And Owaza was happy and so was the old chief, who accompanied them himself, though why he was happy about it Owaza could not guess.

They had marched for almost two days when the chief sent one of his own men forward with a message.

"It is to my friend," he said, "to tell him to come and meet us and lead us to his village." And a few hours later, as the little caravan emerged from the jungle onto a broad, grassy plain, they saw not far from them, and approaching rapidly, a large band of warriors. Owaza halted.

"Whose are those?" he demanded.

"Those are the warriors of my friend," replied the chief, "and he is with them. See?" and he pointed toward a figure at the head of the blacks, who were approaching at a trot, their spears and white plumes gleaming in the sunshine.

"They come for war and not for peace," said Owaza fearfully.

"That depends upon you, Owaza," replied the cheif.

"I do not understand you," said Owaza.

"But you will in a few minutes after my friend has come."

As the advancing warriors approached more closely Owaza saw a giant white at their head—a white whom he mistook for Esteban—the confederate he had so traitorously deserted. He turned upon the chief. "You have betrayed me," he cried.

"Wait," said the old chief; "nothing that belongs to you shall be taken from you."

"The gold is not his," cried Owaza. "He stole it," and he pointed at Tarzan who had approached and halted before him, but who ignored him entirely and turned to the chief.

"Your runner came," he said to the old man, "and brought your message, and Tarzan and his Waziri have come to see what they could do for their old friend."

The chief smiled. "Your runner came to me, O Tarzan, four days since, and two days later came this man with his carriers, bearing golden ingots toward the coast. I told him that I had a friend who would buy them, giving him a little piece of paper for them, but that, of course, only in case the gold belonged to Owaza."

The ape-man smiled. "You have done well, my friend," he said. "The gold does not belong to Owaza."

"It does not belong to you, either," cried Owaza. "You are not Tarzan of the Apes. I know you. You came with the four white men and the white woman to steal the gold from Tarzan's country, and then you stole it from your own friends."

The chief and the Waziri laughed. The ape-man smiled one of his slow smiles.

"The other was an impostor, Owaza," he said, "but *I* am Tarzan of the Apes, and I thank you for bringing my gold to me. Come," he said, "it is but a few more miles to my home," and the ape-man compelled Owaza to direct his carriers to bear the golden ingots to the Greystoke bungalow. There Tarzan fed the carriers and paid them, and the next morning sent them back to their own country. He sent Owaza with them, but not without a gift of value, accompanied with an admonition that the black never again return to Tarzan's country.

When they had departed, and Tarzan, Jane and Korak were standing upon the veranda of the bungalow with Jad-bal-ja lying at their feet, the ape-man threw an arm about his mate's shoulders.

"I shall have to retract what I said about the gold of Opar not being for me, for you see before you a new fortune that has come all the way from the treasure vaults of Opar without any effort on my part."

"Now, if someone would only bring your diamonds back," laughed Jane.

"No chance of that," said Tarzan. "They are unquestionably at the bottom of the Ugogo River," and far away, upon the banks of the Ugogo, in the village of Obebe, the cannibal, Esteban Miranda lay in the filth of the hut that had been assigned to him, gloating over the fortune that he could never utilize as he entered upon a life of captivity that the stubbornness and superstition of Obebe had doomed him to undergo.

ABOUT EDGAR RICE BURROUGHS

Edgar Rice Burroughs is one of the world's most popular authors. With no previous experience as an author, he wrote and sold his first novel—*A Princess of Mars*—in 1912. In the ensuing thirty-eight years until his death in 1950, Burroughs wrote 91 books and a host of short stories and articles. Although best known as the creator of the classic *Tarzan of the Apes* and *John Carter of Mars,* his restless imagination knew few bounds. Burroughs' prolific pen ranged from the American West to primitive Africa and on to romantic adventure on the moon, the planets, and even beyond the farthest star.

No one knows how many copies of ERB books have been published throughout the world. It is conservative to say, however, that of the translations into 32 known languages, including Braille, the number must run into the hundreds of millions. When one considers the additional world-wide following of the Tarzan newspaper feature, radio programs, comic magazines, motion pictures and television, Burroughs must have been known and loved by literally a thousand million or more.